THE MIGHTY HOOK

Shadows of Neverland

The Mighty Hook

Mark Tarrant

4 Horsemen
Publications, Inc.

4 Horsemen Publications, Inc.
1497 Main St. Suite 169
Dunedin, FL 34698
4horsemenpublications.com
info@4horsemenpublications.com

Cover by S Wilder
Typesetting by Niki Tantillo
Editor: Heather Teele

Library of Congress Control Number: 2022942216

Paperback ISBN-13: 978-1-64450-677-6
Hardcover ISBN-13: 978-1-64450-721-6
Audiobook ISBN-13: 978-1-64450-675-2
Ebook ISBN-13: 978-1-64450-676-9

Foreword

The evil Captain Hook! I first heard these words when I was a child. I admit, ever since childhood, I didn't care much for Peter Pan. A high-flying, fanciful, tight-wearing, dagger-wielding lad, obsessed with a young lady somewhere in London. With him, came a cute, little faerie, sprinkling dust on everything like Chris Kattan at a rave.

That all changed when I was in fifth grade. I made a dramatic turn to the macabre, the dark, the exact thing that made those bumps in the night, making me too afraid to look in my closet or under the bed once bedtime hit and most of the lights went out in the house. I was drawn to horror: Frankenstein, the Mummy, Wolfman, Dracula, then movies like *Monster Squad*, *Critters*, *Gremlins*, and then a whirlwind of coming-of-age stories like *Goonies*, *The Explorers*, and *The Last Star Fighter*, even *Mac and Me.*

Needless to say, my horizons were expanding, and my mind was exploding with theories and ideas of who and what could come out at night, or even during the day. Monsters just didn't lurk in the shadows of the night but stood out in plain sight with movies like *Tremors* and *Cujo*. My mind raced with excitement as to what I could do with all this. What could I write about? What monsters could I create?

I started creating all kinds of stories about zombies, witches, vampires, and my most favorite monsters of all time—werewolves!

I met Mark in New Jersey at Fangoria's Weekend of Horrors. What an awesome convention! I was there promoting a little-known horror film titled *100 Tears*, and Mark was there with his book *The Blood Rider* (a book about a preacher turned vampire out for revenge in the Old West). What a hoot! We immediately became best friends.

That was ten years ago. Since then, we have tossed ideas back and forth almost daily. Sometimes, something fantastic finds its way to the front. Something new. Something we didn't know we wanted.

This is that story. I pressured Mark for months, even years, to get this finished. Now it is, and you get to read this masterpiece of horror, action, suspense, and high seas pirate ship battles. Experience a new telling of what really happened on that mysterious island of Lost Boys, guarded by mermaids, zombified children who want nothing more the to drink your blood, and the one man who fought them all, saved the world, and was known only as THE MIGHTY HOOK!

Mark has truly made that youthful, child-like mind of mine smile again!

-- Joe Davison
Actor, Director, Producer, Author, and Amazing Friend

N
W
E
S
MAYBE DEATH?
TREASURE
COVE
LOTS OF DEATH
more death
Rocks with mermaids
INSTANT DEATH

If you have found this crude map, I am most likely dead and you took this from my corpse. This island is full of monsters. If you go looking for the treasure it does exist I have seen it! I drew all I could remember with all the madness around me. Right now I just want off this damned island and want to kill that vampire boy king if I get the chance!
Captain James Hook
Tunnels of DEATH

TABLE OF CONTENTS

Chapter 1

The Angel in the Green Hood

The cobbled streets of Dorchester were silent. The candlelit streets shone, a slick gloss on the brick alleyway paths. A mist of a fine rain had fallen minutes before, and the smell of cool dampness still floated in the air. In the back allies of the city, the streets were dark. Stray cats darted from the shadows. The south end of this quaint town was seedy at best. You locked your doors, as well as your windows, at night with the hope that intruders would think you had little value in your home.

Down one particularly dark and narrow street, a single, small candle in an empty tin box lit the front of the East Street Orphanage. The small building was nestled between a tailor shop and a deserted tavern with boarded up windows. The orphanages were very poor, and the little money given by the churches to feed and help the children was spent quickly or used by the greedy people running it. A quick, chilly breeze blew, rattling the orphanage sign hanging on the front door just a bit.

Inside the building, sleeping on a straw-filled mattress, lay the caregiver of these poor children. Annie Pluming, a large, older woman, sat up in her bed. She looked around the darkness of the small, black room. Her door was open; a small girl in tattered clothing stood frozen.

Annie was quite startled by the small figure in the darkness but had to address the child promptly to show her control. "Mary, what on earth are you doing up? You know the rules. Stay in the room with the others."

The little girl just pointed down the hall.

"What is it child?" Annie asked.

"The angel in the green hood, Mum. He came to the broken windows. He took Sam, Charlie, Ethan, and Paul."

Annie shot up from her bed and quickly ran past the little girl down to the room where the children slept. She entered quickly and scanned the room; it was filled with a dozen small beds, ripped blankets, stained pillows, and sheets. A half dozen children cowered in the corner, shivering like they had seen a ghost.

"Come now, get in your beds," she ordered, walking to the small window which was flung wide open.

One of the children from the corner stepped into the moonlit room. "But Mum, he took them. It's true, the stories of the green-hooded angel."

"Yes, yes, I know you all sneak out at night to run the streets. Now get in your beds. We will find them in the morning, or they will come back through the window when they grow tired," she answered.

The boy spoke up again. "No, Mum. He was here. He came in; he flew in the window and told us to gather around. He told us a story of an island where we could be family. He gave some of us candy as well."

"He was very funny; he made us laugh," another young girl offered.

Annie gave a look of disagreement and shook her finger. "I have heard enough of this. Now back to bed, all of you!"

The children crawled back into bed, tightening the sheets close to their bodies.

"There is no angel in the green hood who will take you away. Those are just stories from mischievous boys and girls who like to run away and play."

She walked to the window and peeked out. She looked down to the windowsill, noticing several gold and silver coins. She was quick to cover them up with one hand, sliding them off into the other.

"That should do quite nicely," she whispered, looking back into the shadows of the streets.

She turned and addressed the children one final time.

"Listen here, I'll have no more lies and stories. If you want a real family, you best learn how to make a bed and clean a house. Enough of the nonsense!"

She closed the window and locked it with a small, wooden bar that ran across it.

"Now get some rest, the lot of you." She left the room and looked down at the handful of coins. *This is more than last year.* She smiled. *Good for him, and good for me.* She went back to her room, placed the money in a small metal tin on her nightstand, and rolled into her bed.

The angel in the green hood was a rumor in many of the street orphanages, but most did not discuss it. The story was always the same: children were taken, beds were empty, and money was made. Tomorrow, she could tell the children that the boys were adopted, and they had a little more money to buy food, while she had much more money to buy wine. With four open beds, she would look as if she was doing her job finding parents, and she could bring in more children and money from the town. No one cared for these children, and a lie covered their losses. Annie rolled over and let out a sigh, falling into slumber with a satisfied grin.

In the mist-shrouded harbor, a wooden boat with only one small sail drifted away from the shoreline with a creak. There, inside the vessel, sat over a dozen boys with blankets wrapped tightly around them. Standing above them, a short, thin figure in brown stockings, a leather vest, and a green hood manned the rudder.

"Take us home!" he commanded as sparkles of light suddenly covered the small boat, and it slowly floated up from the water's currents into the air. It rose higher as the sparks grew stronger, flying off into the night sky as trails of small lights continued to fall into the water below from its thrust.

Chapter 2

WE ARE PIRATES!

Across the clunky wooden boardwalk, Captain Farrell tried his best to help his three men with the large, wooden chest. Two men in front and two, including the captain, behind. Captain Farrell was a tall man with a tight-fitting uniform and soft eyes; when tempered, his lips offered a smirk of arrogance. His men respected him because he was a better man than most.

They walked from the shipyard as sailors, soldiers, and merchants rummaged about the busy port. It was planned to be a quick delivery—supplies and gunpowder. In reality, it was a diversion; it was payroll for the Queen's Navy here in the Caribbean islands. Mixing it in with furniture, crates, and barrels was a creative tactic the Navy used from time to time to make sure their men got their wages so far from home.

Captain Farrell saw a commotion on the docks as several men began to fight. A hulking, black-skinned man with a shaved head and a Spaniard with a red headband were mixing it up in the main courtyard near the docks. The problem was that this was Captain Farrell's path. He let out a sigh.

"We will take the round-about way," he ordered. "Avoid any chance of thievery."

He and his soldiers walked down the dock a few yards and cut down a dirt road behind several of the massive, wooden, mud-baked brick buildings that outlined the harbor.

They followed the back alley road nearly thirty feet to a small intersection when two men stepped from a building, their pistols ready. Rags covered the lower part of their faces. Bandits. Farrell shook his head as one of the men, wearing all black with a feathered cap, stood behind him. The man in black placed his hands on his hips with confidence and shouted.

"Stand and deliver, or the devil may take you!"

Farrell gritted his teeth, "Do as he says."

Farrell turned to face the man in black whose cocky voice gave him away.

"You're not going to get away with this, James," he said.

"Just tell them James 'The Horror' Hook stole the payroll from you. Besides Farrell, I'm not robbing you. I'm robbing the queen."

"You call yourself 'The Horror?' You're a pirate; you don't get to name yourself," Farrell added.

James stepped up to Captain Farrell, leaned in, and pulled down his mask.

"Come on, not in front of my men," he said softly.

"Your men? What about my men?" Farrell grunted, his teeth grinding.

"Fine. Whatever. Just open the trunk."

Farrell opened the trunk with a small iron key. James walked over, pulling his flintlock pistol.

"See, that's how we do it." He motioned Farrell away with his hand and looked inside. Inside were maps, a canister of gunpowder, some candles, and a small envelope.

"Where's the payroll?" James asked.

"Still on the damn boat. See, we knew ilk like you, or other hooligans, might try to rob us, so we were bringing it in with some other items. Only an ex-navy man like yourself would know such a tactic. We have lots to unload: chairs, tables, even a bedroom set. Really James, if you're going to be a blood-thirsty, killer pirate, you have to do more. In fact, if you let us go and help us unload, I will pay each of you a half day's wages and lunch."

James scratched his head, still a bit confused. "That's not what we are; we're pirates, not movers. There has to be something."

He took the envelope from the chest and opened it. There were several gold coins and a letter. He opened it quickly and began to read.

"To the commonwealth of the port authority, use this small amount of coin to hire more local security in case of pirates... Blah, blah, blah... in her service, Admiral Byrd. This proves it; we're pirates, and they know all about James Hook!"

"It doesn't mention *your* name, James; it could be any pirate actually," Farrell grinned.

"If this is about that night with the admiral's wife, I thought she was his personal cabin cleaner! She looked so young. She lied to me."

From one of the alleyways, the hulking black fighter appeared rubbing his shoulder while the Spaniard followed behind holding his shoulder.

"What did we get? Was the fight long enough?" the Spaniard asked.

Farrell shook his head at James.

"Really? That was your diversion to get us in the alley?"

"Well, it got you where I wanted you, didn't it?" James shot back. "Okay, let's tie them up and just go. It's not the score we wanted, but it's enough to have a fun week away from this place."

The other two men began to tie up Farrell and his men.

"James, you're not going to get away with this," Farrell warned. "I am not getting in trouble because of some pathetic, thief-wannabe-pirate. Do you even have a ship? That last one was the size of a raft. Last chance. Help us unload, and we forget this ever happened."

"Look, Wayne, oh I'm sorry, *Captain Farrell*, I am doing the best with what I got. Don't worry about me or my men or lunch; go back to kissing the queen's royal backside."

The Spaniard put a gag over Farrell's mouth and moved him into a corner. After the men were tied tightly to a wooden barrel, the crew of thieves began to leave the alleyway.

"Just remember who robbed the queen this day: James 'The Horror' Hook!" James said proudly.

Farrell rolled his eyes.

The men strutted proudly until out of sight of the soldiers, then they ran like hell itself was at their heels. They merged into the traffic on the port and made their way to a small rowboat tied to a walkway. They all climbed into the boat, packed in like sardines in a can, and the hulking black warrior began to row.

The Spaniard was the first to speak. "So, there was no payroll?"

"Yes, just not with them," James said. "It was still on the ship."

"So ... do we get paid?" the hulking black man asked.

"Yes, Black Jack, just not as much," James said.

"Do we..." the Spaniard continued.

"Hey, hey, enough with the questions. We got some money; we just need a stronger plan. Plus, people will know James Hook and his men are not to be messed with."

"I don't think they will think that," the Spaniard said.

"Well, they will once we do a bigger job and really make some noise."

"Will that captain really hunt you down? How did you know him?" asked a pirate with red hair and thick mustache.

"Parry, if you must know, we were both on the same ship for years in the Navy. Let's not talk about it. He went his way; I chose mine. It's nothing but bad memories. We got some money, we did our pirating thing, so let's celebrate!" James said.

They continued out into the ocean up to a small boat with one large mast and enough room for a dozen men.

"Look, we're almost home, and *that*, gentleman, is worth all the money in the world. There she is: our home, the proud ship, our ship, and our home, *The Conqueror*. She is all ours. No one can boss us around or tell us how to live. We can be free!" James exclaimed.

"Free and hungry," mumbled Black Jack.

The men laughed.

"But still free," James smiled. "Besides, you eat for three grown men."

The big man rubbed his belly with a smile. "She said she is empty."

The rowboat pulled up alongside the small ship, and ropes were lowered down to it. The men began to climb aboard.

One man, with thinning hair who was wearing a pair of glasses, paced impatiently on the deck. He wore all black, a faded, white priest collar could barely be seen. When James stepped aboard, the man walked over quickly.

"How was it? Did you have to kill anyone? Did you get the money?"

James handed the man several small coins before storming off. "Not now, Father Bob. I will be in my captain's chambers; do not disturb me for anything."

From below deck, two men appeared, one tall and slender as a weed and the other the complete opposite, short, thick with a shaggy face.

"Did the fight work, Captain?" asked the short one.

"Not now, Morgan," James snapped.

The taller one asked, "So we don't eat again tonight?"

"No, Drake, we will eat. I have some coin, at least enough for soup and bread. Maybe an ale or two if we go for it watered down at The Crow's Nest Tavern."

"Oh, The Crow's Nest is vile; that waitress spits in my stew every time!" Morgan complained.

"That's because you never compliment her good features," Drake teased.

"She doesn't have any! Even her backside is ten miles of flat dirt road!"

"No, she has a quite nice, round backside if you like a little curve in the road!"

"Bah!" Morgan argued. "She's a horrible girl."

"Well, she's sweet on me," Drake replied.

"She's not; she's sweet on everyone!" Morgan added.

"Enough, you two! It's like listening to an old married couple argue," James murmured.

James handed Father Bob a small handful of coins. The man looked at the coins and back at Captain Hook who was near the steps leading to his cabin below.

"Where do we set sail, Captain?" Father Bob asked.

"Hell if I care, just head west back to The Cove. Maybe a good night of drinking is all we can do." He then disappeared down into the ship.

Chapter 3

Welcome to Your New Home

The cave entrance was ominous as the small pack of young boys marched onward. It looked like the mouth of a skull; large stones in the shape of jagged teeth hung near the entrance. The darkness slowed the boys, but the small man in the green hood persisted. With talk of food and fun, he pushed them deeper into the cave. He lifted a large metal birdcage, and it sparkled and gave light. Inside the cage, a small faint form of a woman with tiny wings fluttered inside. The caravan made its way past several winding tunnels lit with torches.

"Stop here!" commanded the angel in the green hood. The boys complied. He walked to the front of the line and began to address the young boys.

"You are home. You can join us, live, eat, and play forever. You will never need a mother or father. No one will tell you to clean or work again. It's up to you to join us. Stay close to me."

They walked to a large entranceway and stood in front of a great room. Deeper in the great cave was filled with boys. They were all healthy and smiling. Tables of food were in abundance and the boys' clothing was clean. The orphans stood with eyes beaming and mouths open as dozens of boys looked up to them. The man in the green hood set the cage down, lowering his hood to reveal himself to the crowd below. His face was boyish, with blonde hair and deep, green eyes. He smiled, but when he did, large fangs emerged from his thin lips.

"He's home!" a young boy squealed.

The chant began.

"Peter! Peter! Peter!" It echoed down the corridors in the cave as if a king had returned from a mighty hunt.

Peter turned to the new orphan boys. "Now, go! Eat to your heart's content, play with the others, and have fun. We want you to join us. We will give you the chance to be in our family in a few days. So be off, play, dance, and sing! There are no rules but mine, and I command you to be boys forever!"

Peter pointed the boys to a trail of stairs leading to a great room. The boys, now driven by hunger, walked quickly to the tables to eat bread, cookies, and meats, all on fine China with silver forks.

Peter looked over the party with a great smile. He picked up the small metal cage. "See how they love me, Belle? See how I am their true friend?"

The fairy said nothing. She turned her head, refusing to watch the party.

"Oh, come now, Belle. Let's not be like that. You know this is how it's done."

The fairy looked up to Peter, anger brimming in her eyes.

"No, Peter, this is not how it was done; it's not how it should ever be done."

Peter shook the cage quickly and angrily. The fairy tried to get to her feet but collapsed into the bars of the cage. "Why do you challenge me, Belle? Do not make me be mean to you."

Inside the cage, the small fairy was curled into a ball in the corner. She trembled. "I know. I'm sorry. It's my fault."

"Sometimes I think you're not my friend. I just want us to be friends like we were. Remember how we were good friends just a few years ago?" Peter said.

The fairy stood up and began to watch the boys' party carry on; they threw food, chased one another, and laughed. She looked at Peter. He was still the sweet boy, the one who played games and made her laugh. He was still Peter; maybe he was just having a bad day.

"It's nice to see them play," Belle said, holding her elbow that bled just a little.

"Yes, it's good," Peter said, walking down the steps to the boisterous party below.

Chapter 4

YOUR LEGEND GROWS

The Cove. A place to escape from all your worries and woes, whether you are a pirate, a soldier, a sailor, or just needing a good night of forgetting the past. The Cove was a small, village port hidden away on an island not found on anyone's maps. It was only through word of mouth that a person found this place. It had several docks and a dozen buildings; most were taverns, but people could find goods, black market items, and time with a female companion if you were in need.

There was a code of The Cove: Everyone gets along, and no one sells another out—unless they really have it coming.

The Cove took care of its own. The few soldiers who were allowed, many of those in Queen's Navy, had drunk their way out of a bad day alongside pirates and others they may have been chasing after just weeks before. The Cove was a playground for the adventurer, and when someone used their muscle to move on someone, The Cove found a way to make them disappear.

There were fights, there were murders, there were thefts, but no one ever tried to take a man's ship or use this location as a vantage point to take out an enemy. It was neutral ground for pleasure and business. It survived this way because people, both good and bad, accepted the opportunity to all enjoy a warm meal, good drink, and get what they needed at a lower cost than ports ran by the Queen's Navy.

James and his small band of pirates walked the boardwalk, eager to forget yesterday's weak attempt at piracy. There was always new information and gossip here on The Cove. Spending time in a tavern was always fun, and it was almost productive to relax and regroup.

"Shall we visit The Salty Dog, Captain?" Father Bob asked.

"No, not today. I am thinking we hit The Dead Reef," Hook said.

His men stopped walking as he strolled ahead. Realizing he was alone, Hook turned around.

"What's wrong with The Dead Reef? It's better than The Crow's Nest, right?" he asked.

"They don't like us, and it's where the most violent, blood-thirsty pirates go," the Spaniard said.

"Exactly, so we need to learn from them, be around them. They may share secrets or know some great opportunities," replied Hook.

"Or they may beat us and force us out at gunpoint again," Father Bob said.

"That was a misunderstanding ... and several months ago. Plus, we have taken from the Queen's Navy several times. I am sure they will accept us with open arms," Hook said convincingly.

Five minutes later the men stood in the doorway of the seedy tavern. They stood just inches from the bar. The barkeeper had a scar on his cheek, thinning hair, and his hands looked like they were made of stone. He looked the group over.

"Get out," he ordered.

"We have money," James announced. "We can pay." He held up a gold coin.

The bartender looked around at his other customers, a dark lot of pirates from all parts of the seven seas. Many ignored the small group, talking and drinking amongst themselves. Hook slid two silver coins onto the bar. The bartender shook his head but pulled two bottles from under the bar.

"One drink, then you and the others leave. I can't have James 'The Hair Maiden' Hook bringing down our establishment."

"Hair Maiden?" James asked.

"Have your drink and go. I only give charity today because it's my birthday, so I'm in good spirits," the bartender said.

Father Bob took James by the arm and pulled him back as Black Jack, Morgan, the Spaniard, and Drake found a table in the corner.

"Hair Maiden?" James muttered. "How are people to respect me as a pirate if they don't understand my name, or at least try the name I've given myself?" James sank down on a wooden stool.

"Hey, at least they have given you a name," Father Bob said. "That's something." He ran his hand over his balding head. "At least you have fine hair."

Hook looked around the dimly lit tavern; the men here had dark, angry, soulless eyes. He looked back to his small group of men. They had tired eyes, but life was still in them. Maybe he was wrong about being such a man.

Black Jack looked down at James. "He keeps looking at you," he grunted.

"Who?" James asked.

"The Shark, Captain Huxley."

Captain Huxley was a notorious pirate with a crew of over fifty men and three ships. Huxley had made the English fleet and some French ships flee from merely seeing his red and black flag flying high in the air. His reputation was as dark as the flags he sailed under.

James slowly looked over his shoulder, trying to appear nonchalant. He made the mistake of making eye contact with The Shark and froze.

Captain Huxley was tall and lean with a full salt-and-pepper beard set in beads. He wore all black with small patches of leather armor attached to his pants and vest. He always looked like he was going into battle. He gestured, and the men at his table dispersed to the bar. He signaled to Hook.

"He wants me to join him," James said, his voice squeaking a bit.

"Well, do not keep him, or he may run us all through with his saber," Father Bob said. "I told you this was a bad idea."

Hook swallowed hard as he stood up, adjusting his white shirt and walking over to the pirate's table. Captain Huxley pointed to the seat, and James sat quickly. Captain Huxley looked him over for several seconds. James couldn't make eye contact but looked over The Shark's shoulder and cleared his throat.

Captain Huxley spoke, "You are not a pirate. You don't belong in my tavern."

"I am a pirate. I have stolen from the Queen's Navy nearly six times now," Hook objected.

"Indeed, your actions are well known. Stealing crumbs off the floor before the dogs can lap them up. How many men have you killed?" Huxley asked.

"I have killed men. I believe nearly a dozen, but some may have lived. There was one; I think he died. At least he yelled a lot after I stabbed him. In the Navy, I killed several, but that was before I became a pirate, so I don't like to brag about those," James noted, still not looking at Huxley.

"I killed eight yesterday before noon. You are not a pirate. You need to look for something else; open a tailor shop, maybe work the port, or as a fisherman. You have a boat; put nets on it and fish. You claiming to be a pirate and stealing from the queen, bringing more soldiers around, only makes us real pirates look foolish."

"Why can't I say that I am a pirate? I know what I like to do," James pouted.

"Do you like killing men?" Huxley asked.

"Well, no. It's out of self-preservation," Hook said.

"Just because you rob a few of the queen's boats, have a crew, a black flag, and come to The Cove to drink, doesn't make you a pirate. You, sir, are an adventurer, and there's nothing wrong with that. But to continue this charade of being a pirate; everyone on the island knows your failings, your lack of piracy, and your small ship and crew of misfits." Captain Huxley let out a sigh. "I have killed over 100 men. I have treasure buried throughout the islands. I have made the third-most powerful man in her Royal Navy stand on one leg and wet himself in front of his crew before paying me to leave. *I* am a pirate. *You* are not. I think it'd be better for you and your men to do something else. You're embarrassing the rest of us."

"I'm doing my best," James said.

"Look, I could use your friend there, the big, dark-skinned brute. He would be perfect for my third ship, and I can pay him well."

"You're trying to hire off my men?" James asked.

"Some of them are good. The tall fellow may be good for working the ropes, long limbs, a bit skinny though. I lost five men last week to disease and to an ambush. Sure, they are rough around the edges, but I can polish them up. They can be real pirates," Captain Huxley said.

Hook looked over to his men as they drank. They were good, loyal men. "I have to think about it; they are good men. Maybe if you showed me how to be a better pirate?"

Captain Huxley laughed, "I am not a teacher! You learn from experience, from hunger, by passion, by fear! It's failures and struggles that make us what we are, not a fancy coat and hat and some gold taken by a raid. Being a pirate is in the blood. It's the love of the hunt, the quest for treasure, the thought of revenge and taking it. It's the thought of being your own man."

"I'm my own man, and I'm a pirate," James stood up. "Those men are my crew, and that small ship is ours as well. I don't care what people say or think of it. It makes us happy once in a while. No one is going to change my mind on this matter."

Several patrons slowed their drinking, watching as James "The Hair Maiden" Hook addressed one of the most feared men on The Cove.

"Then I guess I will see you out there on the waves of the ocean," Captain Huxley smiled.

Hook stood up straighter now and felt a bit more at ease. He started to walk away when Captain Huxley forcefully grabbed his arm and looked up at him.

"Hook, if you want to be a legendary pirate, where men fear your name, if you want to be what we are, you may go to a dark place, find a fire in you that makes you hate the world and everything in it. You have to go where you are lost and feel like you can never return. You may lose your sanity and humanity at the same time. Fear is not respect, my young friend; it's only fear. Remember that. A good crew, good friends, and the open sea air, that's freedom. My offer for those men of yours will be gone by next nightfall. Think about what is best for them; that's a real leader."

Hook let out a sigh. They were words of wisdom with a back-handed slap of reality. His tone had changed; James had entertained him for a moment.

"Now go and leave my bar. I hope you make the right decision."

James turned and walked past his men. They got up from their corner booth and followed him out the tavern door.

Outside, the small band of pirates looked around the docks.

"At least he didn't kill you," Father Bob said.

James let out a sigh, "Yeah."

Black Jack grabbed his shoulder. "Come now, Captain. We have much to explore and do." The big man smiled as broad as his shoulders.

They pushed James forward, taunting him.

"Pirates drink and pirates conquer, so let's go do it," the Spaniard said.
"Fine, let's go conquer," James said, smiling.
His men let out a small cheer, and they walked down the dock.

Chapter 5

THE KISS OF LIFE

Peter was alone. He walked along the beach as the moon hung low in the sky. The water pushed up the sand with the pull of the tide. He whistled as he walked, picking up stones and tossing them into the water. He stopped near a small cluster of rocks. To the average person, it was just a cluster of large stones sitting on the beach, but to Peter it was more, much more. His mind was sent back.

Memories of the rocks, the beach, the cold ocean spraying its foam across his feeble, dying body. It was here he was given the kiss of life. He was just a boy, 15 years old. The ship went down quickly in the storm, though it tried to get to the island.

Peter did not remember much of his mother and his father. So many years had fogged his once warm memories. He remembered the storm, the waves, the lightening, the ship going down, and the horror as men gave their souls to the sea. He remembered the cold ocean and waking up near those rocks, bleeding and dying.

Peter walked a few steps closer to the cluster of rocks, looking back to the endless dark waters. The ocean, a giver and taker of life itself. He let out a quick sigh, remembering a shadow of a man on the beach as he lay dying years ago. The shadow approached him, said nothing, and bit him on the neck. The smell of the man would always linger in his mind; his muttering was like that of one of his father's night security.

Maybe his father knew and held the man's dark secret, but that went down with him on the ship. After the man fed on him, Peter saw him stagger away, cursing under his breath, his ragged, torn clothing soaked from the sea. Perhaps Peter was not the only one to escape the water's death grip that stormy night. He couldn't remember much more in his dying state. Seeing the man's pale-white skin, Peter considered briefly that maybe he was aboard his father's ship, perhaps an Irishman his father hired out of pity; it made little concern now. The man was gone, and Peter was dying. Peter recounted feeling his neck, the burning of the bite, and falling fast asleep on that beach nearly 130 years ago.

He sat down next to the large, jagged rocks, running his left hand over one of them. It was cold and wet. This place was his new birth, his new life. He remembered how alone he was when he woke on the island and how alone he was for several months until those creatures of magic on the island accepted him, whether by pity or by luck.

Things were better now; he has friends and his new family. His old family was lost in the shipwreck long ago. Very few memories of his first family remain; it feels so far removed. He looked down at his father's ring attached to his thumb. His fingers were still too thin for it to fit. He remembered when his father gave it to him at breakfast before they left the harbor. His mother was not happy about the gift; she said he was too young to wear such a symbol and carry the name. She had hoped to give him the ring on his 16th birthday, but his father chose not to wait. They never saw his 16th birthday or his 50th or his 100th.

He adjusted the ring on his thumb. It was silver with a ruby and on the left side, his family seal. He straightened up, laughing a bit as he watched the sea.

"You won't kill me again," he whispered, "and I will never be alone."

He left the pile of rocks and began to walk the beach again.

After several minutes, he came to a curve in the island. The shoreline turned and caved inward, opening to a cove. There, in the lagoon, a dozen large ships rested below the water. Some lay twisted on their sides, others stuck in the sand. Their rotting, large masts sticking up towards the sky. Once majestic and powerful, these ships now lay battered and broken, a graveyard in the shallow lagoon. The wind blew a cold breeze, and Peter could smell the salty air mixed with rotting wood. He quickened his pace to the ship graveyard and walked out on a boardwalk which led to the wooden monstrosities. He stood at the end of the pier.

He let out a sharp whistle. There was a quick sound of splashing, like a large fish, followed by much more, like a school of fish. There was something in the water. Then came the sound of laughter, splashing, and women giggling. Peter looked into the darkness of the water through the busted ships and saw them. They were beautiful. They shot up from the water, long-haired beauties, their wet hair glistening in the moonlight. The women splashed and danced in the water as their long fish-like tails pushed them quickly back and forth.

"Ladies, ladies," Peter inquired, "is Niviene with you, or is she out dragging sailors to their doom?"

"Oh, you make it sound so horrible, Peter," came a sweet, cold voice.

Peter smiled, turning to see her. Niviene was the ruler of the ocean creatures. Rich, red hair, large breasts, and milky-white skin. Her lips were full and soft. She looked down at Peter as she sat, resting on a sunken deck, her arms folded on the side of a ship.

"I take it you bring good news?" she purred.

"Yes, I am expecting guests in the next few weeks, so I need you and your girls not to bring their ship into the harbor."

"What ship? We do have an agreement to work together, but the mermaids need to eat too," she said.

"I know, and you're all such lovely hosts. This ship will be a Navy vessel. I have a man on the inside, so I can get rifles, gunpowder, and supplies. We can make our island stronger."

"I thought we did not need or care about such things. I thought you just wanted to play. Your quest sounds like that of a man, not a boy," she warned.

"Very true, but how long do you think we can hold this place as men explore and grow? There is talk of growing the colonies. With that will come more ships, more men, more opportunity, and we need to think ahead of such foul men," Peter remarked.

"Peter, you imp, you're actually very cunning for a boy," she giggled.

"I want what's best for the island. So, if you could keep away from sinking and devouring any ships that come close in the next ten days, I will make it worth your while," Peter said.

"We have always kept our partnership, Peter. You protect us from the hunters and their nets, and we protect you as well," she replied.

"I would feel better if you and your friends in the water on the east side of the island do not make yourself seen. It is best to keep hidden below the ships in case of treachery," Peter said.

"Yes, indeed. If they try to go against their deal with you, we will be ready to feast on their bones," she replied.

Peter clapped his hands, "Excellent! Now, I just need to get back to the cave before dawn."

"You came all this way and will not swim with us?" she asked. "We sank a small ship about 100 yards north and have not cleaned it or brought in its cargo."

"Well..." Peter smiled.

The women began to chant to him.

"Come on, Peter. Come swim with us. It's been a while since we played," Niviene said. "How many humans can claim to swim with mermaids?"

"I am not human, not anymore. Let's see what you ladies have done," Peter said, beginning to unbutton his vest.

The mermaids began to cheer as Peter removed most of his clothing and dove into the water. With the women laughing and giggling, Niviene swam quickly from the boat to him. They both swam in place as the women encircled them.

"Do you want to race?" Peter asked.

"You still have yet to beat me, boy," she said. "No human or magical sea creature has yet to beat me."

"You cheat," Peter said.

"I do not cheat," she said, smiling.

"Quickly, behind you, a net!" Peter cried.

She turned to look, but there was nothing. She turned back, seeing Peter off like a cannon ball; he was nearly 10 yards away, swimming and cutting through the water like a razor.

"Peter!" she cried, diving down into the water. The others followed as the vampire-boy pushed hard to the sunken vessel. Peter was only yards away, and he looked over his shoulder as Niviene and the others closed fast. He laughed and kicked again.

He could see the boat on the ocean floor. It was a newer ship with new paint and a fine mast sitting like a corpse on the sand as fish swam around it. Peter let up for one second to admire the ship as Niviene and the others swam past him, reaching the boat.

Niviene shook a finger at him as she touched the boat with her other hand. Peter laughed. The mermaids swam around the ship, disappearing into its hull. Minutes later, they emerged dragging trunks, boxes, and dead bodies of its crew from their watery grave. One of the mermaids swam to Peter and handed him a small chest. He opened it to reveal silver forks, knives, and spoons. He closed it and put it under his arm. Niviene pointed back to the lagoon, and the group all swam back, their rewards in hand.

Peter was the last to reach the shoreline as the mermaids dragged their earnings to the harbor. Some placed new necklaces on one another, others began to show off clothing, and others took the corpses of the sailors and stacked them in a sunken ship for eating later. Peter walked back on the shore with his new silverware.

"You will never beat me in the water, Peter," Niviene said. "Even with your powers."

"True, but you will never outrun me on the beach," he shot back.

"Who would want to run, when they can swim?" she said back. "Besides, I can walk and run."

She swam to the shoreline and splashed her silver and blue tail. Suddenly, the tail split, forming long, fair legs. She stood up like a statue and walked several paces on the beach, her streaming red hair covering her pale, naked body.

Peter began to put his clothing back on as the mermaids continued to play in the lagoon.

"Do you think it's wise to bring men here?" Niviene asked. "We try so hard to keep them away. This island is one of the last places of magic. Here, we trust so few humans. The fact that you are still here after all these decades..."

"It may not be for long, Niviene. They may visit and leave. I do not want them here, but I need their help. Why do you think they are coming to my side of the island? If the others on the island saw or even heard of this exchange, they may run me and my merry group off. Change must come. Having more modern weapons of war for protection can be good for all of us."

"Just be cautious, Peter; you know how treacherous they can be," she said, placing a bracelet on her wrist and admiring it in the moonlight.

"I know. If I feel wary of it, I will kill them all, and we will all feast like kings," Peter said.

He slid his black boots back on his feet.

"Have you spoke with Wolf Lilly?" Niviene asked.

Peter paused. Old memories flashed in his mind. "You mean Queen Wolf Lilly? It has been several years; there's no need. The treaty with your kind and her people is still strong, is it not?"

"She is not my queen. I only look out for the water creatures now. She and I had our differences even before you arrived. You know that Wolf Lilly has no tolerance for dark magic like the Voodoo priestess you saved or humans on our island. I believe that is the cause of this friction between you."

"And how do you feel of her dark magic?" Peter asked.

"I do not fear her. Her power is on humans, not us true gods and ancient creatures. I do not wish her here, however. Remember, it was after her arrival that the elves left for a new land? Oh, I miss them!" she exclaimed.

"Bah, elves! Haughty, arrogant race of creatures to me. They never accepted me," Peter fumed.

"You're a feeder of blood, Peter. You're not human. In some groups, you are a monster."

"Yes, and you and the other sirens eat humans."

"They are mermaids, not sirens. Others love to call us that to get under our skin. I do not eat the flesh of man. I am an ancient. Not one of the fallen ones like the others who swim these waters. When her slave ship crashed into the rocks and she somehow made it to the beach, it was a dark day for our island."

"I could not let her die," Peter said.

"I know. Sometimes your heart is stronger than your head. I understand that you may have felt the same when your family came to this island, crashing in the harbor as well. To see a life struggling, I know why you saved her," she said.

"There was no one else on the ship; they had all drowned. She was clinging to rocks, calling on her gods to save her. I couldn't do nothing," Peter said.

Niviene let out a sigh. "We did not know her to be a woman of such dark magic, this Voodoo power. She has gotten stronger every year. She takes the magic of the darkness, of the dead from the other side. I fear it is changing our island. I know her being here has changed you and relationships with others."

Peter stretched for a second, took a deep breath, and let out a sigh. He looked out at the water.

"I know what you're going to ask, and the answer is still no," she said.

"If I had the sword, I could change the world of man," Peter boasted.

"I gave the sword to a boy-king centuries ago. Arthur and his band of men, as great as they were, still brought darkness and war. I thought so much of him, Merlin did as well, but eventually, power ruins the best of men."

"But you still have the sword?" Peter questioned.

She laughed and shook her head. "I cannot give such a created weapon to the hands of mankind again. The sons and daughters of Adam truly are not worthy of our created gifts. I am afraid it is lost to the waters of the deep."

Peter knew she was lying; she still had the weapon. He adjusted his collar and gave a simple smile. "Such stories of power, legends of ancient gods and magic."

"You have seen the magic on this island. Why would you doubt it?" she said.

"The time of magic is fading, and as man grows in members, he will put it out. They will stop worshiping gods. Eventually, mankind will become his own god," Peter said.

"If that happens, we will flood the earth again and start over, like the creator did eons ago. Why he even created mankind..." she replied.

"Maybe he created us because your kind rebelled against him," Peter replied.

"You boy, have quite an imagination," she said.

"I am not a boy. Do not let my charming boyish looks fool you, Lady of the Lake," Peter reminded her.

"Lady of the Lake sounds so old," she said.

"Well, you are quite old, though your body and face show no signs of it," Peter remarked.

"Ah, charming until the end," she shot back.

"I must return to my throne room; dawn will approach quickly. I will send word in a few days of the military ship. Lots of planning and less time to play for now," Peter said.

Peter waved goodbye and picked up his box of silverware as the mermaids cheered and waved to him.

Chapter 6

When a Man Loves a Woman

James and his crew stood outside the tavern called The Lucky Pelican. It was much larger than most on the island. It had two large, teal, wooden swinging doors and a bar big enough to serve over fifty men if need be. But it was not the drinking that interested Hook, it was one of the owners of the establishment.

"I doubt she remembers you," Drake said.

"Then I will remind her," James added.

"James, she only spends time with pirates, and I mean really well-known pirates," the Spaniard said.

"I told you, we spent several days and nights together a couple years ago, and even last month, we had lunch," James said confidently.

"Lunch? We can have lunch," said Black Jack. "That does not mean we love you or want to do business with you," the big man joked.

"I will be a few hours. Head back to the ship or wander about; I don't care. I will see you all tonight."

James turned and left his men, walking through the swinging double doors.

"Poor man, smitten with a memory," Father Bob mumbled as he and the men left the front of the tavern to see what mischief they could find on the island.

Inside the tavern, music played and women marched trays of ale and dark glass bottles throughout the crowded bar. It was only a Wednesday, but it was filled with people bumping into one another. Instead of anger and dirty looks, people laughed, and the ladies who worked the floor smiled and made everyone feel special. James made his way to the bar and forced his way between several rough-looking pirates. They moved to be polite. He turned around, scanning the room of controlled chaos. She had to be here; she would see him.

Molly was a statuesque woman, graceful, beautiful, and always with a blade strapped to her person. She walked down the wooden steps to the main floor of the tavern. She had sandy brown hair, full and thick, always neat, always perfect. Men stopped talking mid-sentence when she walked by their tables. She was not one to trifle with. Though men wanted to be near her, they knew they could not. She was untouchable to most, and many tried to convince her their time was more valuable than her own.

Not many women controlled their own destiny, but Molly did. It was her girls who served the drinks and spent quality time with the men in port. She was a Madam and an entrepreneur. She kept her mind on business, and business was always good. If you needed anything relationship-wise, Molly could arrange it for a price. She was known to have an ear to listen to what most men called "womanly problems."

She stepped from the wooden staircase and saw James. Her face quickly went from work to a smile, and he smiled back. He walked up like a prince to a princess, feeling as if they were the only ones in the tavern as he looked into her eyes.

"Molly, you look beautiful."

"Why thank you, James. Do you have the money you owe me?"

"Well, no, but I think I will very soon," James replied.

"Oh, James, you really need to get yourself organized. Come upstairs to my office so we can chat a bit, away from prying eyes," Molly insisted.

James followed her back up the steps, away from the loud noise below. He walked with her past a short hallway to a door; they stepped inside.

"I think I have some of the money, I just robbed the queen's..." James began.

Molly slammed the door closed behind them and pushed him against it. She leaned in quickly and began a long kiss. James was surprised, but he did not fight it.

When she did break away for the moment, she smiled, looking into his green eyes.

"We can discuss business later. I have so little time and have to deal with such scoundrels here every day." She kissed him quickly once again.

"Do you want to hear about my last raid?" James asked, her lips pressed against his.

"No, if you continue to talk, then we shall go to my desk and look at my books. Or you can keep your mouth shut and enjoy our time together," she said sternly.

"I just thought..."

"Do not think, James. It does not suit you. You are a good man, and right now I need a good man, not some loud, braggart, dangerous killer," she explained.

He thought about this as her lips grazed his shaggy jaw. Was he not dangerous? He was a pirate. What did she mean by that? Her hands were as focused as her lips as she caressed his shoulders and chest.

"I am dangerous," he said aloud, immediately realizing his mistake.

She stopped and regained her composure.

"James, you have two choices. Choose wisely. If you continue to talk, I will head to my desk, and we will look at your tab and the interest, or you can enjoy this moment with me in my chambers behind my desk."

Hook leaned over and saw a small door behind the office. Inside were pillows, blankets, furs, and a firm bed. He looked down at Molly without saying a word; his grin said what he was thinking.

She grabbed his jaw with one firm hand.

"Good boy," she said, taking his hand as she led him past the desk.

Chapter 7

One of Us

The young boys had spent nearly a week on the island with no bedtime and no rules. They feasted on anything their hearts yearned for: meats, fruits, cookies, and pies. Every night, there was a grand party in the cave with other "lost" boys. Tonight though, they found even grander splendor with chests of gold and jewels, live music, and twice as much food as before. Tonight was a grand celebration. There were whispers of initiations and excitement. New friends were going to be joining them. Some boys looked around in anticipation while others sat around the long banquet tables laughing and talking; many had been here before.

Peter stood on a large chest watching the fanfare. In his hand was the small iron birdcage. Belle tried her best to smile.

"It will be fine, Belle; they will learn. After tonight, they will be one of us," he said, a dull look on his face.

"I don't know why you make me come to the ceremony. I hate it," she said.

"Fine, next time I will leave you back in your cave and blow out the candles, so you can sit in the dark," he said coldly. "Now, help me fly."

Belle rubbed her hands together and pushed a wave of gold and silver dust into the air. It enveloped the young vampire as he laughed.

He placed the cage on the top of the great chest and jumped high in the air. He floated and spun as the boys at the table watched and cheered. He darted around the room, zig-zigging and doing loops, smiling and laughing, and pointing at the boys. He flew back to the chest and landed on his two feet as the dozens of boys laughed and clapped. He took a bow and raised his hand to bring the crowd down a bit from their hysterics.

"Yes, yes, thank you all! My friends, my brothers, today we celebrate the right to join us. You lucky new visitors can enjoy the splendor of our island."

More clapping and screaming arose from the great room.

"Yes, indeed, but you must complete the ritual, the kiss of life."

Many of the lost boys began the chant, "Kiss of life... kiss of life..."

"Trust them, my new friends, trust me. We are your brothers, your friends. Join us tonight and have fun forever!" he shouted.

The boys began to chant once again.

"Now, I know it's a bit different living here on the island with no rules."

The boys yelled, "Rules? Boooo!"

"We are family and have only one rule: That you join us tonight," Peter said once again. "Who will come and take the pledge first?"

A young man about 12 years old ran up quickly and stood next to Peter.

"I will, Peter!" he shouted.

"Ah, see this brave boy is ready to live forever. If you are new to the island, please look at his example. Look at his bravery to join us. Come, all of you new boys; come up here, so we can get a look at you."

One by one, the children made their way to the front of the dining hall until over a dozen boys stood before Peter. The other boys began to chant once again.

Peter bent down and looked into the young man's eyes.

"What is your name, son?" Peter asked.

"Charlie," the young man replied.

"Charlie, you are brave and wise. Now what I have to do will hurt but not for long, like a bee sting. Be brave, okay?"

"Will it be fast?" he asked.

"Indeed, you will feel it quickly, and then it will be done."

"Do what must be done then, Peter, for I wish to be here forever!"

"That's a smart lad," Peter replied, smiling and revealing his fangs.

Peter leaned in quickly as the chanting grew louder. In a quick move, Peter bit down into the young man's neck. Charlie let out a quick scream as the pain burned into his neck. His eyes fluttered, and he fought just briefly. The other boys stepped back, horrified. Peter fed quickly and wiped the blood from his mouth and from Charlie's neck. Charlie staggered back as two lost boys grabbed his frail body and helped him up.

Peter could still taste the fresh, warm, youthful blood in the back of his throat. It was pleasure, a quenching of hunger. Most vampires get to enjoy such a snack, but he could not. He had much more to do. He turned to the tables, and they spun slightly as he tried shaking off the effects of the blood.

"Another one has joined us. Welcome him to our family!" Peter cried out.

Charlie staggered to a table in a state of confusion and sat down, not sure what had happened. Many of the boys rubbed his head and shook his hand.

"Who is next?" Peter asked.

None of the boys stepped forward. One small boy shook and trembled as a puddle formed by his worn leather shoes.

"Now, now, my friends, it's not going to hurt much; let's not be bashful now."

A boy with red hair and freckles stepped up, his hands trembling.

"Ah, good boy," Peter said.

"Will I get to play forever like you, Peter?"

"Yes. You will run and eat and help us make the island fun forever," Peter replied.

"You have been more of a father and friend than anyone back home," the small boy said.

"This is your home now. Forget the beatings, the cold nights, the horrible orphanages, the dark streets."

The boy smiled, walked up, and took Peter's hand. Peter smiled, then leaned in and bit down hard on the young boy's neck. He screamed just like Charlie, and the boys stepped back again. Peter released him to several boys who led him back to the table once again.

Peter wiped the blood from his mouth. The blood was sweet. A week of feeding and playing had made it ripe and strong. He had to be careful to limit the feeding. He couldn't let his bloodlust take over, or he would kill them; they were weak and small. He took a deep breath. He looked down at the remaining children, then over to Belle, who was covering her eyes.

"Oh, Belle, it will be over so very soon." He turned his focus back to the children. "Who will be next to join us?"

Suddenly, one of the boys seemed to wake up between the chanting, the candle lights, and the hysteria. He panicked and ran from the group. He ran from the dining cave to the opening, running past the tables of food and the chanting lost boys. Peter watched as several of the lost boys got up to pursue him.

"No, no, he has a choice. Let him go," Peter said.

The boy scurried to the rock steps, the darkness of the caves in front of him. He looked back over his shoulder to the feast room and then ran into something. He stumbled and fell over. He looked up at a tall, lanky, dark-skinned woman in a black dress. She had long fingernails and rows of braided hair. Her face had strange markings, almost like a painted skull, and she wore bones as a necklace. There were two giant men behind her, one dark-skinned and one pale. Both had dead eyes and carried clubs.

The room got very quiet, a hush from the lost boys. Then came the low chant, "Mama Laveau...Mama Laveau... Mama Laveau..."

The Voodoo priestess waved to the crowds of boys in the dining hall.

"Who loves you, boys?!" she asked with a shout.

"You do, Mama Laveau!" they shouted back.

"That is right!" she said, smiling.

She looked down at the boy, then pointed back to the great room. The boy shot through her legs, but a meaty arm grabbed him by the shirt and lifted him up.

Peter looked at the woman who nodded back.

"Take him away, back to the boat. He will not be part of the family here. He can go back to the cold nights, horrible adults, beatings, and the dark streets. Do any more of you wish to go?" Peter asked.

The other remaining children were scared but found solace in Peter's smile. Food and friendship were not part of an abused orphan's life. None of them moved. Then a large boy, taller than Peter, stepped up. He had blonde hair and a few scars on his face and neck.

He stared down Peter, making him angry. He was about to open his mouth when the boy spoke very clearly.

"I know what you are. I know of the stories of things like you, but I will join you and offer my protection, only if you swear to protect these boys."

Peter stepped back, "I do not remember you on my boat."

"I snuck aboard after following you through the alleyways. I stepped into the group when I saw my chance. You were preoccupied while arguing with the small, glowing woman in the cage. I assume she is a fairy. I thought I would find out if the Green Angel was real or just a lie. Do you think I would let those people in the orphanage hurt them again, let alone have the Green Angel take them? I lost two younger brothers to the abuse of the system. I may not be a man, but I will hurt anyone who hurts them," he said.

"What is your name?" Peter asked.

"I am Edward, and I will swear allegiance to you and the boys, even with your so-called kiss, but only on loyalty of your heart."

"You are wise beyond years. I knew my count was wrong. I detected a new smell in the group, but my mind was elsewhere." Peter glared over to Belle in the cage. She looked away quickly.

"I see you are not afraid of a fight," Peter continued. "How old are you?"

"I am nearly seventeen," Edward replied.

"And you were at the orphanage?" Peter asked.

"Nay. I looked after it as if they were my brothers. You think that fat woman or the men who come around care for us! They used us for money or pity. My brothers and I spent years there. Eventually, only I was left; my brothers died of the sickness. No money for heat, they claimed!" Edward said angrily.

"You will always have warmth and food on my island," Peter reassured him.

"And you will have my loyalty and friendship if you care for them. If not, blood-feeder or not, I will make you an enemy," Edward warned.

Peter clasped his hands together. He was unsure of this new fellow but did like his spirit. He had not turned anyone this old or this big before.

"I do not want you as an enemy, young Edward. You could aid me greatly on this island. You puzzle me at this point. I could turn you or kill you," Peter said.

"In front of the rest of the boys, killing me would be foolish. Some of them know of me and how I fed them when that fat woman went to bed. I slipped stolen food or blankets into the windows at the orphanage," Edward boasted.

"You are a rogue for sure. I will grant you eternal life here but ask your ever-dying loyalty to save these young boys and possibly more in the future," Peter replied.

"Then do what must be done." Edward stepped up with a smile.

Peter gave a nod to the witch. She, her two henchmen, and the boy disappeared into the shadows. Peter looked into the young man's eyes. "Never need to be hungry or cold again, my brother."

As Peter bit into Edward's neck, he did not cry out, only gritted his teeth. He stepped back from Peter, pushing the lost boys off as they came to his aid. With a stagger, he walked back to the table under his own power.

Peter smiled. He was a tough bugger. Anyone who could take the bite and walk away from it was strong, or stubborn. He would keep an eye on him.

"Who is next?" Peter shouted, and the chants began again for the kiss of life.

From the darkness of the caverns, the young man who tried to escape fought as the large man dragged him through the darkness.

"Let me go!" he screamed. "Help me, someone help!"

The witch continued to walk ahead of them and came to another large cave. It was not as bright or as inviting as the feast room. It was cold, dark, and lined with cages. Dozens of cages. There were lit candles, and it smelled like rotting meat. Several men stood nearby, their eyes black and cold like the sky on a winter's night. The boy could not see much but heard the cries of boys and of grown men, cries of sorrow and despair. He let out one last cry for help until a thick, brutish hand raked across his face, and he saw no more.

Chapter 8

The Heart is the Weakness of Men

James stood on the deck of his beloved ship. His men were behind him. They were penniless once again, stranded, adrift in the harbor of the cove.

"So, one week of fun, and now we need a plan once again," James said.

"More like four days," Morgan replied.

"We could go get supplies and food and try another raid?" Father Bob suggested.

"Good, good, but we have very little left," James said.

"We could sail, fish off the coast, and sell it to the Queen's Navy," Drake suggested. "My brother-in-law makes a good wage doing it."

"We are not going to become fishermen, not yet. Let's go back into The Cove and see what I can find for supplies. I will go speak with Molly and..."

A groan came from his crew.

"What? She has always helped us in need," James reminded them.

"Yes, and it's always cost us plenty," the Spaniard said.

"Tell you what, take this last silver piece, go get some food and drink, and I will meet you back here in five hours with supplies," James said confidently.

Father Bob took the coin, and James watched as his crew left the boat and began to walk the dock back to the small coastal village.

He took in a deep breath and jumped from the ship to the dock. His men walked to the south, and he walked north back to The Lucky Pelican.

Three hours later, James awoke in her warm bed. He stretched and rolled his arm, searching for the curvy body of Molly but found only pillows and blankets. He felt wonderful and pushed his head deeper into the pillow. He listened as a door opened, and he could hear Molly talking quietly. Just business, he thought.

He rolled over, thinking about what Captain Huxley had told him. Maybe he was not a pirate. Maybe ending it all and finding a new life with Molly here at The Cove was the answer. Maybe Drake had a point. They had a boat, and he had a crew. It would mean less danger, and they would always have something to eat. Maybe he could find a treasure chest and live like a king with his crew and never rob or kill again. He could take Molly away from The Cove. A dozen scenarios of an adventurous man's fantasy scattered in his mind. He stretched and then sat up. He turned, hoping to see Molly in the doorway. He looked straight at Captain Farrell instead.

"Good afternoon, James. I see you're resting well," Farrell remarked.

James jumped from the bed and staggered to his pants and rapier. Two other men popped into the doorway, holding long-barreled muskets rifles.

"No, James, just get dressed. No reason to bloody up Molly's fine bedroom," Farrell said.

Molly stepped in front of the men. "It's nothing personal. Your tab was getting very large, and Wayne was kind enough..."

"Wayne? You know him as Wayne?" James asked incredulously.

"Look, it's nothing personal; it's business, James, and he paid quite well for your tab."

"Oh, that's how it is? I thought maybe the last few nights, I had been working it down myself?" James replied.

Molly smirked, then shrugged her shoulders. "Maybe some," she said. "James, just get dressed. I have a meeting in a few hours and need this situation tied up quickly."

James cursed under his breath, putting on his pants and shirt. They did not let him put on his boots, so he carried them. He saw Farrell give Molly a small coin sack and kiss her hand. She smiled weakly at him as the door closed.

"Of all the low-down, dirty, back-stabbing horrible things," James said as they pushed him down the stairwell.

"Don't take it so hard, James. She may have sold you out for even less had I not shared her bed last month. She likes a man in uniform," Farrell boasted.

"Oh, that's just wonderful to know. I will sign right up again," James said as they dragged him out of The Lucky Pelican and marched him towards the docks.

Captain Farrell's ship, *The Argonaut*, was grand; it had three large sails and was one of the newest ships in the Queen's Navy. James had enough of Farrell's bragging the last ten minutes. In the true spirit of pride, before he was taken down below to the brig, he was given a tour of the vessel against his will. When they went down below, he was pushed through a pair of swinging doors. There he saw four iron cells, and he spun around quickly. With his hands tied in front, he raised them.

"Now listen to me, Farrell, my crew will be coming, and you have seen how crafty and strong and brave they are. So, I suggest we let this go, and maybe we will let you live," he boasted.

Farrell and his men stood defiant, and they all smiled at his words. James' heart sank, and so did his head.

"They're already here aren't they?" he asked. He turned, finding his men in one of the cells.

"Sorry, James. We kind of got lost on the way to the pub," said Father Bob.

Hook took a deep breath. "I do not want to do this, but listen, if you let us go, I will give you our boat. That's right; she will be all yours, lock, stock, and barrel. You can keep her. Treat her well; she was our home. How is that?"

"It's a great gesture, but you can't give it to me because I gave it to Molly as payment for your capture," Farrell said.

"What!" James exclaimed.

"You had quite a tab, James. A couple gold coins was not enough to sell you out. A ship changed her mind quite quickly," Farrell said.

Hook began to stomp his feet and curse. "You stole my ship for payment?"

They grabbed him, opened the cell, and thrust him in. He slammed into Black Jack and bounced back as the cell door creaked shut.

"Come on, Farrell! Come on, not like this," James pleaded.

"It's nothing personal, James. You're a pirate who stole from my crew and the queen. What am I to do?" Farrell asked.

"There has to be a way. These men do not deserve the gallows; they're a good crew," James said.

"Well, they made bad choices," Farrell added. "Chose a bad captain."

From the swinging doors, a sailor stepped into the lower deck. "Sir, I just got a message from Admiral Thompson. He sent it here to be delivered personally to you."

"Admiral Thompson?" Farrell stepped from the cell and took the letter. He broke the wax seal on it and began to look it over.

"It looks as if returning these men to the jail in the harbor will have to wait. They need us in a couple days with something." He folded up the letter and placed it in his pocket. "Looks like you and your men will have a few more days away from the gallows yet, James."

"Come on, Wayne. Let's talk about this. Captain Farrell, let's make a deal," James said.

"It's a bit late, James. I have to follow the protocol and rules. I offered you and your men a chance just days ago," Farrell reminded him.

"There was a time when you liked adventure and breaking the rules," James said.

"And it always got me into trouble, James. Always," Farrell replied.

"Because you always got caught!" James exclaimed.

"Because you always left me! You always saved your own neck! I am surprised you have a crew considering your merits of friendship."

"People can change. I have changed," James explained.

"I was your friend, James. Now, it's duty over mischief."

Captain Farrell and his men left the brig. Hook looked out from the cell bars.

"So, what now, Captain? What do we do?" Black Jack asked.

"We do what I hate doing: We sit and be patient," James answered.

Chapter 9

The Host with the Most

Peter sat alone at a table in the great feasting hall. Scattered about were the lost boys, sleeping and dreaming. It was close to dawn, but from inside the deep caverns of his underground kingdom, natural light made its way through hairline cracks in the stone ceiling. Belle sat in her cage, eating from a large slice of apple. She watched Peter with every small bite.

Peter was reading; he liked to read. He liked to read news about other lands and history. He made it a point for the lost boys to read and learn. Many laughed and fought back, but Peter knew how to entertain and make history a story. Once he got several of them to read, the others fell into step.

"Have you been following this story about the colonies? How they continue to fight against Britain?" he asked.

"We fairies try not to get involved with the follies of mankind," she answered.

"Typical fairy, ignoring the big picture. No wonder those on the other side of the island wiped out your small village," he said, smiling.

Belle stopped eating. "You said I could go free. You said you would help me find the others."

"I will, when you and I are friends again. I am sure your kind still exist somewhere, just not where I needed them to be."

"You're a monster; you have no right."

"You had no right to tell them of my plans. That's why we are no longer friends, and you rot in that cage unless I need you." Peter tossed a chicken bone, striking the cage and sending Belle cowering back.

Peter continued, "I miss talking to people who have vision, not fantasy creatures who think they know what's best for people. We are still not friends."

Belle built up a little courage. "If I ever get out of this cage, I will..."

"You will what? Fly away? I hope you do, so I don't have to hear you cry anymore. I keep you in that cage to protect you! There will be a time soon when I no longer need you, and then you can be alone on your merry way. Maybe some magical creature will eat you once we are gone," Peter warned.

"They would never eat us. They are like us," she replied.

"There is no more *us*, Belle! They were all slaughtered, and only I saved you from their fate, remember? Besides, the mermaids do not like you. I doubt the tribe on the other side of the island likes you either. Wasn't it them who destroyed your village and killed your friends? Be glad I made the treaty with them, or who knows, you could be in a stew by now," Peter stated.

Belle began to cry.

Peter said, "Always with the crying like a sad orphan. Not here on my island. Here we dance and play and live forever."

A shadow moved across the feast room at the entrance of the cave. The Voodoo priestess appeared. She stepped with the silence of a tombstone and made her way to the table. Belle covered herself, hiding underneath a small, torn rag.

"I received this today; they should arrive in just a couple of days," the witch hissed.

Peter stood up and took the letter from her. He opened it and began to read. "Yes. Good," he mumbled. "They will deliver what we need."

"What if they try to take advantage of us?" Mama Laveau asked.

"That has been all arranged. The mermaids will be in the harbor to take their ship. I am hoping they are men of their word. If I kill an admiral and sink his boat, others may come looking for his remains. If they venture to betray us and we do kill them, we will just leave earlier than planned. It will take weeks to get word. Then the entire British Navy can come here and bombard this place, and we will see if the creatures of magic can fair against weapons of war."

"We will be set up in New Orleans before the first ship pulls into the cove. Those wretched mermaids can deal with the cannon fire and muskets without our help," the witch said.

"I wish them well and hope no blood is spilled, but this island can be their tomb. We have greater plans," Peter said. "How are the new guests?"

"I checked on them before I came to see you. They are resting. However, two are fighting the fever, and may not make it through the transformation," the witch replied.

"So, two out of the twelve will not join us. Next time, I need to bring back more children. If the two start to show signs of rejecting our gift, take them to the Pits of Despair and leave them with the others," Peter said.

"One of them is the bigger child, the one called Edward," the witch replied.

Peter paused, rubbing his jaw. "I was hoping..."

"You may be a vampire, but he is nearly a man. I was surprised that you even tried," she said.

"He had a spark. I could feel it. A loyalty and aggressive nature I liked," Peter said.

"There is still a chance he could transform. It's only been a few days, but you know how this goes; not everyone can be like you," the witch reminded him.

"We should have more boys and your zombies to leave the island on schedule if we are short-handed. We will still find a way. Do you think word of our venture has traveled to the other side of the island? Does Queen Wolf Lilly know of our plans?" Peter asked.

"Still a bit attached to her, are you? She is of the world of magic and ancient ways. I am sure she knows. She has spies all over this island. I caught a couple of her soldiers snooping around the beaches. I do not know why she insists on coming into our domain," the witch replied.

"Because she can. Because she thinks I will be the boy she met years ago. She is weak. Once we finish our plan, we will leave this island, and she and her people can try to take it back," Peter said.

Belle sat up. "You really want to leave the island? With everyone?"

"Yes, and that is all you will know because you talk too much," Peter replied. "I will make sure my men are in position for the transaction, and in place for other activities if they present themselves."

Mama Laveau smiled and looked at Belle in her small cage. "Everything is good and on schedule, but we will talk more in private. I think I have a way to help our cause grow. We can discuss it later after this little venture."

Peter stood up, took Mama Laveau's hand, and kissed it. "I love a woman with vision. See that, Belle? Instead of crying and whining, 'All my friends are dead... I'm in a cage,' she has a plan; she has vision. You could learn a lot from Mama."

Belle wiped her eyes, and the Voodoo priestess smiled.

"Dark magic is always the strongest magic," she said, "but you know, some of your kind's dust does wonders for my brews, very strong magic indeed. Why do you think you cannot leave the cage? It's my magic that keeps and protects you, little winged one. Controlling such men took so much work, but a little fairy dust with the right mixture here and there keeps them stronger and more aggressive than I thought possible. The zombies I created years ago would never move and function so well."

Peter let out a yawn.

There came a knock, and they looked up. Edward stood in the doorway. He was pale and shaking. "Peter, I am ill. I do not feel well."

Peter looked at the Voodoo Queen. Their eyes said everything. It was common that not all boys turned.

"Edward, it's a side effect of the kiss. You must lie down. Go back to the sleeping hallow and rest. We will come to you in a few minutes," Peter assured him.

Edward smiled, "Ah rest. Indeed. Thank you, my king!"

Peter smiled and watched as Edward stumbled away back to the caves.

"He is not changing; he will transform," the Voodoo Queen said.

"There must be a way. Use your magic; try to keep him," Peter pleaded.

"Peter, we have tried before, remember? At least three times. We saved a few, but in the end, the results are the same," she said.

"I know. For me, try to use your magic. He has a great heart, and we need bigger, stronger, loyal boys. They move faster than your zombies," Peter remarked.

"I am surprised you wish to have boys taller and bigger than you. It's very dangerous to give them power," she said.

"If they are loyal, they will stay with me. Can't I have a few, close bodyguards?" Peter asked.

"Bodyguards? Do you feel threatened as of late?" the witch asked.

Peter flipped through the maps on his desk. "America will be hard. I think having some security, boys like Edward, could aid me."

"And what of my magic and men?" she asked.

"A boy and an ex-slave woman with money and power in a new land? We will be a target for sure. We may need to make allies quickly, and I need to find some bigger boys or young men to aid us. As much as I like our family, it must grow," Peter replied.

"I trust our plan and my magic. I will do what I can with Edward, but even with my magic, he may be gone already. I will go make a sacrifice to my Iwa spirit, and he will aid me. He has guided my path ever since I left that horrid plantation. It was he who guided me here to this island," the witch said.

"I think the storm guided you here, and without me hearing your cries, you would have died on the rocks," Peter murmured under his breath.

"Ah, yes, but my Iwa put you near me and has set us on a great path. I will have my revenge on the plantation owners and free my sisters. My Iwa has shown me the light."

Peter let out a huge yawn, exposing his fangs. He rubbed his watery eyes. Even vampires needed rest.

"Please forgive me, I must retire. All this reading has made me tired. Give the new children until nightfall. The ones who do not heal, place them in the pits, but do try to save Edward. We could use him in our plans. He is smarter and stronger than most of the boys we rescue."

Peter stretched and picked up the iron birdcage.

"Time for rest," he said.

"Sleep well, Peter," Mama Laveau said.

"I always do," he replied with a grin.

Chapter 10

NOW YOU WANT ADVICE?

James stood on a beach. The ocean crashed behind him. Before him lay a giant pile of treasure. Gold coins, jewels, goblets, and fine necklaces. A treasure chest the size of a coffin with gold handles sat in the center of the pile. He walked to the chest and placed his hands on it. He caressed it slowly and looked down at an iron lock. He pulled his pistol and shot it, shattering it. He slid his pistol away and knelt down to open the treasure chest. He slowly opened the lid; it creaked. Suddenly, several small bloody hands shot from it with the sound of laughter.

James stumbled back and the lid closed. He stared at the chest as blood began to seep from under it. The red ooze poured down the beach towards him; he heard chil dren laughing.

"James wake up," came a voice.

He stirred quickly and looked around. It was dark; his face rested on the iron bars of his cell. His mind was still cloudy from the dream.

"James," came a voice again. He turned to find Farrell standing, holding a candle, bringing dim light to the brig.

James slowly rose to his feet as his crew snored loudly behind him.

"A bit early to ask what I want for breakfast, Farrell?" he joked.

"Always with the wise tongue. I want to speak to you in private."

Captain Farrell walked over and held out a pair of iron shackles. "Put these on and come with me."

James took the handcuffs and slid them on his wrists. Farrell unlocked the cell, opening it only enough for Hook to squeeze by. Black Jack rolled over in the cell with a snort. The Spaniard opened one eye but relaxed and drifted back to sleep with the rest of the snoring crew.

"Come with me to my chambers. I need your thoughts," Farrell said.

"Will there be food? I'm hungry; you have not fed us very well," James complained.

"I will feed you and give you some food for your men. Just quickly, I do not have much time," Farrell replied.

James followed Farrell from the brig up the steps. Now most men would think to seize the moment and attack, but James was smarter than most men. For whenever your captor wants to talk, there must be a great reason. This was not the time to try to escape but to see what his old friend may be willing to do for him and his crew.

Farrell's chambers were small, neat, and tidy. There were several maps on a wooden desk and a bowl with fresh fruit. Farrell sat down in a throne-like chair with the maps in front of him. Hook took a banana from the silver bowl of fruit and began to open it with his chained hands.

"As you know, I have been called away from returning you to the military outpost on the island of Saint Marcus to meet up with Admiral Brady. We are meeting with him today to discuss this so-called mission," Farrell stated.

"What does that have to do with me and my men? You want me to thank you for giving us a few more days away from the noose?" James said, biting half the banana into his mouth.

"They want us to meet here," Farrell said, pointing to the map. "It does not make sense; this island is not on my other maps, and I heard rumors back at The Cove. After asking a bit, even the pirates avoid this area. They say there is an island, but no one has ever returned."

James swallowed and took another bite.

"Let me see this map." He took it from Farrell's desk and studied it. "I have sailed by this area once, but the fog was so thick, we moved east. So even if there was an island, we would have never seen it. Who gave you this map?"

"It was delivered by Brady's men. Our instructions are to meet, take some of my men aboard his ship, go to this island, and leave my ship and the rest of my crew back in case of any trouble," Farrell replied.

"Trouble?" James asked.

"Yes. They claim Spanish pirates, but I do not like such a task. This island, this mission, why did it not come from the queen herself? I believe Admiral Brady has gone rogue," Farrell said.

"Well, that's quite a story. You may find yourself with a pirate mutineer on an unknown island," James said, smirking.

"I have concerns. What would you do?" Farrell asked.

"Oh, now you wish to know my opinion?" James said, sarcasm in his voice.

"James, sometimes a man in my position cares more for his men than the title of captain or his allegiance to a government. You have a good crew, and I care for mine as well," Farrell said.

James rubbed his chin and looked over the map. "Brady knows something, and he isn't letting you in until you're there and it's too late to get out. I suspect there is something he wishes to gain from that island. You could be bait, or muscle. I do know that island is not on any map, so I would be cautious with your men and your loyalties to this Admiral Brady. He has you by the short hairs, indeed. If you decline, he can report you. If you agree and stumble into a pirates' struggle unknown to the Queen's Navy and lose a ship or two, it could destroy your career." Hook took an apple from the bowl. "I would hate to be in your shoes."

A set of keys landed on the desk. James looked at Farrell and bit into the apple.

"You and your men come with me. Act like my crew, and I will grant you freedom," Farrell said.

"You are joking, right?" James asked.

"James, my affection for my crew is as strong as your affection for your crew. If Brady is just using me and my men as a small group to sail under the queen's flag for his personal gain, I want to know more. I want more eyes watching and ears to hear what I can't. Having your ship there can only aid us. Try to be diplomatic while he tells my crew and I what to do. I do not trust him or this so-called mission to an island no one will speak of."

"So, we go with you willingly, and if everything is on the level, you set us free after we break from Brady's hands?" James asked.

"Yes. You have my word. No one knows you were captured, and to be honest, James, people do not care. You're not worth that much," Farrell said with a sigh.

"Well that depends on who you ask," James said. "What about my ship?"

"I can't help you with that. I will place one of my men aboard to guard it back at the Cove. I can't just give you your ship back; I just bought it. I may use it as a wedding present for a certain aristocrat back in England whose daughter Emily winks at me and enjoys naked swimming in the harbor when her parents travel abroad. A ship, even one as small as *The Conqueror,* would be a great way to gain family favors. But if you're free from the noose, you can try to find a way to get a new ship," Farrell said.

"So, you're offering freedom, a fresh start?" James asked.

"It is a fresh start. Go speak with your men. We meet with Brady in a few hours. I will make you my lieutenant. Just stay close to me and learn all you can. It could save your crew and possibly mine," Farrell replied.

Hook took the set of iron keys from the map-covered table and began to leave the captain's quarters.

Farrell spoke out again, "James, remember your military training; I need you to play the role."

James' head sunk, but he turned around and smiled. "Yes, my captain. As you command."

Farrell frowned, "Do not overdo it. I know when you're lying."

Farrell took the bowl of fruit and a plate of pastries and handed them to Hook. "For your men."

"Aye, aye, Captain," James said, smiling.

Farrell rolled his eyes, and James left the through the door.

Mama Laveau looked at Edward's pale body. He moaned. He was strong, but even after she prayed and put curses and symbols on his body, the curse of the vampire was not holding. She had given him all kinds of medicines and incantations like she had on a few of the boys of years ago, but Edward was not healing. His body twitched, and his teeth clinched. Near the bed were the remains of a small goat which had been cut in half. Symbols on the wall, still wet from fresh blood, flickered in the candlelight. Peter walked into the room and watched the young man fight on.

"Is there hope?" he asked.

"Not for this one, I am sorry, Peter," she replied. "I used several spells to help, but my magic is not for the powers of the changing. Not everyone can be transformed into a vampire. Some do not have the strength."

The Voodoo priestess made her way to a large wooden cabinet with several shelves. She opened a door and placed a bottle back inside. There were a dozen glass jars containing the remains of mummified fairies, their bodies dried and frozen like suffering statues.

"I was surprised the crushed bones of such creatures were as strong as the fairy dust," she said.

"But their bone dust cannot save him?" Peter asked.

"No, Peter, I tried. I even reached out to the other side, to my demon, but he gave no quarter," she said.

"Peter? Peter..." Edward called out. "I can't see, but I hear you..."

"It's the fever, Edward. I am here," Peter reassured him.

"I am feeling better. She gave me soup and..." He tried to sit up but fell back down into the pillows.

The Voodoo priestess looked at Peter. "He must go."

"Then I will take him," Peter said abruptly. He slid his fingers to the ring on his thumb and turned it. He did this when his mind was racing a bit. It helped him focus.

The two of them watched Edward rest for just a few seconds longer.

"You know, Edward, maybe we should go outside, get some fresh sea air instead of this stuffy cave?" Peter suggested.

One of Edward's eyes opened. "Maybe fresh air. Yes," he slurred. He rocked up to a sitting position, and Peter helped him to his feet.

"I will let you two go for a stroll, and I will bring you more soup when you get back," Mama Laveau said.

"I liked the soup; it was filled with warm chunks of meat," Edward murmured.

"Yes, she does an amazing stew," Peter said.

"She hides the fish taste quite well. It was fish, right?"

"Yes, we eat a lot of fish on the island," Peter said, smiling. He glanced at Mama Laveau, who smirked, and the two boys walked from the cave.

"I have had such thoughts of late," Edward said, "but I am not able to control my thoughts the last few hours. Am I going mad from this fever, Peter?"

"No, no, you're just sick my friend. Some fresh air, more of the stew, and you will be joining us in great adventures on the island," Peter replied.

"Indeed, we must protect the other boys. I hope they are not as sick as I am," Edward remarked.

"No, they are fine. They'll be glad to see you when you're better," Peter replied.

They continued to walk the caverns. Peter would talk of his great plans and of the feasts and wonders of the island, and Edward would cough and suddenly shout out things like a madman. The turning had finally broken him.

Peter and Edward came to the great cavern. There were lights from the ceiling, chairs, a pathway, and at the back of the cavern, a cliff. There were signs that read, "Danger, Turn Back." Edward could not read them but wiped the drool from his lips as the room spun. Peter helped Edward hobble towards the cliff.

"You, Edward, are a good young man. I am glad we met," Peter said.

"What's happening to me, Peter?" he asked.

Peter's eyes sunk. "You are sick and will not get better. You will go crazy and become something I cannot have running around in my part of the island."

"I do not understand." Edward looked down past the cliff. It was dark, ominous.

"I am sorry, Edward," Peter said.

"You said you would protect the boys. You said you would help me. I was going to help you?" Edward pleaded.

Peter looked into his deep, green eyes, and suddenly, they went black.

"You lie, Peter! You are a liar!" He grabbed Peter by the neck, and Peter struggled to fight him off. Edward was strong and violent. *Maybe the Voodoo Queen was right about turning older young men into vampires.* Peter broke Edward's grip and kicked him quickly across the chest. He stumped back and wobbled at the edge.

"Peter, what is happening to me?" Edward shouted. Peter stepped up, and using one finger, tapped him on the forehead, and he collapsed over the edge into the darkness below. There was a crash, followed by the stirring of many whispers. Peter adjusted his black vest and walked away from the Pits of Despair.

In the darkness, Edward lay sprawled out on broken plates, furniture, bones, and rocks. It was dark, but he could hear movement. The smell was cold, wet, and like death. His back hurt. His breath was short.

"Is it yum-yums?" came a high-pitched voice.

"Yum-yums?" said another. "We have new yum-yums?"

Edward regained his footing. Now, as he looked around the darkness, his vision grew stronger, and his lungs filled with air once more. His hearing caught the sounds of the voices and of footsteps. His hand shook as he picked up a piece of wooden table leg with nails in it. Something was coming; fear set in. Then, suddenly, his fear stopped, his eyes gleamed, and his mouth opened. He let out a small growl. He didn't feel sick any longer; he felt wonderful, strong, and in control. He was hungry, extremely hungry. He stood tall on the pile of trash and placed both hands on the wooden table leg.

"Are you yum-yums?" a voice asked.

"No. You are yum-yums!" Edward shouted from his drooling mouth and ran into the darkness, swinging the table leg in fury. There were several screams followed by silence.

James moved his collar from his neck. The uniform was tight and itchy. Admiral Brady stood near Farrell, looking at a map with two of his yes-men behind him. Brady was older and thin, with no facial hair, and a uniform tailored specifically for him. His medals and insignias shone, even in the dim light of the room.

"Like I said in our letter, this is a private affair handed to me from Lord Charlton, who is right underneath the queen herself. So, we will conduct ourselves as if we were under the flag of Britain itself every step of the journey," Brady said.

"And what are we doing on the isle?" Farrell asked.

"That is a need-to-know basis, young Farrell. Just know everyone will be rewarded for their service, under her majesty, of course." Brady walked from around his desk and put a cigar in his mouth.

"Smoke?" he asked. James began to raise his hand, but Farrell knocked it down quickly.

"No, thank you," Farrell said. "So, where do you need my men?"

"It's just an easy job, shouldn't be any trouble. You and a dozen of your best will come with me to the island. I want your ship, *The Enforcer*, to stay back away from ours. We are to pull into their port near dusk and deliver the cargo," Brady said.

"So, a night delivery?" Farrell asked.

"Yes. Like I said, we need to keep this quiet and in secret. Don't worry; we will be off the island in less than a few hours. It has all been planned out. Just keep your ship back in case of pirates or those pesky Spanish. I don't know why you even bothered with that small ship. Your ship and men are watching the rear. If this goes well, it will be a great day for the Queen's Navy," Brady replied.

"That is all you need us for?" Farrell asked. He glanced quickly at James, who stood like a statue, looking over the map.

Admiral Brady smiled. "Well, I do need you and your lieutenant to come to shore as well. I am sure more of our presence will help aid in the transaction."

"I understand. I will do as you order," Farrell said. "I will return to my ship and get things in order for tonight."

"Excellent. Be back to my ship at 8:00 p.m. to go over the final stages of the mission," Brady said. He took the cigar and lit it. "Gentleman, I bid you good day."

Farrell and James left the captain's quarters.

"The man is more barracuda than flounder, I can tell you that," James mumbled under his breath.

"Aye, James, indeed," Farrell replied. "Now you know why I need you and your men close to mine. I know your group is worth two dozen fighting men, and what this admiral is doing goes against everything the Royal Navy does. Why, I bet it involves pirates, or worse, maybe guns and goods hiding in the shadows."

"A man like Brady is well connected. Even with his dirty schemes, it would be hard to convict or even suggest such behavior," James added.

"I worked too hard and care too much for my men to have some pompous elitist bury us for a chest of gold coins. Royal Navy or not, I am not dying for him or his schemes," Farrell replied.

"Now I see the man I used to drink and fight with," James said.

Farrell shrugged his shoulders. "I respect the uniform, James, but I love my life and my crew more."

The island cove was buzzing with excitement as Peter stood on the dock. The sun was down, and the moon was just rising over the black ocean, its glow casting shimmers of light on the endless waters. Several of the lost boys ran around carrying boxes and cloth satchels. One boy lit several torches near the dock, lighting a path to the shore. Below, the mermaids splashed around playfully.

"That's good my friends; let us make our guests feel warm and welcome!" Peter shouted.

The Voodoo priestess strolled to the pier. "Everything is in place, Peter. The banquet, the food, and my men."

"Excellent. This will be a great celebration and a start to our path, to our plan," Peter replied.

"Do you trust them? This Admiral Brady?" she hissed.

"Not a hundred percent, but I am hopeful his greed will keep him and his men alive. I do not wish to bring more of the royal fleet to these waters until the time is right and the advantage is ours."

"You plan on killing them all?" came a squeaky voice. Mama Laveau and Peter looked down at the iron birdcage. Belle stood defiant, glaring at the boy vampire.

"Why, Belle, I had forgotten you were there," Peter said.

"You should leave the little bird in the caves; she can only cause trouble with her mouth," Mama Laveau hissed.

"Now, now, let's all be friendly," Peter said. "This is a great day for us. The first steps in a new life. Belle, I have no desire to kill anyone. My hope is they come through on their word and leave our island before midnight."

"I will go and check on the Great Hall once again," the Voodoo priestess said and began to walk away from the harbor.

"Peter, oh Peter, do you have time for a swim before they arrive?" Peter turned as the mermaids splashed in the lagoon.

"No, I am afraid not, my beautiful friends. Possibly after the guests leave," he said.

The look on their faces was like a pouting child, but they quickly giggled and splashed water on one another.

From the water, Niviene launched herself high into the air, splashing water. She descended to the pier. In the descent, her large, deep blue and green tail faded and legs appeared. She landed on both her nimble feet. She walked with confidence to Peter. Mama Laveau glanced over at her but quickly looked away. Niviene saw it. How she hated such dark magic on their island. Humans with power from the other side, dark magic; it was always a crutch to make humans feel like gods. She refocused on Peter, the once crying, small boy whom they found and let live.

Peter smiled and gave her a quick hug and a kiss on her pale neck.

"Everything will be wonderful tonight," he assured.

"If anything doesn't go right, my girls and I will make sure they never leave the harbor," she replied.

"I know I can trust in you," Peter said. He took a small pocket watch from his jacket and looked at the time. "Excellent, only a few hours to go, my friends. Let's make it wonderful."

Chapter 11

THE DELIVERY

On the deck of the Admiral's ship, *The Royal Oak*, Farrell looked back to his own ship, *The Argonaut,* sitting in the dark waters a mile away. James stood near, looking as well. He had left Father Bob on Farrell's ship, knowing the old man was not as passionate about adventure and possible trouble. He then looked at Black Jack, the Spaniard, Perry, Drake, and Morgan. His crew was ready though they looked almost humorous in their Navy uniforms.

"I just want this to be over; I do not trust this so-called mission. The quicker we get back to my ship and sail away from Brady and this strange island, the better," Farrell noted.

Brady and his men left his chambers and walked out on the deck.

"Are you ready for glory?" Brady asked.

"I am ready to follow orders," Farrell said.

"That will do. We sail a bit south of the harbor. There, we will make the delivery," Brady informed.

"Not wanting to overstep my rank, but my curiosity has me at a quandary, Admiral," Farrell said.

"What are we delivering and to whom?" Brady stated smugly.

Farrell's blank face was as a good as a "yes, please."

"Guns, powder, and cannons. Weapons to help a small group of rebels fighting an evil here in the waters off the coast, or so I'm told," Brady remarked.

"Are we arming allies or enemies?" Farrell asked.

"We are arming the highest bidder," Admiral Brady said, "and everyone profits from it, from the Queen's Navy to our cook. Just do your part, and everyone will be happy. Why should pirates be the only ones who get rich?"

James said nothing but gave a grim smile to Farrell.

The large ship floated deeper away from Farrell's boat. The fog, like thick storm clouds, was waiting for them just a hundred yards away. The ship slowly cut through the strange murkiness; all the men on the deck looked and peered forward. Far in the distance, small mountains stretched up to the night sky. The dark jungle was thick, like a stone wall across the beach. James squinted at the cove's skull-like hillside.

"Well, that is promising," he mumbled.

"Just your eyes playing tricks on a cluster of rocks," Farrell added. "Men always see what they wish if they stare out at the seas too long."

"That is not a busty tavern wench holding a pitcher so..."

"Enough, James!" Farrell snapped.

Brady looked over his shoulder at the two grown men and gave a sneer before turning back to the island.

"Steady as we go," Brady announced. "Just some evening mist."

Within seconds, they were through the fog. There, a mile away, was a large, ominous island. It had a rocky coast to the right, and in the darkness of the night, only shadows of the trees and mountains could be seen.

"There!" Brady said, pointing. A lagoon lit with dozens of torches brought life to the darkness. "Bring her around," he ordered.

The ship began its journey to the lagoon, gliding carefree on the still water.

"I am not saying we should be foolish to trust these pirates or mercenaries, but they do know how to welcome guests," Admiral Brady said.

"Should we actually go into port or stay back and bring the goods on smaller boats?" James asked. He watched the men scramble and the commotion on the pier.

"Nonsense. If we do that, they will think we do not trust them. They have a dock and a pier, and they are expecting us. Where did you find your lieutenant, Farrell? Some pirate island?" Brady said with a laugh.

The ship slid into the harbor, and men threw ropes to the pier. A half-dozen men in black cloaks and hoods began to tie the ship down. They placed a plank from the deck down to the dock. Farrell, James, and a half-dozen men walked down the plank to the wooded pier. There was splashing in the water. James looked down but only saw the fin of what he believed to be a large fish. He paused for a second, squinting at the dark water, but then he continued down the ramp. The small group walked to the beach, past the men in black robes.

The first person they saw emerging from the mist was Mama Laveau. She came out of the darkness with two large men, one on each side. Their faces were dull, and they carried swords attached to their belts.

The Voodoo priestess was smiling. "Welcome to our island, Admiral Brady."

Brady was taken back for a second. "I thought I was to meet a man, Peter?"

"You will meet Peter; I am his liaison. He will be here shortly. He has a flair for entrances," she said.

"Oh, well I can assure you I have seen it all, being from the royal courts," he said, smiling.

"Indeed," she said back coldly.

"We have brought all he has requested..." Brady began.

"Save your tales for him; I am just his messenger. You may begin to unload your ship at your convenience," she said.

"I will unload my cargo after I have met the man and gotten paid," he shot back.

"He will be here shortly, as will the payment," she replied.

James looked around. The men in robes moved sluggishly as if asleep while they walked. There was more splashing from the harbor.

"I do not like this. Something is wrong, something... unnatural," James whispered to Farrell.

"Yes, I feel it too," Farrell replied.

Mama Laveau looked over her shoulder as a shadow began to move across the rocks from the torchlight. "He is here," she announced.

A looming shadow appeared, created by the torchlight. As the shadow moved forward, it continued to grow as all eyes fixed upon it, waiting for this arrival of a tall, grand entrance. Instead, the small boy-like frame in a green hood appeared on the beach. Behind him were a dozen children. He walked like royalty towards the admiral, his head high and his stride strong. From behind came a small whispering chant of, "Peter, Peter." He stopped short of Admiral Brady and his men, and the chants got louder. He pulled back his hood to reveal his boyish face. The chanting stopped.

"Good, you are here; we can celebrate!" Peter said. "I love making new friends."

"You are Peter?" Brady asked, confused.

"Yes, my good man, and you are Admiral Brady, I assume?" Peter asked.

"Yes, I am. I did not know I would be dealing with a boy," Brady remarked.

"Ah, yes. Indeed, I am a bit young, but I do have what you came here for. It's not about whom you do business with, as much as what you get paid," Peter said with an impish smile.

"Indeed," Brady said, still caught off guard.

"Would you care to dine with us first? I have a great feast prepared. The boys and I have slaved on it for days," Peter said.

"This is your army? These boys ... these children?" Brady asked.

"Yes, they and the men you see working. They are my family, my brothers. All on this island are my family, and we wish to have you join us to celebrate this night," Peter replied.

"We did not plan on a meal, just to sell guns and powder," the admiral said.

"I am not like most leaders, as you can see by my family. You doubt me, like most men, so let me show you that I am a man, or a boy, of my word." He raised his hand and several of the boys walked forward with small chests. They opened them and sat them on the beach. Gold coins and gems of all sizes glittered in the moonlight.

"Go ahead check it if you wish; it is all there," Peter said.

Brady motioned to Farrell, who took a handful of the gold coins and looked them over. They glimmered in his palm.

"Spanish markings, Spanish gold," Farrell said.

Brady smiled, "If you steal and fight the Spanish, you must be with us."

"I can assure you, they put up a terrible fight, but not as much as the Queen's Navy," Peter boasted.

"You seem very wise beyond your years," Admiral Brady said.

"The world is a hard place, Admiral. Sometimes you can't simply be a boy and play; you need to grow up fast. May I suggest we leave the loot here to go and have our feast? Afterwards, we can do business. I am sure your men could use a good meal, and my boys worked so hard on it," Peter said.

"So be it. You want to feed us, then we shall eat. We will do our business after. But let me leave most of my men on the boat; only my crew with me now will dine. Over our meal, we can discuss possible other business as well? The more men, the more whispers and secrets escape," Brady remarked.

"You speak the truth. I will bring them some baskets of bread and meats, but we shall eat in the hall. Please follow me," Peter insisted.

"Begging the admiral's pardon, if you want, I will stay with the ship," James blurted out.

"Nonsense, Lieutenant Hook! Come join us; enjoy the bounty and hospitality of the young man," Brady stated. "We will not stay long."

"If your lieutenant does not wish to partake, he is free to go," Peter said.

"Nonsense. He will dine with us. Won't you, Lieutenant Hook?"

"I do love a good ham," James said, smiling.

"We have great meats on the island, boar the size of cows!" Peter said. "Come. We have business and pleasure to enjoy." Peter then turned, and with the boys, he began to walk back down the beach. The admiral and his crew followed.

"If you think you're getting out of this, you're crazy," Farrell said. "If I have to go, so do you."

"Profit clouds your admiral's judgment; this is not right. A boy-pirate, the children, the woman in black. She has the markings of a witch, a Voodoo priestess. I have seen them, heard stories. My first mate, Black Jack, his aunt was a Voodoo priestess. Some are good, some are evil."

"Everything alright back there, Farrell?" Brady asked.

"Yes, just listening to Hook's ramblings," Farrell shouted. He turned his attention back to James. "We follow orders, dine, laugh, smile, and get out," he said, gritting his teeth.

"You know I do not do these events well. Remember Paris?" James asked.

"What was his wife's name?" Farrell asked.

"I do not remember, but I remember her telling me she was not married on that occasion as well. Those French women have the most exquisite lingerie," James added.

"Just smile and keep your mouth shut. Luckily, I have not seen an attractive woman here to cloud your judgment," Farrell added.

James glanced at Mama Laveau and shuddered.

Admiral Brady and his entourage entered the torch-lit cave which held the dining hall. There before them were a dozen tables and a feast fit for royalty. Peter took a seat at the head table in a large throne-like chair. More of the lost boys arrived, bringing pitchers of water and wine. Peter sat smiling, watching the celebration unfold.

"My guests, enjoy our hospitality, eat, drink."

The men did as suggested, taking seats as rich foods were brought on silver trays and placed on the tables.

"My friends, my brothers, these men have brought us our freedom, our chance to grow and live." Several of the lost boys smashed their fists to the table, crying with joy. One boy began the chant, "Peter... Peter..." and the room became loud once again with his name.

Peter stood up, "Now, enough! Eat my brothers!" He then took a giant turkey leg, held it up, and took a ravenous bite from it.

Brady and his men began to fill their plates as well, eating rolls, meats, and fruit.

James sipped from his golden glass, his plate empty.

"You do not dine?" Farrell asked.

"What if it's poison?" James said.

Black Jack was across from Hook, and half his mouth was already filled with wild boar. "James, if it is poison, we die tonight with a full stomach, or in a few days, we die from a rope, choking on our own weight."

"Good point." James grabbed a slice of ham from a silver platter across from him.

"Did you not tell them I would let you go if you came with me?" Farrell asked.

"Yes, but none of us believe you," James shot back. He took a bite of the ham.

"You would not take my word?" Farrell asked.

"Well, it's not you personally. It's that you're one of them. You work for the government," James added. He swallowed the barely chewed piece of pink meat.

"Oh, so because I work for them, I have no truth?" Farrell asked.

"No, not exactly. But we're pirates; we do not trust anyone, let alone a power-hungry crown that spreads its forces to enslave and conquer others," James replied.

"Here we go again," Farrell said.

"Look, my men and I, we just want to be free, sail, plunder, and live. That's what this Peter character is doing. Look at him; he is living," James remarked.

They watched as Peter laughed and talked to a lost boy.

"So, you would take his word over mine?" Farrell asked.

"I do not know, but I trust him over your admiral, that much is certain," James replied.

"You are something, James; I don't know what, but you are something." Farrell then ripped a leg from a roasted chicken and placed it on his plate. "For the record, I will let you go. Not trusting an old friend is just silly."

"That's the part of it, my friend; you're an old friend, and that's why we are here together now. I trust you not to take us to the noose."

"But only this one time. If you steal from me or her majesty again, I may have to bring you in."

"I know. You will keep your word; that's all a man has really. More than gold, women, or wine, if a man can't keep his word and have his crew believe in him, he has nothing at all."

"I am glad we are talking again, James," Farrell remarked.

"I am too," James said, raising his glass. "To old friends, the future, and change. And if you ever want to try being a pirate..."

Farrell laughed but raised his glass and struck the goblet.

"Time will tell, Captain James Hook," he said.

The next hour was filled with stories around the tables as the men and boys ate and drank. Peter did a ten-minute, one-man play as entertainment to everyone's surprise; even Admiral Brady clapped his wrinkled hands in admiration.

"To Peter! If he cannot rule the seas, let him rule the theatre of the world!" Brady shouted. The men laughed and lifted their goblets.

Peter made his way over to the admiral and sat down as the men were filled with food and drink.

"This was wonderful," Peter said cheerfully. "We should get to our business and send you and your men on their way. We have other plans that you may be interested in, and we can pay much more as well."

"I would like to speak with you more on that. If you have more funds, I can supply whatever your group needs," the admiral informed him.

"We have plenty; money is no object," Peter replied.

"I see," said the admiral. "After our business is finished, maybe we can have another meeting for a larger opportunity."

"That would be most helpful; we have much bigger plans," Peter said.

"As long as they do not fire at our ships, I think we can make arrangements," the admiral said.

"No, you do not bite the hand that feeds, Admiral," Peter said. "We have no discord with the Royal Navy."

"Indeed. You are quite a pirate leader, Peter," the admiral replied.

"Let me go and get something from my library. I want you to see our plans. Maybe you could shed some light on my ... strategy?" Peter asked.

"I would be more than happy to," the admiral said, smiling. "Always willing to give advice."

Peter left the hall quickly, a smile on his face. The admiral signaled to one of his men who leaned in. The admiral whispered in his ear for a moment; the soldier gave a nod, then a smile. James watched as the two men began to talk.

"What's he doing?" James asked.

"I'm not sure. Should I go ask?" Farrell suggested.

"It may be nothing," James said. He had one eye on a piece of chocolate cake and one eye on Admiral Brady.

Peter returned with a map under his arm and a book and placed it by the admiral.

"I am unsure of this map," Peter began.

"Before we discuss it, can I send my men back to start unloading and getting things ready?" Brady asked.

"Yes, by all means. Let's get this done so we can ... play," Peter said.

The admiral let his soldier go and began to unroll the map. James watched the man leave the room.

"He sent someone back," he said.

"Probably just to start the delivery," Farrell said.

The admiral looked over one of the unfurled maps. "It looks very good to me. Of course, these places here by the coast are a bit off by the colonies."

"From what I read and hear, war is coming to the colonies," Peter said.

"Bah, just a rumor of some angry brats in a new land. Think of it as nothing. Now I see your angle, Peter; you could pirate and supply for the war effort?" the admiral asked.

"No, Admiral, I do not wish to get involved with any of that. However, I could be tempted to help one side or the other with supplies. Maybe have a dock or port in the new land?" Peter asked.

"You are very ambitious for a young man of what, fourteen or fifteen years of age?" The admiral asked.

"Something like that, admiral," Peter replied.

"Let's head back to the shore and finish our business. I will see what I can do to aid you with your plans," the admiral said.

"Excellent," Peter said.

The vampire-boy-king then stood up on his chair. "Everyone, your attention please. We must return to the beach to finish our business; then, we can return to our festivities."

Sighs from many of the children could be heard.

"I know, I wish to play more as well, but it won't be long," Peter said. "Follow me, my brothers."

Peter jumped from the chair and let the children out of the feast hall. The admiral and his men trailed behind, full from the feast.

Chapter 12

THE TREACHERY

The beach was quiet as Peter opened the first crate. He gently pulled a musket rifle from the wooden chest and looked it over.

"Amazing. Simply beautiful," he noted. He then looked to the other ten crates and seven other boxes marked with the word "Powder." Five small, moveable cannons stood in the line next to the powder boxes.

"You have kept your end of the deal, Admiral," he added. "We wish to thank you. In time, maybe more deals can be brought to the table."

The admiral smiled slyly as his men took several small boxes of gold and treasure towards the ship resting in the harbor. James and Farrell stood yards away, watching as the excitement on the beach was slowing.

"There may be other times for us to work together again, young Peter," the admiral said.

Peter motioned to the lost boys, and they began to surround the gun crates. The men in black robes assisted them in moving the cannons.

The admiral looked over to the ship docked just yards away. James saw the movement. The admiral then removed his hat from his head.

"Today though, my boy, is the last you will see," he said.

James looked at the ship. The cannon doors opened, and several men with muskets lined the deck. Peter's eyes opened wide, and before he could give a command, the admiral pulled his pistol and fired a single shot, striking the young man in the chest. Peter fell back into the crate of rifles and collapsed to the sand. The admiral then gave his order.

"Fire!" he cried.

James saw the men on the ship move into place.

"No!" James shouted. It was as if time stopped then quickly started up even faster.

It was too late; the barrage of cannon fire and muskets echoed and screamed across the beach. Explosions of sand and blood filled the air. The lost boys ran for cover, but there was none as muskets ripped them down. It was a quick massacre; the children and those in black hoods fell to the beach and to the pier of the dock. The guns slowly faded as the life of those on the beach snuffed out; the last robed man collapsed to the sand.

"Cease fire!" Brady commanded. The gunfire stopped and the smoke cleared. The admiral looked around. "Excellent. We cleaned up a pirate and made a small fortune. Farrell, be a good lad and take your men back to that horrible feast room. See what other treasure you can find."

Farrell did not move; he stared at the bloody beach, the dead small boys.

"Are you mad?" he shouted.

"No, sir I am not. These were very bad pirates, and we did a great justice for the queen. They may not ever know the bounty we found on this cursed rock. I told you everyone would win," Brady replied.

"You butcher!" James yelled.

"Oh, come now, Lieutenant. If you and your captain do not like the arrangement, maybe we can leave you on this island," Brady remarked.

James could no longer control his rage and ran at the admiral. He tackled him, striking him several times before a gunshot and two large sailors pulled him off. The admiral got to his feet.

"I see we will have to have some discipline for your men after all, Farrell. Now go take your men and search this island for more treasure, or I will have you hung like a traitor when we get back to the queen's soil," the admiral remarked.

"Sir, I do not understand," Farrell said.

"What is there to understand? We found some pirates, we killed some pirates, and we take what we want. We helped the Queen's Navy and pocket the rest for ourselves. I told you, everyone wins."

"Oh, not everyone," came a thunderous voice. Peter was sitting on a chest of guns, his head down, the hood covering his face. The burn marks on his chest were caked in dry blood. "I told you, never bite the hand that feeds you. You bit me, so now I feed on you."

The admiral looked down at his revolver. Did he miss?

"My brothers, my sisters, do not let one of these men leave the beach alive," Peter shouted.

The dead lost boys sat up, their eyes now black and teeth showing fangs. From the water, a thrashing of what could have been a thousand fish.

"What is all this?" Admiral Brady whispered.

"This is how we deal with traitors," Peter said. He jumped from the crate and knocked the admiral to the ground. He stood over the admiral with his small hands clenched. "We fed you! We gave you everything you asked for, and you turned on us. You have shown the greed and guilt of mankind. Was I not hospitable? Did we not treat you as one of our own? I even performed for you! Is this how you give affection, by shooting me? The worst part is that I trusted you, going against my better judgment. I thought you saw opportunity, and now you have made my plans even more difficult." Peter smacked the admiral hard across the face. "You played my hand. I do not have a choice, even if it means changing my plans." Peter looked to the water. "Take the ship my lovelies."

From the shallow waters in the port, the mermaids emerged, grabbing men near the ship and dragging them into the water. The admiral looked over his shoulder. His mighty ship rocked and churned as its men were flung from the deck. Niviene shot from the water and landed on the deck, her fins becoming legs once again.

"Take the legged men back to the bottom of the lagoon!" she commanded. "Mankind has shown his treachery once again."

The hooded men in black staggered to their feet as the witch appeared from the shadows. She joined Peter near the admiral.

"I told you they could not be trusted," she said.

"I know. I was weak. I trusted but not again," Peter said.

"Would you take my advice?" she asked.

"Yes," Peter replied.

"Do not kill them all. We could use strong backs, and now that others in the Royal Navy may come, we should speed up your plan. More workers to get the work done faster. We can use many of them for our journey back to the colonies of America," she replied.

Peter grabbed the admiral by the collar. "Not this one. This one is mine." He leaned in and bit down deeply on the man's neck. The admiral screamed in pain. Farrell and Hook saw the feeding and went back-to-back, pulling their guns.

"Bloody damn vampires!" James shouted. "You did not say anything about vampires."

"I didn't know!" Farrell shot back.

"My crew, my ship, vampire children. I would have taken the damn noose, ya bastard," he said angrily.

Several of the lost boys surrounded Farrell and Hook.

"I can't do it; I can't shoot them. They're just boys," Farrell said.

"Boys who are going to eat you, ya stupid bastard." Hook fired, and one of them fell back to the sand.

"Drop your weapons!" Peter shouted.

Farrell dropped his; James tightened his grip.

"Yes, you sir. Drop it or I will repeat what I did to your admiral."

"He was not my admiral!" James shot back. "I am a pirate, not one of these men, and I will die a pirate's death with a blade or gun barrel in my hand."

Peter moved like a shadow and stood before James. He looked him over. "You do seem a bit wilder than these dogs. I do not know if I like that or not."

"Look, Peter, is it? King Peter or Peter the Brave or Peter Vampire-King? I mean you can't just be Peter, right? We all want a great name or title; I get it. I do not mean to brag, but I have a pretty great name in some circles. You know, a title for a middle name?"

Peter looked puzzled. "I do not really need a title; Peter is fine. What kind of an arrogant, lost soul do you take me for? Besides, it's not what they call you, it's what you answer to, right?"

James thought for a second, dissecting his own ego, but started to speak again. "Great. Okay, Peter, I just want my men, my crew, and to get off this island. I was brought here under a lie at gun point, and I do not plan on dying because of that bastard! I just met that son-of-a-bitch admiral this morning. I am not with these men. I am a pirate," he said boldly.

"Your uniform says different, but your eyes, yes, your eyes are not of a man who follows orders," Peter said.

"Look, let me and my crew go, and we'll leave and never come back. We won't tell anyone. We won't even think about this place again," James pleaded.

Peter tapped his lip. "Hmmm," he grunted, "you did strike the admiral, and I liked that." Quickly, Peter ripped the pistol from James' hand. "No, I trusted one man today, and it cost me. Take these men and the others to the caves."

Several of the men in black robes surrounded the remaining men. James watched as Black Jack, the Spaniard, and two dozen men were marched off the ship. Farrell and James were placed in a line, and the men were all tied with ropes on their hands.

"You're making a big mistake, friend. We could have made a deal," James said as Peter walked past him in line.

"Oh, there are deals still to be made. I hope you choose the right one." He then continued to walk from the line with Mama Laveau by his side. "This does affect our plans, but look at the supplies and the new grand warship we now have for our journey," Peter said.

"She is a wonderful ship," Mama Laveau replied. "It will get us to New Orleans with ease. Just remember your promise: the first target is the plantation of William Morris. I want him to feel the whip and know how a slave bleeds."

"You will have your justice, my friend. Together, we'll change the world, one location at a time. I just hope war doesn't break out too quickly with the colonies. Damn greed. The war could slow our plans," Peter said.

"Or it could aid us. As men die and bleed, we can conquer. We will be hidden by the shadows of the war," she replied.

"Hmmm, very true," Peter said.

Peter and the Voodoo priestess led the train of captured men down the moonlit beach into the jungle. The dark, monstrous caves stood still like an ancient god waiting for more sacrifice.

Chapter 13

Welcome to My Island

The torch-lit caves were humid. The smell was of death itself. There were several wooden cages of bamboo and rope. Inside their cells, men were broken and still. Their faces were hidden down, their clothing tattered and worn. James, Farrell, and the other captured men walked past the cages in a single file line. They walked past what could soon be their future.

The men were led down the hall: James, Black Jack, and Farrell all in a line. James quietly fought the ropes, his wrists squirming and fingers fighting. In some ways, iron was better for keeping a man like him from escaping. It was always a challenge, but James continued to try to wiggle his hands free enough to get a weapon. They were marched and then stopped in front of a large, bubbling, black cauldron. The burning ambers blazed beneath it as a burgundy, thick ooze bubbled inside. The stench of death was much stronger near the hellish stew. Mama Laveau stood near the great iron pot with Peter to her right, his hands folded and his face cold.

"You lucky devils have been spared today," he began. "You came here to rob me and kill my brothers, so now you will be given a choice: join me or die."

None of the men spoke. Their eyes wandered a bit from the pot to the cages. Mama Laveau took what looked to be a small doll with wings; it was, in fact, a mummified fairy. Its frail body was grey and brittle. She crushed it in her slender fingers, dropping the bones, wings, and dust into the cauldron.

"I need men. Strong men like you can help me with my dream, a dream of living forever, playing, and enjoying pleasure. Why must we always fight and kill, when we can laugh and enjoy life? Who wants to grow up and become what you men are? Slaves. You are slaves to men, to your kingdom, to your captains and royalty. You will never change. So, I ask you, why not be a slave for me? My crew and I are not slaves; we are friends. We work together for a better world, a world where no one has to grow old or grow up. Sure, some work must be done, and some need to sacrifice a bit more. But here, on this island, we have found paradise, and you will too. Imagine no more pain, no more suffering, no more hunger. We can give you that," Peter promised.

From the back of the line, a skinny man spoke out softly, "Will there be pay?"

Peter laughed. "Yes and no. You see, our plunder, our gold, we share it. But we do not give everyone a working wage. No, we share as we need. Bring him to me," he ordered.

Two men in black robes grabbed the young man in a royal uniform and dragged him in front of Mama Laveau and Peter. They pushed him down, and he fell to his knees.

"Do you wish to serve, to join us, to never be a slave again to a country or king? To never be hungry or cold? To just be alive?" Peter asked.

"I... I..." the man began.

Mama Laveau took a large wooden spoon and dipped it into the dark cauldron. The broth filled the spoon, and she lowered it to the young man. He fought for a second, but slowly opened his mouth and took a deep sip. He coughed and choked and fell backwards, being caught by the two guards. They raised him to his feet, and he let out a small sigh. He turned and looked back at the line of men. His face was blank and his eyes dull.

The witch stepped in front of him, grabbed his jaw, and looked him over. "He will do. Stand on one leg," she ordered. He did. "Now raise your left hand." He did. "Now what sound does a cow make?" she asked.

The young man opened his mouth and a low guttery, "Moooo," emerged.

"Now run that man through," she ordered and pointed.

The newly transformed zombie picked up a sword near a small table and slammed it quickly into a uniformed man standing in line. The man clutched the blade and looked at the zombie.

"Thomas, how could you? I introduced you to my sister, you bastard," the dying man said, crumpling to the ground. He let out a slow death rattle, staring at the friend who struck him down. Thomas pulled back the blade and stood still, waiting for his next order. James watched in horror, as did the others.

"She uses the dark spells of Voodoo," Black Jack said. "She is evil, not a true priestess of the religion."

Mama Laveau's ears burned, and her head cocked. She walked up to Black Jack and looked up at the giant man. There was a thin cord with a small bag hanging around his neck.

"I see you are of the faith by your gris-gris bag. Tell me, what charm were you given?" Mama Laveau asked.

"I will not tell, for you are an abomination to the spirit world, working with dark magic and with a drinker of blood."

She ran her thin hands across his thick chest. "You are such a prize specimen; it would be a shame to kill you."

Black Jack did not move as she ripped the necklace from his body. He glared at her.

"You will join me," she said. "You will all join me, or I will sacrifice you to my Iwa! And he will feast on your soul's essence for eternity!" She walked back to her cauldron, bent down, and picked up the wooden ladle.

"No, not today," James said under his breath, his hands working the ropes faster now. Black Jack watched from over his shoulder.

He whispered, "I am ready on your word, Captain."

"We die on our feet, not on our knees," James said angrily.

Farrell looked back. "Are you mad?"

"Am I mad? Look around you; this is madness," he whispered.

Peter looked back to the line. "Do we have more volunteers?" he asked slyly.

Only silence answered back.

"Very well. Those are your choices gentleman: the brew or the grave. So, step lively and keep it moving. I will make it fast, but if you choose the grave, it will be a slow, painful death."

One by one, the men stepped up. James looked back over his shoulder at Black Jack, and his eyes told it all. Farrell looked ahead; two more before it would be his turn. More men staggered and fell from the evil stew, mindless and lost. James stepped up, cutting in front of Farrell.

"What are you doing, James?" Farrell whispered.

"Just be ready to run like the devil is on your heels," he whispered back.

The man in front of Hook swallowed fast and began to shudder. Two men in black robes yanked him from the cauldron.

Peter's eyes met with James once again. A wry smile formed on Peter's face, and he let out a small chuckle. "Your fate, my spirited friend," he said as Hook stepped up. "Maybe in another world, things would be different, but this is my world; you will join me or die."

Mama Laveau steadily approached James, bringing the large wooden spoon with its red rusty, slick ooze to his lips. Peter watched with excitement, another man he could break. James opened his mouth, and suddenly broke his rope bonds, grabbed the wooden spoon, and slammed it quickly into the witch's left eye. She fell back, screaming. He tackled the young vampire.

From the chaos, the remaining pirates broke from the line and scattered like chickens in a farmer's pen. Black Jack grabbed the two men in cloaks, slamming their heads together as they dropped their weapons. He cut his robes and tossed the blade to other pirates and sailors behind him. Farrell stood still, unable to move or think. Peter and James rolled across the floor until Peter ripped Hook from his grip and tossed him off. When Peter looked around, the witch was still reeling in pain on the ground, and the new captives were running back into the caves. Black Jack ran quickly, picked up his necklace, and took off running behind James.

Peter ran to Mama Laveau to help her. She thrashed in pain as the wooden spoon protruded from her eye socket. He knelt beside her, looking at the wooden spoon. He ripped it out quickly, and she cried out again.

Peter stood up. "Capture them! Alert the others!"

A man in a black robe walked to a large hanging bell and began to ring it, sending its sound throughout the caverns. Peter turned to see Black Jack and the Spaniard running towards the caverns to join James.

"I'll skin you alive, pirate!" Peter screamed and began to run after them.

Farrell began to run the opposite way, but three men in robes cut off his escape. He threw a punch, but the man he struck just stood his ground. He backed up and looked for another way to run, only to back into the witch. He turned around, looking at her bloody, one-eyed face.

She grabbed his face, whispered a dark curse, and Farrell collapsed to the dirt.

Peter was now to the caverns but saw only the shadows of the three pirates escaping into the darkness. He began to run again when the witch called out, "I have their friend, my master!"

He stopped and turned to see the witch dragging Farrell across the ground by the back of his jacket.

"They will not get far in the caves," she said, "and we can learn more of our new enemies by getting information from this one."

Peter kicked the ground. "Trust is so hard to have these days. Now, I will lose more time hunting them and cleaning up this mess." He put his hands on his hips and looked at Farrell. "Bring me Belle so that we can figure out how to stop this mess from spreading. I may have to fly tonight."

"Dawn will be here in just a few short hours," Mama Laveau replied.

"I know, but I can find them quickly if I leave now," Peter replied.

"May I suggest someone else go hunt them so we can regroup? Let them go for now. Let them run off into the caves; my pet will do the work for you," Mama Laveau replied.

"You mean…?" Peter asked, but he knew what she meant.

"Yes, he will hunt them while you round up the others," Mama Laveau explained.

Peter rubbed his chin. "This is why I do love your council. You bring my haste and whimsy for revenge into focus."

The witch smiled, "I will free him to track your enemies."

"Is there anything I can do for your eye?" Peter asked.

"Bring me the hand that dealt the blow as a trophy, if it's not too much to ask," the witch said. She covered the eye socket with one hand as it bled.

"You will keep his hand; I will keep his head," Peter said, smiling. "Let the beast hunt. I will see to the others and his friend. This so-called pirate is a troublemaker. We will end him soon enough and continue on our plan."

The witch smiled. She took a cloth from a small leather sack on her belt and wiped her face. She staggered a bit as she walked past several wooden cages to a dark cave opening with iron bars. Something hissed and moved in the darkness.

"It is time, my friend. Time once again to hunt and find these evil men." She grabbed a rusty, heavy chain and began to pull it, sending the iron bars up. When they reached the top of the cave, it came forth.

Thick scales and jagged rows of faded yellow teeth appeared first. Torchlight caught its bright yellow eyes. A great beast of an alligator, nearly twenty feet long, its body thick and strong. The claws on its stump-like feet were black and long. The creature stepped out, and the witch knelt down to tickle its scaly chin. It let out what could be described as a hideous purr. It liked her. She walked to the cauldron, grabbed the broken ropes near the ground, and returned to the gator. She lifted them to his flaring nostrils; the warm breath of a great beast pushed back on her cold hands.

He sniffed the ropes. She muttered another curse and blew her breath on the great scaly beast.

"Find this man, but do not kill him, for he is ours for that pleasure," she commanded him.

The great beast then marched off towards the darkening caverns, its thick, lumbering tail swaying with excitement of the hunt.

Chapter 14

RATS IN A MAZE

James, the Spaniard, and Black Jack collapsed against a cavern wall. It was dark, and their breath was short.

"Farrell didn't follow; he did not make it," Black Jack grunted, bending over, hoping to get more air.

"We aren't going back for him. Not with only us. We are going to get out of these caves and off the island. Then we will deal with rescuing that slow bastard," James said. His legs cramped, and he slumped over.

The Spaniard was cursing under his breath in Spanish and broken English.

"I know, I know. I saw it too," James said. "A vampire, a damn vampire, a Voodoo woman. I don't know what's happening on this island. Did you see the mermaids? They ate everyone! This island is cursed, and now, we know why."

"That woman is using dark, bad magic, Captain," Black Jack said. "I have seen my aunt work with voodoo to heal, not for evil, not like this. It's bad juju. You should never use our religion to bring forth the dark side! She is nothing but a witch and coward!" He stood up, almost knocking his head on the ceiling of the cavern. "Alright, let's think this through. We have to get out of the caves first, but we have no idea where we are. We can go blindly forward or…?"

"You want to double back and sneak out?" the Spaniard asked.

"Like we did in the raid on Morris Island?" James asked.

"Well, it worked," Black Jack aruged.

"The guards were drunk, and there weren't vampires, witches, and cannibal fish-ladies near the boat!" James said angrily.

"So, we lay low until dawn, right? He can't be out in the sun, correct?"

"I do not know if that witch has such bad magic. Who knows her power," his first mate grunted.

"We need to stay positive," James said. "Let's do what they would never think us to do. We head back, hide, find our way out of this maze, and get to the beach. If we must, we swim off this island."

"What about the mermaids?" Black Jack asked. "I do not swim good."

"One thing at a time," James said angrily.

"Then we come back for Farrell and the others?" the Spaniard asked.

"If we get off the beach alive, we will think of something. He and the rest may be dead already," James said. "Come on, let's go."

The men walked quickly and quietly back into the caverns.

When Farrell awoke, he was tied to a towering, wooden stake near one of the witch's cages. His vision was blurred, but after the splitting headache faded, his eyes could make out shapes in the dim torchlight. The witch wandered from her pot to him. A large, raggedy leather patch was now strapped over her left eye socket. Herbs and moss dangled from behind the leather.

"Good, you're awake. Now I can really hurt you," she hissed. She took a leather whip from a crate and walked around him. "You will tell us all about your plans with that admiral," she announced. She cracked the whip, and Farrell straightened up. The sound echoed in the cavern.

"There is nothing to tell; I knew nothing of any of this!" he cried out.

The witch smiled and walked around him, slower now. She ran the whip's end gently across his shoulders and neck. "I wish I could believe that, but I cannot." She pulled the whip again, cracking it but still not striking him. "The so-called pirate who took my eye, do you know him?"

"Who do you mean?" Farrell asked, playing dumb.

This time the whip struck Farrell across the back, cutting open his shirt.

"You know of him. He and others fled. Do not tell me you do not know your own officers," she said.

Farrell swallowed hard. How long could he hold out and for what? Death was coming for him; she had all the time and tools to do it.

The witch stood in front of him and grabbed his jaw.

"Do you see this face? Look at my wound; he took this from me. Quit lying. I want truth, and I shall have it, either by this whip or black magic," she said, smiling.

"Ah, good; he is awake," Peter said as he walked quickly into the cavern. "I thought he would never wake up." He looked at Mama Laveau's face. "Are you blind? Is it permanent?"

"I will find a way to heal. It may cost a few sacrifices of the men we captured, but a spell may heal me if I spill enough blood for my Iwa," she informed him.

"Take and use whatever you need from our prisoners. We will get you on the mend. I do bring good news. We have rounded up the others; they are dead now. Four men actually got to the shore, but Niviene and her girls brought us their bodies. So, where do we stand with this poor excuse of a man?" Peter asked.

"He claims he does not know the man who took my eye," she replied.

"Really? They stood so close on the beach and spoke so much before that dog, Brady, double-crossed us," Peter said angrily.

"Brady double-crossed everyone! No one but he and his men knew what he was going to do!" Farrell shouted. "We had nothing to do with it."

"We?" Peter asked.

"Yes, we, my ship and my crew. We were escorts to assist in the shipment. We knew nothing!" Farrell protested.

"Wait, there is another ship?" Peter asked.

Farrell swallowed hard. He blew it already. "Kill me quickly, and I will tell you what you want; leave the ship alone. They never came to the island or to your borders. They stayed far off. They have nothing to do with any of this."

"We could use another ship. Send the mermaids out past the fog. See if it's true, or if he is a liar," Mama Laveau said.

"I am no liar, witch! I'll be damned if I do not beg for the lives of my crew. I am a good captain!" Farrell shouted.

"I will spare the crew if you tell me of this so-called pirate who stood with you," Peter said. "How does a man with such a story wear a uniform, and why was he with you?"

Farrell said nothing.

"Send a message to Niviene. Tell them they can feed on a ship just outside," Peter started to say.

"No, wait! I'll talk, just spare my men," Farrell said.

"Tell me all you can, and I will consider it. If you're honest," Peter replied.

Farrell swallowed hard. "I want your word. You will spare them and not send your beasts on that ship."

"I always keep my word, Captain. It's you and yours that do not. Had Brady just left with his gold, you would not be here. Remember that!" Peter scoffed. "Tell me what I need to know."

Farrell let out a sigh; he was desperate now to save his crew. "His name is James Hook. He is a pirate. He is trouble with a blade in either hand. He is very skilled and very dangerous. He was under my care as a prisoner, he and his men; I captured them. When Admiral Brady asked me to accompany him here, I did not trust him, so I asked Hook to play my lieutenant in case things went wrong."

"Aha, so he *is* a pirate? Hook, that's his name? Why would you ask a pirate to help you?" Peter asked.

"We were friends long ago in the Navy. We did several missions together under the British flag," Farrell replied.

"So, he is not just a pirate but a warrior as well. Interesting," Peter remarked with a look of admiration.

"There, I have told you everything. You know his name and why he is here," Farrell stammered.

Peter walked around Farrell, thinking.

"My problem is that if Hook causes more trouble, I need leverage. The bad news is that I am sure your ship heard the fire on the beach, and they will come by dawn if someone doesn't report back to them. If they stay at sea, they will be spared. If they come to our island, be assured, they will die. For now, I am much more interested in this Hook character and making him suffer. I think you may have just saved your own neck," Peter replied.

Farrell laughed. "You are mistaken. He won't come back for me or for anyone. Not the James Hook I know. He is far off on a beach, building a raft, miles from here."

Hook, Black Jack, and the Spaniard crept carefully around the giant feasting hall. Three of the lost boys snored soundly on the tables. They crept past the tables lined with the remains of the great feast. Black Jack stopped and reached for a large turkey leg, but James grabbed his arm.

"No!" he said in a loud whisper.

Black Jack frowned.

James pointed to several swords laying on the tables. "Get those," he whispered.

The three men grabbed the steel and continued around the feast room, stepping gingerly around plates, goblets, and food scattered aimlessly on the floor.

"Do we go back to the left or right? I don't remember," James asked. "I wonder where that tunnel up to the stairs leads?"

"There is no time for curiosity, Captain," the Spaniard warned. "Choose a path, and we will follow you."

There was a clang and a growl.

"What was that?" Hook asked.

Three lost boys rolled over and sat up, their eyes still weary from food and drink.

"Quickly, hide!" Hook urged his men.

The three men squatted down behind the chairs and tables.

One of the boys stretched. "I am so tired," he said. "Was that the alarm?"

"We should find Peter to see if he found all those bad men that attacked us," another said.

"Why do we always have to work when we could play?" the third asked.

"Because Peter asked us to. Besides, we play all the time. It is Mama Laveau's men who do all the work," the first boy spoke out with a yawn.

There was a growl again. The boys looked around. The giant alligator emerged near the stairs, sniffing the air.

"The hunt!" a boy said. "It must still be going. They released the alligator. Oh, how exciting! Let's go find Peter and tell him they may be close."

"Why should we tell Peter when we could find them ourselves?" asked the second boy.

"Because it's not the rules of the hunt; that's why. Let's go," the first boy reminded him.

The three boys then ran from the room quickly, down a cave entrance.

"I love the hunt!" a boy squealed.

The great alligator moved slyly down the rock steps and entered the throne room. The three men popped their heads up and saw the great creature.

"That is a beast we can't fight," the Spaniard said.

"Oh, but a mermaid, witch, or vampire? Yes, that we can," James said sarcastically.

The creature made its way into the banquet hall, sniffing the air. It was close. Its tail thrashed, knocking over several wooden chairs.

"Those boys will tell that vampire-boy-king the gator is here; it won't be long," James said. "We need a plan."

Black Jack reached up to a table and grabbed a turkey leg.

"That is no plan," the Spaniard said.

"Not me, you idiot. That thing wants to eat," Black Jack said. "If we feed it, maybe we can get away."

"Ah," said the Spaniard.

Black Jack stood up, and the gator moved quickly. He tossed the turkey leg, and it struck the alligator on the nose. The beast opened its mouth and brought the meat to its teeth. In one bite, the leg was gone.

"I think it will take a lot of turkey to slow it down," Hook warned.

The Spaniard carefully took a platter of ham and tossed it at the giant alligator. It snapped and swallowed it as well.

"Maybe we should split up," the Spaniard said. "It will confuse it."

Suddenly, the beast charged and knocked the table over, spilling plates, food, and goblets to the floor.

"Run!" Hook shouted.

The men scattered quickly, but the speed of the beast was just as quick. The Spaniard slipped in a puddle of gravy on the floor as the creature rapidly approached him. He raised his sword and slashed down, cutting the beast across the nose. The alligator knocked him to the left, and his weapon flew from his grip. The eyes of the giant beast glared at him. On the steps, Black Jack and Hook continued to scramble. They turned back, their swords ready, as the beast began to bear down on the Spaniard.

"Run! Do not look back; I will slow him," the Spaniard yelled. Suddenly, with a mighty bite, he was cut in two, and his body and head were inside the beast. He cried out once and then went silent. The alligator thrashed what remained of him, sending his lower body crashing into a table.

Hook and Black Jack did not look back. They ran to the steps and down into another cavern. The alligator smashed his way past several tables, eating any fallen food that hit the floor.

Farrell sat in a cage, his back and chest showing through the tattered uniform. Blood had seeped from his wounds, turning the white shirt to a washed-out pink. His face was bruised and cut.

"I believe you will find this cage much more relaxing than the flogging post," Peter said. "If I require more information, please do not hold out again, or I will let her do her magic. And let me promise you, I would take the whip over her dark spells."

"I did not hold out," Farrell replied weakly. "I told you everything."

"There is always tomorrow," Peter said, smiling.

Just then, the three lost boys stopped short of the cave entrance. The witch looked over, annoyed.

"Mama Laveau, may we enter? Oh please, please!" one shouted.

The witch raised her hand, nodded her head, and they ran past the cages to Peter.

"Oh Peter, we saw the great beast hunting. It was wonderful! He is so amazing!" one boy said.

"You saw him? Where? Near the shore? Or in the caverns?" Peter asked.

"He was in the dining hall. We were going to follow him but wanted to tell you first. Those are the rules of the hunt," the second boy claimed.

"You boys have done well. On the next play day, I think we all deserve more hide and seek and more bread pudding too," Peter replied.

The boys smiled. Peter turned his head and frowned. "One million miles away? He is here, almost within a sword's swipe of my throat!" he barked at Farrell.

"Well, he should have left. The James Hook I knew would never stay. Unless..." Farrell replied.

"Unless what?" Peter asked.

"Unless he thought he could backtrack and outsmart you by sneaking away under your nose. That's the Hook I know as well. He is very unpredictable at times. That is another reason he was let go from, or in his words, 'left,' the Queen's Navy," Farrell replied.

Peter was enraged. He grabbed the cage, shaking it angrily. "I will kill you both and eat your bones!"

"Can we watch?" asked one of the boys. "It is so fun to watch you kill them."

Peter turned his head back to the children "Of course. First, take me where you last saw the great beast. We will return to the feasting hall."

"Hooray!" yelled the boys.

Peter looked at Farrell. "I will come back for you later. As for your ship, your crew..."

A man in a black robe staggered into the cavern. He walked to the witch and whispered in her ear. She smiled.

"Ah, apparently several small boats have come ashore near the lagoon," she said. "Most likely a scouting party to see why the first never returned."

Peter clasped his hands together. "Wonderful! Now, I do not have to spare them, and I keep my word because they came to my island."

"You would have killed them anyway, you cowardly boy," Farrell said.

"No," Peter answered with a smile, "but I would have killed you. Come, my little ones. Dawn is coming, and we do not have much time. First to the hall, then we search the caverns and the beaches. We may have found fresh blood and another ship for our journey," Peter said.

Peter, Mama Laveau, the vampire boys, and several men in black robes quickly left the witch's cave.

Farrell let out a sigh and looked at the other men in the cages; their will and bodies were broken a long time ago. "Good luck, James," he mumbled.

James and Black Jack were exhausted; their sprint had now become a slow, stumbling walk. The caves were an endless maze.

"My legs have not ached like this since I was in the Navy," James panted. "I am not as young as I once was."

"Nor am I, but I will rest when I am dead, Captain," the big man agreed. "My gris-gris is for luck, and I feel we may have a chance to get away. I believe you can get us off this cursed island!"

James tried to catch his breath. "We owe that crazy Spaniard a proper pirate burial at sea if that creature left anything of him. That damn beast ripped him in two. This island takes men's souls. I never saw Drake or Morgan get off the boat; I am sure those mermaids had their way with both of them. Ghastly way to go, even as a pirate."

The big man leaned against the cool cave wall. "I think we took a wrong turn; these caverns all look the same." He looked at Hook, and his tone changed. He held his gris-gris in his huge hand. "Will you come back to free Farrell? Would you risk your life for an old friend who did you wrong?" he asked.

There was a quick pause as James stopped to think.

"He actually never did me wrong. Now, as I think back, I may have been the problem in a few of our adventures. I would come back for any of my crew. The thought of any man being here, trapped, tortured, enslaved, bothers me to my core. If I have the power to rescue Farrell, I will return."

The giant black man put his heavy hand on Hook's shoulder. "That's why I follow you, James. You're a good man and a good friend."

"You throw that word 'good' around too easily, my big friend. Let's go and find a way off this wretched place," James insisted.

"Agreed!" he replied.

The two men walked swiftly, using only the small torches on the cave walls to light the way. They went on for several minutes before finding a fork in the tunnel that led to a brightly lit cave. They walked in slowly with their swords drawn. It was a hollowed-out cavern; inside, piles of gold coins, chests, and jewels lined the walls. In the center of the treasure room was a large oak desk covered in maps, papers, and a few thick books. Gold candelabras lit the room, making the gold give off a dull shine from every angle. Behind the desk stood a towering, makeshift bookcase, made half of wood and half of what appeared to be large bones. Thick volumes of different-sized books lined the shelves.

They walked in carefully and began to look at the treasures.

"Great ghost of Poseidon," James said.

"There is enough treasure here to have your own small country. Or buy one," Black Jack said.

"Aye, or a year of turkey legs for a very large first mate," James joked. He walked to a pile of gold and plunged his hands deep into it. He lifted handfuls and watched the gold and rubies fall through his fingers. This was the score all pirates, all men who wish to hold power, could ever want. As a boy, he went hungry; as a pirate, he also went hungry. With this wealth, he and his men would never be hungry. They would never have to plunder or steal. They could be free to do and see anything. He could be the richest pirate who ever rode the waves of the seven seas. He watched the last coins fall and land back in the pile. *Freedom*, he thought. He looked over at the desk. *Freedom built on the slavery of other men*. He walked from the pile of money to the desk.

"What is it, James?" Black Jack asked.

"This much money and power, it's for something, something evil!" James exclaimed.

"What do you mean?" Black Jack asked.

"They spoke of a plan, of ships, of war. You said it yourself, there is enough here to own a small country, or buy one. If this boy, Peter, leaves this island with all this gold and these children and the men controlled by the witch, he will enslave hundreds." Hook began to look through the maps and the writings. "He's planning much more. This island is his port. I believe he wishes to expand."

Hook moved some of the maps, and there were three large rubies the size of small apples being used as paper weights. They shined and sparkled. He had never seen jewels this large. He took them off the desk and dropped them in his left boot.

"I thought you were not taking the booty?" Black Jack asked.

"I need to get my ship back from Molly if we are going to return. Call it a business expense," Hook said.

"Turkey leg money," the big man said.

"Exactly. Come here and look at these maps," Hook said.

Aboard *The Argonaut*, Father Bob looked from the deck at the waves of fog. They had heard the cannon fire over three hours ago, but then silence. No one had returned. Three small rowboats had gone out, but they had not returned either. He adjusted his glasses and looked out again.

A young man, no more than 22 years old, stood with his chest out on the deck of Farrell's ship.

"We will wait five more minutes, then we will go to the island," the young man commanded.

"By what authority?" Father Bob asked.

"I was put in charge of this vessel by Captain Farrell, and I will not wait any longer to see if they are in trouble," the young man replied.

"They may be exploring or partaking in a feast or working on a new deal. It is best to wait," Father Bob pleaded.

"We heard cannon fire, and I am not one to run from a fight," the young man assured him.

"No, but you should not run into unknown danger," Father Bob said. "No one knows this island, and unless you were given the order to aid them, I would wait."

"Listen, old man, this is not your ship; you are not part of my crew, just some ragged old pirate. I will heed your advice like that of a seven-year-old girl," the sailor spat.

"My friends and my crew are on that island as well; I too worry. But in times like this, it is better to learn more and wait before making a rash decision," Father Bob said.

The young sailor stared at the fog, and then turned back to look at Father Bob. "I have made a decision. You are not part of our crew, and you will slow us down. We will be bringing *The Argonaut* to the island."

Minutes later, Father Bob sat in a small rowboat, his hands tied loosely in thick rope. He watched as the ship sailed off towards the island into the fog. He began to fight with the ropes and curse under his breath.

Peter looked around the banquet room; it was a mess. Flipped tables, bloody gator prints up and down the stairs, broken furniture and food scattered about. He looked back at Mama Laveau, several of her men, and a dozen lost boys.

"We will clean this up later," Peter instructed. "Right now, we must find them."

"I will take the men to the shore to take care of the landing party, Mama Laveau said. "The beast will continue to hunt them. Maybe you should rest. The sun will rise soon, and you need to stay in the caves. Do not worry about one troublemaker."

Like a spoiled child, Peter threw his hands up and kicked a table. "I want this pirate, Hook, and I want him now!"

"You need to feed; you're moody," Mama Laveau said.

"I am not moody; I do not need to feed. I need to stop this man so our plans may continue."

"Peter, you are thinking blindly. We have gained another grand ship and a dozen strong men to help us in our plans. You are too focused on a man you can't control, a man that does not matter."

Peter's head sank, like being scolded by his mother. His mind wandered, and he remembered how his mother had scolded him the night before his father's ship broke to pieces the night of the storm. These sentimental thoughts would sometimes creep into his mind but washed out quickly like the tide.

He sniffed the air; he could smell the men. He slid his hand down, once again playing with the ring on his thumb, thinking, analyzing. He could hunt better than the alligator, who may or may not have given up after feeding on most of the food on the banquet room floor. Peter was still crafty and full of brilliant deceptions.

"You are right; I will retire to my office. Maybe feed, read, and let you and your men do what needs to be done. This whole night has been a burden on me."

The witch smiled, "Mama will make it better. Come with me to the shore, my children. We have work to do."

The Voodoo priestess, a dozen robed men, and the remaining children walked to the back of the large banquet room and headed into the caves.

Peter walked past his throne-like chair, sliding his hand across it. Behind it were the caverns. He walked up to the opening of the cave; a gentle breeze blew, and he sniffed the air again.

"You can run, Hook, but you cannot hide," Peter said with his head in the air. He chuckled to himself. He would cherish this, the ultimate game of hide and seek. He stepped into the darkness with a grin.

Back in the treasure room, Black Jack pointed at maps as Hook flipped through hand-written pages.

"I wonder if there is a map to this island," Black Jack said. "If we can escape and have a map, returning would be key."

"How can a man so big, be so smart?" Hook said, grinning. "If all these caves and land are detailed somewhere on a map, it would help us get out."

"You can't just get off this island," came a woman's voice. "Well, not this side of the island."

Both men turned, drawing their swords. They did not see anyone.

"It's a ghost, a female phantom," Black Jack said.

"I am no ghost, you big bull," came the voice again.

"Show yourself, treacherous, vile woman!" James huffed.

"I am down here, stupid man," the voice replied.

James scanned the room, then looked down. There sat an iron bird-cage, half-draped with a silk, jewel-coated sheet. James and Black Jack knelt down to look at the small female inside. She glimmered, and her wings fluttered.

"What in the world?" James asked.

"What?" she asked. "Have you never seen a fairy?"

"No. Then again, I have never seen a vampire or a mermaid until this night either," James replied.

"There's no map to the island. Peter has it all in his head. He decides who comes and goes and where and why," she explained. "This is his part of the island."

James leaned in closer to the cage to get a look at this magical creature. "How do we get to the shore? How do we get off this place?"

Belle was silent. She could not betray Peter. They had been friends for so long.

"Tell me, little woman; tell me," James begged.

"I do not know if it is right. I do not want to hurt him," she blurted out. "He was good once. He was a dear friend."

"You won't hurt him by telling me anything. He won't know."

Black Jack removed the necklace quickly from his bull-like neck and dropped it discretely into an opening at the top of James' right boot without him noticing.

"I will say, there is a way, but you must go through the Pits of Despair. They are so awful and treacherous."

"Fine. Pits of Despair. How do we get there from here? Just point us out, and you will never see us again," James replied.

"I can't betray him; he said he cares for me. I talk too much. I won't hurt him more," she replied.

"Why are you in a cage? Why are you hidden away?" James asked.

"Because she knows her place, Hook," came a strong voice.

James stood up quickly and spun around, as did Black Jack. Peter walked into the room, his head held high.

"I admire how far you have come, how you have avoided my great beast. Your spirit is strong," Peter said.

"We just want off the island," Hook replied. "I told you, we have no business here with you. We were brought here."

"I know why you were brought here; Farrell informed me. I know all about you now, Captain James Hook."

"Is he dead?" James asked. "Did you torture him to talk?"

Peter laughed. "He broke like every other man does. And if you wish him to live, you will drop your sword and surrender to me."

"What do you want with the new world?" James asked.

"Oh, you have rummaged through my desk; how nice of you," Peter spat. "Did you help yourself to my gold and my tobacco as well?"

"I just wanted to know the plans of a boy who does not want to grow up and thinks he can be a man," James replied.

Peter chuckled. "A boy who thinks he can be a man? A boy who wants to play all day, indeed."

He walked past his desk, and James and Black Jack stepped back cautiously, even from this small-framed vampire. They watched every subtle action and motion in his body.

"You can't win," Peter warned. "You can't escape. You can join me or die. Those are your choices. If you want to know my plans for the colonies, for the new world, then join me. I could use men like you. Maybe, make the magic not so strong? You could be one of my captains? I could still use good, strong men like you and your large friend."

Peter bent over and picked up the iron birdcage and placed it on the desk. "So, Belle, my sweet Belle, what did you tell them?" Peter asked.

"Nothing, Peter, nothing at all," she chirped. "I was good. I promise."

Peter placed his finger over his thin lips. "Secrets," he said. "Friends do not keep secrets."

He then took one hand and shook the cage violently. Belle was thrown around the cage, slamming into the small iron bars, screaming.

"Hey, come on!" James shouted. "She didn't say anything. Leave her alone."

Peter stopped and looked at Hook. "Tell you what, why don't you tell me what you think my plans are, and I won't shake the cage again."

James was confused. Peter lifted the cage up by his face and smiled.

"Why do you care what I think?" James asked.

"I would like to know what others think they know," he said back.

His tightened his grip on the cage. Belle grabbed tight the small bars, waiting to be shaken. She looked with squinted eyes at James.

"Okay fine, I looked at your stuff," James blurted out.

"And?" Peter asked.

"And you're going to try to take your work to the new colonies and set up in the port of New Orleans. That's all I got. So, what? You move there, start selling, whatever, big deal. Now how about you let us go? I'm sick of your games."

"Games? This is not a game, Hook. It's a plan for a greater life," Peter said.

"No, it's a game. I know the game. People with some power, some authority, trying to act like they are better or bigger than others; it's a game. You're no different than Brady or any of those people in the Queen's Navy or the man who wields money over the poor. It's a game, because you're just a boy. A spoiled, rich child who thinks freedom is a game. I will not play it with you. Never have, and never will. Drop the cage and tell me how we get off the island," James insisted.

Peter laughed, "I am a boy? A spoiled child?" He placed the cage down and drew his sword. "Let's see how you play a game with a spoiled child."

Peter jumped to his desk, moving his blade with ease. Black Jack stepped in front of Hook and pulled a small dagger.

"Typical," Peter said. He jumped down from the desk and began to strike at Black Jack, who deflected the attack, cutting and slicing. Peter yawned, defending the big man's blade with one hand. It was a quick slash upwards that tossed Black Jack's blade from his grip and sent it to the floor.

"Now what, big man?" Peter asked.

Black Jack moved forward, and even with his vampire speed, Peter moved to his left, thinking the strike would come from a fist. But Black

Jack thundered his huge head forward with a head butt, and Peter fell backwards. Peter was quickly put in a bear hug and thrashed wildly. His strength was like nothing Black Jack had felt before. As he groaned and tried to hold on, the boy-like vampire broke free and struck him across the face, sending him to the ground.

Peter jumped on the big man and threw several blows across his face and body. Black Jack blocked several with his huge arms; suddenly, the arms stopped, and his bloody face went still. James lunged and stepped up, but Peter was already awaiting with his blade and knocked Hook's away.

"I may have the small body of a boy, but my true power is in my speed. We will fancy how you are with a blade now, Captain Hook; I do hope you're a better swordsman than a pirate," he sneered.

Peter began to thrust and swing, and Hook countered, stepping back. Each blow of the blades gave James a numb hand, for Peter was as strong as two grown men. Belle watched from her cage, covering one swollen eye with her trembling hand. Hook was backed into a corner, a pile of gold behind him. Peter had his blade out, ready for another attack.

"You are much more fun to play with than most who come to my island, Hook. It's been a pleasure. Now, I must fulfill a promise before I kill you."

Peter slashed and stabbed. Hook blocked and parried; suddenly, Peter's sword moved much faster, and James could not see the attack. In a flash, he watched in horror as his hand, still holding his sword, was sliced from his arm; it flew high into the air and landed in a pile of gold. The pain was not quickly felt; the mental image burned more than his wrist. He pulled his hand in as blood trickled from his forearm. His eyes watered.

"Now, now, this will be quick," Peter said, smiling. "I already have a place for your head on my desk."

Hook could see the power, the madness, in his eyes. His smirk, his spoiled sense of entitlement. James was seething, and he gritted his teeth.

The death blow was coming.

Peter leaned in and whispered into his ear, "All you ever were, all you could have been, I am taking from you forever."

"Run, Hook, run!" came a great thunderous voice.

Peter turned and Black Jack bull-rushed him, slamming him into the desk, pinning him. His sword fell to the floor. Hook wasted no time; he grabbed Peter's sword and ran from the room. Black Jack swung his thick arms, giving a wild attack, driving the vampire-boy across the desk. The birdcage fell to the ground and rolled. Belle hit her head and blacked out. The giant man struggled to physically overpower the boy. He knew every second that Peter was not on his feet, Hook would be running, so he fought harder. He wrapped Peter in a bear hug once again and rolled him off the desk. They crashed to the floor, but Black Jack would not let go. Peter was desperately shaking and thrashing. He bit down on the big man's forearm, and Black Jack let go just enough for Peter to break free. Black Jack slid on his back and began to crawl on his hands and knees, trying to leave the office. Peter rose to his feet and marched at the big man.

Peter picked up James' hand, which still held the sword, from the nearby pile of gold. He grabbed the handle of the blade over Hook's pale hand.

Peter chuckled. "In the end, you may die at your captain's own hand!" he joked and collected his breath. "No, not today. I believe Mama Laveau will have use for you. We have big plans and could use a strong back for them."

"I would die for Captain James Hook any day," the big man grunted.

"Well, my strong friend, today is not that day," Peter replied.

Peter raised the blade over his head, struck the big man across the temple with the sword handle, and Black Jack stopped moving.

Chapter 15

WELCOME TO YOUR DOOM

Hook ran, stumbled, staggered, and crawled through the dimly lit caves. He did not know where he was going, or if he had made a wrong turn. He only knew that he was weak and tired, his friends were dead, and he was being hunted. He had to keep moving. The smell of blood hung in the air; his shirt sleeve was stained from his severed hand.

He came to a cavern; inside, it had a concave ceiling with thick cracks stretching across it, letting in the stars and the moon light. He staggered more though the cavern and fell to his knees in front of another small cave. There were wooden signs and a pile of decorated skulls with paint and feathers. The words on the wooden sign warned in white lettering, "Do Not Play Here," "Pits of Despair," "Warning," and "Go Away!"

Hook peered into the small cliffside. It dropped down; there was no light, rope, or ladder, but it was the only way out of the cavern. He rested and ripped the sleeve off his white shirt to wrap his wrist. He sat back, took several breaths, and watched clouds form in the dawn sky far above him. The daylight was piercing the cavern room. He could now see flowers and grass amongst the rocks and dirt floor. There was life in a room of death. He heard a stirring from across the great cavern and saw a shadow. Peter had found him.

He leaned over the cave entrance, trying to slide down, hoping to find a bottom in the darkness, but he fell for several feet with a crash below, landing hard on what he assumed were rocks. The sword he stole from Peter fell from his grip on impact and disappeared in the darkness. He looked up and a thin beam of light was piercing down into the pit he had just ventured into. He got to his feet and looked down at the dozens of skulls, bones, and tattered clothing that broke his fall. His back ached and his arm was numb as he staggered into the darkness.

He felt around with his good hand, located a shallow enclave, and crawled inside it. He was exhausted; there was nothing left to give. He needed rest. Within a few short seconds, as much as he fought it, his mind and body answered the call. He blacked out as his beaten body, crumpled and worn, was hidden in the darkness of the cave walls.

Peter walked into the large cavern, the sun now spreading its light into the cave. The entire cavern was illuminated and alive. Peter stood on the edge of the sunlight. He could see the signs and the Pits of Despair. No one had ever returned from the pits. These were the catacombs where those who did not change from the vampire's bite or the dark medicine of the witch were left to die. The things in the pit were uncontrollable and animalistic, wild beasts feeding on whatever fell or made its way into the pits. It was a great dumping ground for bodies, trash, and those who did not change.

Peter was tired; he had never had to fight so much as he had in the last several hours. Still, he had much to do, and he wondered how the ships and the hunt on the beach had gone. He stepped a few inches closer towards the sunlight and put out his hand. It began to smoke and smolder.

He sniffed the air, hoping to find the scent of James Hook, but the stench from the pit clouded any smell of anything alive. He pulled his smoking hand back.

"If you did make it this far, Hook, you will wish you let me kill you," he said. He then turned, disappearing back into the caverns.

Belle woke up sharply and looked around the treasure room. Everyone was gone; maps and blood were scattered across the floor. She leaned on her cage door, and the door shifted. She looked at the door lock; it was cracked from the fall. She knelt to examine it. She pushed and it moved more. She looked back to see one of the hinges was broken. She pushed again, and the door opened with a creak. She was free! She could leave, fly away. She could get away from Peter. The rustling of voices came, and she panicked. She pulled the cage door closed and pulled on the hinge to make it look as if nothing had moved. The Voodoo priestess and Peter entered the office treasure room.

"I can send my men into the pit to search for him," she suggested.

"And risk losing more men? We have only enough for our new ships," Peter said.

"You do not know if he even went there. He may have fled, and the beast may pick up his scent," Mama Laveau said.

"I know how to track men," Peter retorted. "I am almost positive he went that way. If he went down into the Pits, he is as good as dead. He is missing a hand, and his spirit, if any is left, is broken," Peter informed her.

"If you like, I could send men to the other side of the island in case he finds a way out or is still hiding close by. We just cannot let them be discovered by the Queen Wolf Lilly," she insisted.

"Yes, double the guard and let the mermaids know as well. Do not worry about Queen Wolf Lilly," Peter said. "She cares not of our side and our business. The treaty is still good, even with the fairies gone."

He started to pick up maps and books from the floor. "Look at this mess," he whined. "It's going to take me hours to get organized again." He bent down and saw Belle, but she lay still, acting as if she were sleeping. He walked to her cage and looked inside.

"She is as tired as I am; I'll let her rest." He walked away from the cage and placed a stack of maps on his desk. "Timing is important, you know. If we sail for the coast of the colonies too soon or too late, the outcome could vary. We need the war as a backdrop to get a stranglehold on the area. New Orleans is the only place I believe to do this. We can run ships, slave ships, weapons. We can buy anything we need to become a powerful force in that region as the two countries fight amongst themselves. When one becomes a victor, they will have to come to us if we own and run all the ports."

"I just want revenge," Mama Laveau said. "That plantation owner, Silas Barns, killed my mother, enslaved my sisters, and took my child. So many beatings and whippings. I swore if I ever got back to the colonies, I would destroy him and his family."

The Voodoo priestess' mind was now back on the plantation; she could hear the screams and feel the crack of the whip on her skin. She shuttered and swore under her breath. "He sold me to that other slave ship for the cost of a box of tea. He knew in time I would try to kill him, so he sold me away and now punishes my family."

"You will see him dead or have him as your slave in due time. I swore this to you years ago," Peter said.

"I know. I need to be patient; I just do not like to be. Oh, to see my sisters and my little one again, if she is still alive. My heart has no time for patience," she pouted.

"Now *you* need patience?" Peter laughed. "That's what you lecture me on. That's amusing."

"Peter, sometimes your sense of humor is boorish. I crave my family and revenge for love," she replied.

"Love is funny sometimes. It makes some men weak, and it makes some men strong. I guess it depends on what you love. Maybe I shall write great books once we are established in New Orleans. I am a gentleman with such wit," Peter suggested.

"Things will look better tomorrow night; I think we all need a good rest," Mama Laveau said.

"I agree," Peter replied.

She turned to leave the treasure room.

"Oh, I almost forgot," Peter said.

She turned back and Peter tossed her Hook's cold, pale hand.

"See, I do not break promises," he said, smiling.

"You are a boy of your word." She wandered back towards the cave entrance, admiring the hand. "I will find a nice place to display this trophy," she said as she left the room.

Peter let out a yawn and rolled out another map on his desk. His eyes blurred from exhaustion, and he shook his head. He was tired. He walked to small candelabra near the bookshelf, and with a mighty blow, blew the light out of the room. He lay down on the floor next to the iron birdcage.

"Do not worry, my sweet Belle. A few more weeks and I will set you free, I promise." He rolled over. Belle heard but could not believe him. She stayed quiet, acting as if she were asleep with a small snore.

Chapter 16

YUM-YUM

James was lying in Molly's bed. It was warm; the pillow was crushed into his face. He lay listening as she hummed sweetly. He opened one eye and saw her half-naked body walking across the room. He felt a small biting on his arm and leaned over to see a small, tan puppy licking and biting at his forearm. The puppy played and jumped, then licked and nipped at him again.

He laughed.

"When did you get a puppy?" Hook asked.

"I didn't get a puppy James," Molly warned. "You need to wake up. Someone is trying to eat you."

"Eat me?" he asked.

ames awoke with a start and looked down in the darkness. A small, childlike creature was gnawing at his bloody wrist. Its breath was heavy. Its hair was matted, and its skin was flaking from its young face. It stopped and looked up at him, eyes dull black like a piece of coal. It took a step back, hunched over, and pointed at him.

"Yummy..." it hissed. The child-like creature then dove on him, beginning to gnaw on his bloody rags.

James tossed the child off and saw a rusty broken sword amongst bones and trash which was scattered across the ground.

"What kind of hellish creature are you?" he whispered.

The boy hissed and ran in circles, striking itself in the head.

"Yum-yum-yum!" it cried. It stopped and stared angrily at James. "My yum-yums!" it yelled one more time and charged James with its fanged mouth open, letting out a war cry.

James picked up the broken sword and slashed quickly. The creature collapsed into the wall and fell to the floor. He was fixated on the small thing; it wore grey cotton pants, a soiled brown shirt, and had bare feet. It looked almost human but wild like a beast.

If it was a boy at one time, it was no longer. He looked down at his stump-like wrist, then at the darkness of the caverns. The cliff was too high to climb. Below him, the pile that broke his fall was full of trash and bones.

He began to sift through the trash, finding broken cups, plates, clothing, and broken furniture pieces. He found a few small candles. He was desperate to find anything he could use; he knew he did not have much time. What if there were more of those things down in the caves? He took the candles, a broken fork, and some worn rope. He gathered them in his arms and left the trash pile. His wrist was throbbing. He could see light through cracks in the roof. He saw the dozens of possible animal or human bones scattered about the cavern in the dim light. That sole creature was not the only one. He tightened the grip on his sword and began to push on though the darkness.

Belle was awake and did her best to make the door on her cage look as if nothing happened. Peter might sleep until dusk, but he was known to only nap. She had little time before he may attend to her cage.

She was right to assume he would wake and not wait for nightfall. He rolled over with a stretch and sat up, looking to the cage and at Belle.

"Lots to do today, Belle. I will return. I must go see if the new prisoners, I mean guests, are taken care of. Plus, we now have two new ships. That gives us four ships to use when we all leave the island for New Orleans. It is quite wonderful, is it not?" Peter asked.

"I am so happy our plan is coming together, Peter. Though, I thought you would let me stay with the other magical creatures on the island," Belle replied.

Peter stood up and grabbed the cage. He straightened it. Belle looked to the door and lock, hoping he did not see the damage.

"I know I said I would set you free," Peter said, "but we may need your magic when we get to the new world."

Belle frowned. "Peter, you promised."

"I know, but let's wait to see. I may not need you at all. Just be patient." He then placed her cage on the desk. "Besides, how do you know there aren't others like you in the new world? It could be a great adventure for all of us."

"But you promised, and you always keep your promises," Belle reminded.

"I know, but I may have to break it, just this once. Only because I care so much for you. You are a part of our family," Peter reminded her.

"But Peter..." she began.

"Enough!" he shouted. "I do not want to hurt you. I do not want to break my promise, but you continuously push me. I have to go."

The boy vampire stormed from the treasure room. Belle knew she had to escape, or she would be going with them.

Peter was not the friend she once had years ago, and his word and promises were empty now. Her small, trembling hands reached for the door of the cage. She pushed lightly and with a creak, it swung open. It was there: Freedom. To be away from him and that terrible witch. She just had to step out from the cage. She wondered, *Will he hunt me? If he finds me, he will punish me or even kill me?* She grabbed the small door and closed it tightly. Her head sunk, and she began to weep.

Deep in the Pits of Despair, James lit a candle using a flint and stone. He tied broken pieces of wood and rope to his stump-like wrist, so his hand was now a small torch. The light was little, but it gave off enough illumination to give a path; he could move forward in the darkness.

In the shadows, Edward was watching. He would take several steps, stopping and starting as James did. James did not like being hunted. Edward was studying the prey, not to attack him, but to learn. The other creatures ran and made noise but not Edward. With such little light and the loss of blood, the shadows played tricks on James' mind.

As he lost focus, his other hand clung tightly to the sword with such fever that it continuously went numb from the overuse of the muscles in his hand.

It was not that James was brave or foolish, but fear and staying battle-ready can wear one down. Hook was near the end of his rope. The shadows moved, and he heard small footsteps running or walking behind him. Or were they in front of him?

The sounds in the caves could confuse the best hunters and trackers. He swore he could make out children laughing or crying. James always excelled at hunting and tracking but took pleasure in escaping to live another day. That, and making women laugh, he could make happen with little effort. Some called it charm; others called it luck. Either way, now, in the shadows of the caves, James felt neither charmed nor lucky. He moved on, step by step, hoping that every tunnel continued, for a dead end may be his end.

Farrell watched from his cage as Mama Laveau tossed various plants into the large, black cauldron. The smell started as a warm soup but finished like spoiled meat. She mumbled under her breath, focused solely on the strange brew. Farrell knew he and his men were lost, but he smiled slightly. As long as Hook was not dead, there was a glimmer of hope.

"You know, the Navy will come looking for us," he stated.

The Voodoo priestess continued to stir.

"You can't lose two ships and not have a search. You killed an admiral," he continued.

"We have time. Your Navy will not arrive for several weeks; by then, we will have left," she said with a grin.

"It may be only a few days. I was to report to my superiors in two days with Hook and his men. When I do not go into port, they will start searching," Farrell remarked.

Mama Laveau stopped.

Farrell knew he could do nothing to help his cause now except give false information, hoping to irritate and complicate their plans.

"I was not serving under the admiral; I was asked to join him, secretly. So, unfortunately for you, I am sure the Navy will come looking in days, not weeks."

"You lie," she said angrily.

"Why do you think my ship stayed back from the beach? Or why my men came in hours later to rescue us? They were not part of the admiral's plan. When we do not come to port, they will assume trouble, maybe pirates, and send ships quickly. Maybe even put out a reward?" Farrell asked rhetorically.

"Your ship was not that big. You and your crew are not important," she hissed.

"Maybe not, but if they fear pirates or war, the ships in the area will search. Either way, you will have company much sooner than you like," Farrell remarked.

The Voodoo priestess stormed over to the cage, and Farrell fell back. "No matter how many men search, you will find yourself in my cooking pot, and parts of your body will accompany us to the new world. We have more men, more dark magic, more ships, and now weapons. And we have Peter! You underestimate him because of his small body and child-like appearance. He is very wise and cunning. Our plan is good, our strength is growing, and you sit in a wooden cage, about to be part of a meal for my living-dead soldiers. You have nerve and foolishness in your veins!"

"A vampire-boy and dark, island magic can be halted by men with will," Farrell said.

Peter walked into the cavern. "Oh good, he is awake and chatty. What do you speak of now, Captain?" Peter asked.

"Men of good character. Men who want freedom," Farrell said.

"Those are good traits in men, but I plan on using other traits, such as greed and power. Those outweigh such good men. Look at your own country, look at history, power struggles, war. But if you're cunning, if you're patient, if you are prepared, you can take it all. And we will," Peter stated.

"Just how do you plan to take it all? If I am to die, I would like to hear your plan, strictly as an outsider. With my military history, I am curious. Telling it to blood-feeding children and mermaids cannot give you confidence," Farrell insisted.

"I like that you stall your death by trying to play mind games with me. It is humorous. Maybe we shall keep you alive for my personal entertainment, removing a finger or limb and then hearing what you have to say," Peter said with a grin.

Farrell went silent. Peter looked at the captain and grunted, then turned and walked to Mama Laveau and the bubbling pot.

"Did you kill him yet?" Farrell asked.

Peter stopped walking and turned around. "The island will feed on him, and he will wish he died from my hand."

"So, he lives," Farrell clasped his hands together. "Even a creature like yourself could not kill him."

Peter ran to the cage and grabbed Farrell by the coat, shaking him. "Who is this Hook!? Why does he live, and why do you doubt my island will kill him?" he asked angrily.

"If you give me some water and some bread, I will tell you tales of James Hook and how he has avoided death and capture and has more luck in him than the entire land of Ireland," Farrell offered.

Peter let go of his coat. "How do you kill him?"

"I do not know if you can. I know he has escaped death more than a dozen times, and the more you upset him, the more vengeful he becomes. I would not want to be on the pointed end of a sword held by the mighty James Hook," Farrell replied.

"The Mighty Hook indeed!" Peter scoffed. "I took his right hand." He pointed to a glass bowl where James' pale hand rested. "He is a good fighter, but luck can only sustain life so long. It will run out," Peter said angrily.

"His only weakness is a curvy woman with a pretty laugh. Until you find his corpse, I would never think his luck had run out," Farrell warned.

Peter turned. "We need to send out search parties. I want that man found and brought to me tonight!"

"You think he could survive the Pits?" the witch asked.

"At this point, I believe he may. Let's be ready if he emerges and tries to flee our island. Have Niviene patrol the water with her mermaids. We will sweep the beach and send your men into the jungles," Peter said.

"If he does emerge from the Pits, what if he gets to the Jungle of Light? What if she finds him? She and her man may find out your plans of the island and the magic I have been using. Queen Wolf Lilly was born a child of the ancients, and my magic is disdained by them. They do not know the true power of the other side of the unseen world," the witch cautioned.

"Their kind hates what scares them. Why do you think she refuses to see me these last few years? She is afraid of your power and mine. We must stop him before he gets close. I do not need those savages aiding him or slowing down our plan. We are too close now. A one-handed, broken man will not stop us. Come, let's go to the beach; I will summon the children," Peter insisted.

Peter and Mama Laveau walked quickly from the cavern, disappearing into the darkness. Farrell let out a sigh.

"I thought I would get some water and buy James some time. I was wrong on both counts." He slumped back into his cage. "Good luck, Hook."

Every new dimly lit cave room and turn chipped away at James' heart. The candle he had tied to his bloody stump was withering to a smolder, and the sounds of small, quick feet echoed around him as he trudged on. The small cracks in the ceiling that allowed sunlight to cut through were few and far between. He kept his blade in front of him and spun around slowly every few steps, knowing there were things in these caves that man or beast would rather not see again.

He continued to another fork in the caverns. *Right or left, life or death?* The question burrowed deep in his mind, but he knew if he did not choose, death would come faster. *One foot in front of the other, James,* he thought, turning left. There was a burst of childlike laughter, then screaming. He quickened his pace down the tunnel, looking back over his shoulder. Those things, the little beasts, were closing in. Were they hungry or were they hunting him as a game? In the shadows, Edward continued to track and study. He was not like the others.

Hook moved on, and then a smell hit him; it was water, the ocean. He walked faster, and suddenly, his boots became wet. He had walked into a large lagoon in the cavern. The water became deeper with each step. It was a dead end. Small holes in the cracked ceiling showed the sun was going down, and the remaining light sparkled off the dark water. He looked down at the water; there must be a tunnel out towards the ocean. He could smell the salt in the air and the pounding of the surf; he was close. He began to walk faster, and the water rose past his knees. Suddenly, the laughter grew louder. He turned, and there were half a dozen small, pale looking children with fanged teeth, black eyes, and tattered clothing. Their staggered walk and monstrous faces showed that if they were once human, that part of them had died long ago.

The children hissed and ran into the water. Two of them jumped, knocking James back into the shallow pool. The candle went out, and Hook swung his blade in a fury. The closest child felt the sting of the blade first and sank into the water. The others fell back momentarily, allowing James to get to his feet. The salt water dripped on his shaggy face; the sea was close. It was behind him, or at least behind the rock walls of the cave behind him. The remaining children ran into the water with their hands reaching, hissing and splashing angrily.

James tightened the grip on his sword and advanced with several quick strikes. Three more of the creatures fell back, screaming and bleeding into the water. One of the children grabbed a small, bloody limb from the water and ran off with it, holding it in its hands and teeth like a stray dog with a fresh bone from the butcher shop. Hook stepped quickly to his right and thrust the sword, stabbing another of the small ghouls in its chest. He held it under the shallow water as it kicked and splashed.

He looked around, hoping more of the children were not coming. Only one watched him. Another was standing near the rocks, feeding on the arm. The little creature stopped fighting and went still, and Hook pulled the sword from its pale body. One of the small creatures hissed and looked around. It was alone.

"Not so tough without your..." James began, and the boy jumped from the water and knocked him into the water. He bit James' neck and head like a wild dog.

James grabbed him and tossed him off, sending him skipping across the lagoon like a large stone. The creature got to his feet and screamed angrily. James' broken blade lashed out, cutting the creature across its small chest. It whimpered and tried to get back to the shore, but it was only a few feet away when it stopped and began to float in the water.

James watched its body gently move in the current. The water was moving; there was a current from outside the caves. He looked to the shore as the last little creature fed and walked from the shallow water, back to dry land. The little monster was not paying attention, only gnawing on the arm piously and humming. Hook's shadow rose over him, and it stopped. He looked over his shoulder and smiled.

"Yum-yum!" it said and lifted the small, bloody arm to share it with James.

"No, thank you," James replied. He made his blade work again, killing the small boy-like creature.

He sat on the ground, surveying the damage of the bodies strewn about as they moved with the tide in the lagoon. He laid back, his hand still gripping his blade. He looked up at the sunlight disappearing from the ceiling cracks. He did not have much time. He waited several minutes to regain some strength, then sheathed his broken sword to his belt and walked into the water. He took a deep breath and dove into the darkening depths. He swam down close to 20 feet. It was nearly black, but he felt the rocks and returned to the surface. He took another breath and went down to feel around.

There was a break in the rock wall, and the water pushed him backwards. He heard out in the darkness but could only see a couple yards deep. He returned to the surface and took a deep breath. He had two choices: die in a deep tunnel or be attacked and eaten by whatever was in the caverns. He may not get a second chance at the tunnel, and the light was leaving with every moment he waited. He held his breath one more time and shoved off, deep down into the lagoon.

He found the entrance of the cave and used the sides to push and kick ahead, saving his strength. His air was running short as small air bubbles left his nose. He scanned the water but saw no light or end. He pushed forward harder and quicker as his lungs burned and his body ached. He reached for more wall to push in the darkness but found none.

He swam and kicked in the darkness. The water pushed back harder now; he had to be close. He had to be near the ocean. He looked up and could see the sun setting, the last of its light on the top of the water. It was only a few feet away.

He pushed the air from his lungs, shot up, and broke from the water. He gasped loudly, filling his lungs again. He thrashed for a minute before calming himself and floating on his back. He looked around. He was in a lagoon with small plants and trees; 200 yards away was sand and the ocean.

He reached up towards the sun as it crested over the dark water and let out a sigh. If night came, Peter and his minions would find him. He had to hide again.

He floated to the shore and collapsed onto the lagoon's sandy beach. He looked at the stars for a moment as they started to fill the sky. He had to rest; he had nothing left. He needed a moment to catch his breath again. He closed his eyes and began to drift off. He thought he was dreaming because he heard the most beautiful laughing from young women. They laughed again. He kept his eyes closed, hoping this was all in his head and he was back at Molly's.

"What do we do with him now?" a young woman's voice asked.

"I do not know how much a soaking-wet man is good for," said another and more laughter began.

James peered with one eye open. In the lagoon, three beautiful women swam towards him. Their skin was soft, their hair was glowing, and their smiles were beautiful, except for the fangs.

James cursed under his breath. He had seen what they could do to a man. He shook his head and sat up.

"Oh look, he lives," one of them joked.

"Do we tell Niviene or Peter?" asked another.

"Or do we keep him for ourselves?" the third one said. They all laughed at that.

"If I am going to be your plaything, you need to know, I bite back," James said.

"This son of Adam, he bites back?" one said. "I like him."

James had always been a charmer, but these were not just women. As good as his silver tongue was, he knew they would rather have it served, with his heart, on a platter. He winced as they came closer to the shore and rose from the water. All three were topless, curvy, with seaweed decorating their upper shoulders.

"I think we scare him. Not much fight in a one-armed man," said the leader, who had a seaweed tie in her blonde hair. The two behind her giggled.

James got to his feet. "I may only have one arm, but that's not what I need to handle the three of you," he said smiling, staring down the blond in the front.

She smiled, showing her fangs a bit more. "Unbelievable! The confidence of this human male. It is a shame we have to kill him."

"Well, in my defense, against three beautiful women such as yourselves, killing me with pleasure is the most horrible way I can imagine dying. So, whatever your plans, whatever you do, please do not use your charms and those lips against me. I believe your exotic powers would break my heart and soul. Please do not use your beauty to kill me," James replied.

The two behind her laughed, and a small blush rose on their porcelain faces.

"Enough, male mortal," the leader said. "I see you are well-versed in speaking and have had your way with many human women in the past. We do not crave such a thing."

"No, why would you? The touch of a strong man, his passion pressed hard against your frail lips. The feeling and adrenaline of lust, like war that beats dense in a man's chest. Have you even kissed a real man or just killed them?" James asked.

"That is none of your business!" she spat.

"Oh, I see the one in the back, with the red hair. Yes, you have kissed a man and liked it," he remarked.

The mermaid looked away, almost embarrassed.

"You amuse me. Maybe we should take you back to Peter alive," the leader said.

"Oh, we do not want to do that," James said, then peeled off his shirt.

"What are you doing?" she asked.

"Look, if you're going to kill me, then do it. If not, I am coming in the water to show you what a man's kiss is like."

"What? No, wait!" she blurted out.

James dove in the water and swam to the mermaids. "If I am to die, it will be in the arms of beautiful women, not some boy who thinks he is a god."

The mermaids were frozen. James swam close and looked at the blonde leader. He slowly caressed her straw-colored hair.

"You may take me to the bottom of the sea and feed on me, but my last moments will be spent holding a beautiful goddess close to my chest and feeling her lips on mine," he said.

The two behind her swam closer; they now circled Hook.

"Do it," he said. "Kiss me or kill me. I do not care which. But know this: I am not afraid to kiss you or have death take me if I have lovely creatures such as yourself near me."

The mermaid shuddered, and he leaned in and grabbed her hand, pulling her close. He kissed her hard. She started to back away, but he held her close. He broke from the kiss and looked at her.

"Do you wish to drown me? I am ready," he said.

She smiled. "I can always bring you to Peter when we are done with you."

The other mermaids laughed and the two behind him kissed his neck.

He grabbed her hair and kissed her again. He felt their cold hands across his chest. He closed his eyes, kissing her harder. She bit his lip and it bled.

"Mortal men are so weak," she whispered in his ear. "Breeding with us kills most. I hope you have the strength."

She swam back a couple feet and looked at him as the two behind him rubbed his shoulders. "How long should we play with him, girls?" she asked.

"At least until he is at death's door, if he can handle it," the one with red hair suggested.

"Oh, I can handle it," Hook said. He looked out into the lagoon. He thought he saw movement, but his judgment was not very clear as the blonde pressed up against him and kissed him. She pulled back and smiled.

"I will not try to hurt you too badly, human. But it will be something to take to your deathbed, even if it's only a few minutes away," she said.

"Do what you must," Hook said.

He could not win against such powerful creatures, but maybe he could buy time. Besides, he enjoyed doing this even more than pirating.

She kissed him again and grazed her fangs across his neck. He turned red. She smiled and looked into his eyes. "I will make it worth dying for."

She kissed him hard, and the unworldly pleasure struck him. His mind swirled with emotions, but it stopped as quickly as it had started. He could no longer breathe. It was if he were drowning. He opened his eyes and was captured in her gaze. Suddenly, her face went blank. There was a *swoosh,* and she screamed, looking at him. Hook tried to push back and swim away. She turned, showing several arrows protruding from her back. The other two mermaids began to swim as arrows flew, striking them. They dove and swam. The one with red hair rose to the surface and tried to catch her breath, and three arrows struck her. She kicked her fins and floundered in the water.

The blonde turned to Hook and grabbed him by the head. She slammed her head into his and punched him several times in the face. She tossed him, and he crashed to the beach. James was dazed as he saw more arrows strike the blonde mermaid, who hissed and splashed. She jumped high in the air and dove into the water as arrows struck her.

James looked to the beach, and a dozen men wearing buckskin and holding bows and torches approached. They surrounded him. His head pulsed, and it all came crashing down on him. He looked to the moon, and a beautiful, tan woman with long black hair, wearing a bone necklace, looked down at him. Her eyes were wild and warm.

"I had them right where I wanted them," he said.

"I am sure you did," she assured him. James smiled and blacked out.

Chapter 17

STRANGE DAYS AHEAD

It was the smell of cooked meat that woke James, the scent of roasting fowl. His eyes opened slowly, and he sat up and looked around. The sun was rising in the east, and he sat under a tree on the beach. There were a dozen men by a large fire. One of them was roasting two small birds over the flames. James shook his head and tried to get up, but he realized he was better sitting for now.

He leaned back. His body ached, and his forearm throbbed. He looked at his wrist. The wound was redressed and covered in strange, dark-purple plants. He sniffed it; it was sweet like a berry, but still strong like medicine. One of the men pointed to him from the fire, and two of them with the woman in buckskin walked towards him.

"You are very lucky. I do not know of any man to escape from Peter's side of the island," she said.

James tried to get up, but he staggered and fell back to his butt. He stayed down. "His side?" he asked.

"You must have a lot of questions, so let me start by telling you my name. I am Queen Wolf Lilly, the leader of our tribe. We live and guard the west side of the island. We hunt, fish, live, and survive. We have been here for several generations. We have always known of the dark magic on the other side island but have stayed away from Peter, his witch, the mermaids, and the abominations of his blood feeding lost boys. They have polluted the magic of this ancient land."

"Why don't you fight him? Kill them off?" James asked.

"It is not that easy. When I was a girl, this island was a paradise with magic and power, peace and life. Many things have changed since Peter came into power, he and that witch. Now we and other creatures of magic stay on our half of the island in the deepest parts of the jungle. I am afraid time and the power of magic are faltering. We were on a hunting party, saw your little adventure with those scaly-skinned harpies, and thought maybe if we save you, we could learn more of what Peter has been hiding. We have a treaty with him and those devilish fish women, but we know he is planning something. If we must kill a few to find out, so be it," she explained.

James let out a sigh. "He is killing, enslaving, and planning on doing a hell of a lot more. I have to figure out how to get back, save my friends, my crew. If any of them are still alive at this point."

"Your crew is as good as dead," Queen Wolf Lilly said.

Hook tried to stand, and this time did momentarily before falling back on the tree. "Well, that sounds very encouraging, but I can't let them die for nothing. He killed my crew; he took my friend hostage. He has a Voodoo priestess, an army of living-dead, and he is controlling men. He enslaves them. Have you seen the children? They feed on blood. And the caves, what are those things in the bloody caves?"

"We do not go into the caves, even on the outside of the island," she said.

"Well, damn right! I mean, what are those things?" he asked.

"They are what happens when dark magic does not hold on humans, mindless feeding creatures. What is your name?" she asked.

"I am James Hook. I am a pirate. Well, I am not a pirate. I'm just... I don't know what right now. I am the captain of the ship, *The Conqueror*. My crew and I were taken against our will and are now stuck on this island. He killed my friends and has some locked in a caged, and I want him dead!" James replied.

"Well, James Hook, I can tell you he is very strong. Unless you have a small army, he will kill you, and your friends are going to be his puppets to control," she said.

"I have to stop him. My crew did not die for nothing, so I could escape. They gave their lives, so I could get closer to escaping this damn island," James said angrily.

"If you are to escape this island, you will need a ship. I do not know if one of ours will get you where you need to go, but in time we could build one," she said.

"I do not have time." James felt a sharp pain in his side and fell over.

"You have many wounds, Hook. You need to heal," she said.

"I need a ship and a crew, and I will take that monster to hell," he said angrily and felt his side.

"Rest here. You are safe for a while. Our village is a day's journey to the east. In a few days or weeks, we may..." she started to say.

"We do not have days or weeks. He is planning something to leave the island and go to the new world with all his vampires, living-dead, and whatever else he can pack up. I saw a fairy, yeah, a fairy. She had wings and talked. I think I am going mad on this island," he said and sat back down.

"You are not going mad, James Hook. This is a magical island, and Peter was not always the monster you see. We were friends as children, as young children." She went on, "I met him over 50 years ago, before the witch, the slave-trading, the mermaids, and the horrors of darkness, when he was just a boy. A cursed boy with a need for blood, but still, we spoke, played, and at one point, loved."

Hook rubbed his eyes. He was still so very tired.

"He was good and fun, but he changed. He became violent, angry. My family forbid me to go to the other side of the island. One night, under a full moon, I confessed my love and kissed him. He laughed and said he had no plans on being in love or having love, but he said we could play and be friends forever if he gave me a kiss on the neck. I ran home and never returned to that side of the island. A treaty was bonded years later. We were both present but neither spoke. This island has many magical elements and creatures. The fairies were killed off by something a few years ago. Some said pirates, but no humans come to this island without our knowledge. I believe the Voodoo woman, the one who has caused pain for all of us, had something to do with it. She even had the mermaids conspire against us! We were all together once, an island of magic and creatures of legends. The treaty has kept things civil on the island for nearly a decade now. We do not bother his side of the island, and they say they do not come to ours," she explained.

"So, in all that time, you still have not spoken?" James asked.

"I believe he has tried or visited me in my dreams. But the witch came years ago, and the island changed. Peter changed even more. Now, we stay to our side, and so do the good things of this island. If he is leaving, this is good for us and the others. This island can once again be a home for all magical creatures," she replied.

"Well, it won't be good for people in the colonies. He is going to sneak in, take over, and make life hell for people. I have seen his maps and plans; he has ships and a small army set up," James said.

"I wish I could do more to help you, but it's not our battle, James Hook. If it's true that he is leaving, my people and the magic creatures of this island will finally be free from him and the witch," she replied.

"You helped save my life from the mermaids, so I know you have a good conscience," James said.

"We regret killing any magical creature. Maybe we hunt them because they kill our fisherman? Or because they come to our side of the island to seduce our young warriors only to feed on them? That treaty is ignored by many, but having it makes others feel safe. If they do plan on leaving, then maybe the world of magic will get to control the whole island once again," she explained.

James let out a sigh. He would not find an ally here, only rest.

"Take heart, Hook. If you do get off the island, you can know you did all you could and still have your life. Your stump hand will be a remembrance of the evils and troubles this place has, and how you are the only man to get away from such a creature as Peter.

"Things like Peter should be stopped and destroyed," he said.

"If what you say is true, he is very powerful now. I will not risk my warriors and magic when he may be leaving anyway. His choice to leave only helps us," Queen Wolf Lilly said. "Come back to our village, rest, get your strength back. We will help you get off the island, and then you can start a new life. It's the best thing you can do."

"And what of my crew? What of their memories, their sacrifices?" James asked.

"We all have ghosts in our pasts and dark memories that we must let go of. Life is not always fair, Hook," she remarked.

"I do not want fair, I want revenge! I want my hand back! I want my crew back! I want to make sure he does not do this or bring the horrors of this island to others!" James shouted.

"I admire your heart and courage, but sometimes in life, you cannot beat the enemy. It is time for you to rest; come back with us," she implored.

"I do need rest. I need a damn ship and a damn crew, so I can kill that vampire-boy-king! Then I can rest!" James said vengefully.

"You will die if you keep pushing this hard. It's foolish," she said.

"I would rather be thought a fool by a stranger than a quitter by those who sacrificed everything for me to live and fight on," James shot back, gritting his teeth.

Queen Wolf Lilly signaled to her men with a quick hand motion, and they began to walk down the beach. She stopped and looked out to the water. A small boat was approaching.

James rose to his feet and peered out as the little boat bobbed and slowly made its way to the shore. It was a rowboat.

"Maybe fate or luck has found your ship, James Hook." She then walked away to join her men.

"Father Bob," James said.

The old pirate brought the boat to the sand and climbed out.

"We are in need of a captain," he said.

"And I am in need of a ship and crew," Hook said.

Father Bob walked to Hook and looked him over. "You live. And the others?"

"Lost to the island. I will tell you more on the row back to The Cove," he replied.

"All?" Father Bob asked.

"Yes, all, Father Bob. There is a great evil on the island which no one could be ready for. Now, help me on that beautiful boat and get us off this cursed land," James replied.

Hook leaned on Father Bob, and with a limp, the two made their way to the rowboat. Father Bob helped James in, and he sunk back. Hook looked back at Queen Wolf Lilly. She let out a sigh. She snapped her fingers, and two of her warriors placed several canteens, two satchels of fruit, and pieces of meat in the small boat.

"May the goddess of the sea get you back safely. I hope you take my advice, and you and your old friend stay away and never set foot here again," she said.

"Thank you for your kindness. You will see me again," he said, smirking. He raised his stump-like hand. "This is not over; the memories and sacrifices of my crew will be avenged."

Father Bob pushed the small boat from the shore and climbed in. Hook took a piece of fruit and began to eat as the old man rowed. Father

Bob could see Hook's face was dark. He knew his captain; now was not the time to talk. It was time to row. James kicked his boot. There was something in it. He took his one good hand and struggled to pry his boot away from his foot. He pulled off the boot and shook it. Black Jack's necklace fell out, what he called his gris-gris. James lifted it up and looked it over as Father Bob continued to row.

"Lucky charm indeed," he said. "We will need more than luck to return and kill that creature." He took off his other boot, and three rubies rolled out to the floor of the boat.

"Great Joseph and all the saints!" Father Bob exclaimed.

"I may still only be an adventurer and thief, but I think this could help buy us some vengeance," Hook said.

Father Bob picked up the giant rubies. "Aye. I think it could buy you a small army if needed."

"That is my plan," James said. He laid back in the rowboat and closed his eyes. "To The Cove Father Bob, to The Cove."

Niviene was livid, her hands in tight fists as she walked past the dock. The only surviving mermaid sat, bloody and clinging to a wooden beam on the walkway. Peter stood nearby, as did Mama Laveau.

"Two more of my girls, my family, killed by her. You could have wiped her tribe out years ago. They have come into our part of the island and now this. This is an act of war!" she said angrily.

"Technically, your girls were trespassing on their side of the island," Peter said. His tone was scolding.

"There is no side. This was our island at one point. We swam free between the caves, the lagoons, and had total freedom," she replied.

"And you will again, very soon. We will leave, and then you and your kind can set up war against them and the others if you wish," Peter said.

Niviene walked with a huff to Peter and looked down at the vampire-boy-king. "You brought this on us. We took sides. We helped you against the magical creatures of the forest. The elves left, the fairies were killed by pirates, and now, we are enemies of anything on that side of the island."

"You chose your side years ago, Niviene. I have kept your kind safe from pirates and harpoons, nets, and slavery," he shot back.

"This island could have been all ours if you did not have a crush on her as a youth. You could have turned her. You could have made her your queen, but no, you wanted to play. You wanted to be friends and run around all hours of the night. And now, you grow tired of the island and small conquests. Your dreams of a future may be grown-up, but your way of getting them is still childish," she lashed out.

Peter blinked and instantly, his small hand held a blade to her neck. "Do you wish to die today?" he asked.

Niviene knocked his hand away. "You would threaten me? You can convince mortals of your power and strength; I do not fear you."

"I do not want you to fear me, Niviene. I want you to respect me and follow my orders," Peter replied.

Niviene walked to the water and jumped in. "You're nothing like Arthur or the ones before him in the times of magic and of the ancients."

She went to the wounded mermaid and began to caress her hair.

"I need you to obey me," Peter said.

"I will not obey you any longer. Not at the cost of my girls. You are losing your edge, Peter. This plan of yours is killing what we all had. Your endless lust for power has driven you to madness."

"It's not madness; it's survival," Peter stated.

"We survive on this island just fine, but your new plans bring men and trouble. This one man, this Hook, has vexed and beaten you," she reminded him.

Peter walked to the end of the dock and looked down at the warm water.

"He has not beaten me; he has fled. He will not return. Our plan to leave this island will continue. We now have ships, men, and weapons. We can move into the new world. Do not worry yourself, Niviene, of our plans; you will not be needed. Go take care of your mermaids. Live in the past with your legends and talk of ancient times. If I wanted that damn sword, I would have taken it from you by now. You gave it to a boy-king to help rule a small island, and he is a hero? I plan on ruling the world. I can become a god without it! I just hope you and your girls can avoid the nets and spears of men when my protection of this island is over."

Peter walked back to Mama Laveau, and they both turned to walk towards the caves.

"She is scared; she may come back to us," the Voodoo priestess suggested.

"No need. In a few short weeks, we will leave, and she can fend for herself like they did before. Bragging of her power in the times of kings and magic. She bleeds like men, so she can die as one, not some demigod of ancient times. '*Oh, look, I can live in the water and on land; oh, I am special.* I grow so weary of this place, of old magic and old ways of thinking. America will find us our true fortunes. We will see how she and her kind like to be trophies or hunted as folly for lonely sailors," Peter replied.

They walked into the cave entrance. Peter heard the boys laughing and playing from the dining hall.

"I think spending some time with my friends will do me some good," Peter said.

"And what of that man, Farrell?" Mama Laveau asked.

"His threats are as empty as his pockets right about now. No one comes to this island, even if they are looking for a ship. Your magic keeps the fog blanketing our side, and Queen Wolf Lilly has her own magic to protect her side from visitors as well. Farrell or Brady are not worth much to the Navy. Everyone is expendable," Peter stated.

"Like Niviene?" Mama Laveau asked.

"Yes, like Niviene. You and I, however, we're partners. We will do what we must to get what we want," Peter said.

"Do you think Niviene could cause trouble for you and your ships before you leave?" Mama Laveau asked.

"If she does, I will put out the traps and lock them away. She has nerve speaking to me like that. I have a mind to make an example of her to her girls if she does not conform and apologize," Peter stated.

"We could use her one last time to bring in another slave ship. Now, with such a large fleet, we need a few more men," the witch added. "Why not apologize, keep her close, and when you get all you need from her, then set the traps? We will leave the island with a full crew, and she and her maidens can starve or be hunted off."

"Do we really need more slaves?" Peter asked.

"You killed many of the men on both ships, Peter. We need more crew," the witch replied.

He let out a sigh. "Fine, I will go and make amends. We have spent this much time in planning, no need to have it come unraveled due to a small snag in the plan. I will go see her tomorrow night."

"Excellent," Mama Laveau said. "What to do with Farrell, now that Hook is gone?"

"Feed him to the creature, or maybe we can use him for a game with the boys, a good hunt after a good meal. Yes, we will use him for a game, he and a few more. Before we leave for our journey, one last hunt on the island to celebrate. I like this idea! A grand party, a goodbye party for us all!" Peter said joyfully.

"It will be done," she said.

It took nearly six days for the small boat to fight and chug its way to The Cove. Both Hook and Father Bob were sunburnt, dehydrated, and starving. When they were within distance of seeing the pirate island, it awoke their need for survival, and both men, without saying a word, pushed hard, rowing and looking to the island for moral support. Father Bob would take small breaks, removing his glasses and squinting, hoping they were getting closer. Hook focused more on his stump-like arm and the fury that burned within him.

The small ship slid into the coastal beach past several large ships, and both men dropped the oars and dropped their heads. Father Bob began to whisper a prayer, and Hook begrudgingly said, "Amen," when he was done. They staggered from the boat onto the beach as other pirates and sailors walked the boardwalk, trading and going about their mid-day routines.

They walked slowly into the line of shops and taverns. A rain bucket was against a brick building, and both men splashed water and drank slowly like horses at a water trough. With some of their strength returned and their faces and hair dripping with cool water, the two pirates caught their breath and looked around the shipyard.

"What do we do next, Captain?" asked Father Bob, the water dripping from his shaggy chin.

"I find a crew, we get our ship from Molly, and we go and kill that boyish hell-creature," James replied.

"So, all or nothing?" Father Bob asked.

"Isn't that the only way, dear Father Bob?" James asked in return.

"Only way we know," he replied. "I have a silver coin in my boot; it's all I have. I will find us a room, some food, and other small supplies."

"Go find Molly and do not say of our adventure. Just get a room. I have to see a man about an army," Hook said.

"How's your arm?" Father Bob asked.

"It's healing, but it will never know the satisfaction of holding a sword or the caress of a firm woman's flesh, and that bitters me to the core," James replied.

"There are a few doctors on the island. We could..." Father Bob started.

"No, Father Bob. Go to Molly, and get a room," James insisted.

"Aye, Captain." Father Bob walked off quickly, and Hook looked down at his stump-like hand.

The Dead Reef was quiet, and the sunlight seemed to flutter from the small windows. The patrons, all worn and seasoned men of the sea, sat sipping their drinks from almost-clean goblets. Huxley sat in the back of this well-known, well-guarded tavern. Two young, busty women, one on each side, caressed his beard and giggled quietly. He smiled as one whispered in his ear.

The door of the tavern flew open with a creak and a slam. James stood in the dim light. His face was red and cooked, his clothing cut and shredded, and his stump-like arm hung to his side. He looked like a starved dog coming in from a storm, a stray dog you would not want to approach for fear it may make a meal of you. What little sound there was in the tavern was cut short as men stared at him.

He stepped in, walked past the bar and patrons, and approached Captain Huxley's back table. He stopped short and looked down at the legendary pirate. Some men slid their hands to their knives and pistols. Huxley made no sudden moves.

"You have the look of a desperate man, maybe even a pirate. But you also have the look of a man called James Hook," Huxley said, smiling.

The men in the tavern laughed. Hook stayed focused, never breaking eye-contact from Huxley, who noted the cold stare and deep focus. He looked at the pink and red rags wrapped to Hook's arm where his hand once was.

"Seems like you have been out pirating, by the looks of your hand," Huxley remarked.

James glared down at him.

"What is it you want, Hook? My time is more important than your adventures," Huxley said impatiently.

"I want you to help me kill a boy. A very powerful boy, his witch, and their army of living-dead," James replied.

Captain Huxley was taken back. "My, my, what a story indeed. A boy, a witch, and the undead. Are there mermaids or magic wizards as well?"

The bar erupted with laughter.

"No wizards, but yes, mermaids, and they eat the flesh of men," James said.

"This is a fantastic tale, young Hook. Indeed, one of your best. Go on, for my amusement, " he said, taking a sip of ale.

"I need you and your crew to come with me to the island to kill a vampire-boy-king and his army before he spreads his conquest to other lands, including the colonies in America."

Huxley clasped his hands together. "My boy, this tale is amazing! Oh, tell more!"

"Will you help me or not?" Hook said angrily.

"Hook, even if I believed your tall tale and thought for one minute you were not delusional from the loss of your hand or sunstroke, how would you pay me? My services are not cheap. You have no boat or collateral. Where is your crew?" Huxley asked.

"My crew is dead, murdered by the creatures and evils of the island. The island of fog, on no map, to the south, between the straights of Aphrodite's bosom," James informed him.

Captain Huxley sat up. "The island of fog..." he murmured. "The island is cursed. There are evil creatures like no man has ever seen. So, how do you intend to persuade me and my crew to join you on this fool's quest to a cursed island to save the world?"

Hook slammed his hand on the table and slid it away. Three large rubies the size of a baby's fist stared back at Captain Huxley. They shone and sparkled, even with tavern's limited light. The grizzled pirate pushed the two young women away. "Be gone, ladies; the men have business to discuss."

The two women scampered away, cursing under their breath.

Hook began, "I know of a room bigger than this tavern with boxes of gold and jewels, enough to make a wealthy man a king. If you hear my plan and give me just five more minutes of your time, you may have one of these gems. The rest are for my ship and supplies. I aim to go back to the island to kill a vampire-boy and his army. I need a crew of men who are not afraid to kill."

"My men kill like breathing air," Captain Huxley said, smiling.

"Your men may not survive the island and the horrors on it," James replied.

"You challenge the bravery of my crew and my skills?" Huxley said. "My dear James, what has become of you? Reckless, daring, and willing to do anything with no fear of death, even from my blade?"

"Will you join me, or do I go back alone and kill everything on the island that took my crew and my hand? It's your choice: Fight for glory or sit in this dark tavern reminiscing about days of former glory? I will give you half the loot if you help me get vengeance for my loss," James said.

"I have heard of such an island. I have seen it. When I was younger, I avoided it. Your name does not become legend by dying early in your pirating career. I saw it once, and we went far away from it. We sailed hard into a storm to avoid its pull. I lost eight men in that storm, and one ship was nearly destroyed, but we did not go to the fog or to that island. I have heard no ships leave its shores," Huxley stated.

"If you come with me, we can leave its shores with treasure, the likes men have never seen," Hook said. "I know the island's caves, the creatures, and the one who commands them. I can get us to the treasure room, and we can kill every hell-spawn that walks the island."

"How many men do they have?" Huxley asked.

"They have well over 100 men, both living and dead. The children are blood-feeders, and there are mermaids and other mythical creatures," James informed.

"I have three ships and 70 men. Will that be enough?" Huxley asked.

"Depends on how they are led and the strength of their will," James replied.

"My men do not fear anything, and we have fought and won against the greatest, both in the Queen's Navy and Spanish Armada. They will be strong. You had better be right of the treasure, Hook, or you will be buried on that island and never leave it," Huxley warned.

"We sail in three days," James stated. He took two rubies off the table and stormed out. Huxley took the remaining ruby from the table and looked it over. It was beautiful, flawless and cast shadows of red, even in the dim tavern's light.

"In three days, gentlemen, we seek fortunes, glory, and death!" Huxley shouted.

The bar interrupted with shouting and banging of goblets.

Chapter 18

THE EMPOWERMENT PROXY

Belle had been fighting with the thought of freedom and the broken door for days. Her cage sat on Peter's desk, and still, he had not seen the broken latches. She, however, was broken in her heart about leaving him. She sat in her cage, looking at the door. Where would she go? When could she do this? Freedom was just inches away. The witch walked by the cave entrance of Peter's office and stepped inside. She looked at the small fairy who covered her face with her little hands and peeked out.

"Oh, so shy, so scared. Do not fear, little one. Peter and I have plans for you when we get to the colonies. Maybe we will get you a larger cage with more water and a mirror so you can see yourself," Mama Laveau laughed and left Peter's office.

Belle watched her leave and crept to the door. She waited a couple minutes before pushing the cage door lightly. It opened just a crack. She waited again and yanked it closed. All this time in the cage, she was still safe inside. *Maybe Peter would change. Maybe the new plan... a new cage... new promises*. No. She shook her head. She knew they were empty.

Belle placed her hands on the cage door and pushed again. The hinges popped, and it opened just enough for her to fit though. She took a deep breath and pushed passed the door and hinges. She stood outside the birdcage and fluttered her wings. It felt like love, like a warm crash of empowerment and freedom. Freedom to smile, laugh, and be who she was meant to be. She smiled and jumped from the desk, flying high into the air. She flew in circles and dove, flying like a hummingbird. She laughed to herself and shot out like a shooting star from the office into the caves. She was free!

Chapter 19

BAD FRIENDS

Queen Wolf Lilly followed the tracks of blood and violence, broken twigs and bloody grass. She had found three bodies and heard the screams near the village. She ran harder into the jungle. One hand gripped a spear, the other held a long, stone dagger. She stopped quickly to listen; there was a cry from a man in the darkness, then silence. She ran ahead and came to a small clearing. Two more of her tribe lay dead, their bodies slashed and their chests cracked open, exposing ribs and muscle tissue. She wandered around their bodies. She collapsed to her knees and began to weep. Peter watched from the shadows. He tightened his grip on a cloth sack. Blood dripped from it.

Queen Wolf Lilly stood up and within a split second, hurled the spear into the darkness. The spear grazed Peter across the shoulder, and he fell back.

"Do not hide from me, boy!" she screamed. "You come into our lands and murder my people! Only you would have such nerve. If this is for the mermaids, they were trespassing on our lands and have killed many times before. We hunt them like a tiger or bear. This... this... Peter, why have you done this?"

Peter regained his footing. Even with his vampire powers, he knew she was quick, one with the wind and nature. He had gotten what he came for. He did not want to speak with her; it had been too long.

He was not the boy he once was, but still not a man capable of finding his justifications for his actions, other than selfish pride. That was his only solace in the dark now as she walked in circles and screamed at him. His ego and pride grew and boiled inside. He had a plan, he had a goal, and he had everything to make it happen. His eyes, however, met hers for a brief second in the moonlight. She reached for him in the darkness, and his ego and pride melted for a moment.

"I am sorry," he whispered.

She was frozen, lost in the gaze of a friend lost years ago. He blinked and the friend was gone, and the murdering monster was back. She pulled a stone dagger, but Peter had slipped away in the darkness like a breeze. She wiped a tear from her eyes and gritted her teeth, knowing her childhood friend was truly lost forever.

The iron birdcage was hurled across the office and slammed into a bookshelf.

"That traitor!" Peter screamed. "That wretched, horrible creature!" He walked over and lifted the birdcage and caressed it.

"Oh Belle, why did you leave me? Why did you run away? We were friends; I loved you." He caressed the door and it wiggled open.

His mood changed suddenly, and he threw the cage again, smashing it against the rock wall. He stormed back to his desk and sat down, sulking. He scanned the maps and books on his desk. They had such plans. He was going to show her so much. Mama Laveau slid into the office.

"Is everything alright?" she asked. "I heard crashing."

Peter lifted a weak hand and pointed to the cage. "She left. She just left us. I thought she cared for me. I thought she was one of us."

The witch walked behind the young vampire-boy and placed her hands on his frail shoulders. "She was, but she made a choice, Peter. I am surprised she stayed this long. The dark spell I used to keep her from fleeing the cage wore off years ago. She just continued to believe it was there and quit trying to escape. The only thing keeping her trapped in that birdcage was a small pin in the door that never closed right to begin with! Weak-minded and suggestive to the end, I guess."

"Nevertheless," she continued, "we are so close to our goals, our dreams. I know how you cared for her, but remember who your true friends are. As you get closer to your dream, some people may fall away. Some people are trapped in their lives, not by magic but by a broken door, afraid to try to leave. They are weak, Peter. They do not have the heart, the drive, or the vision that you do. Do not let one small creature who walked away make you feel regret or treat your loyal friends differently. You have me, the boys, and even Niviene and her sirens for a short while," she reminded him. "Focus on the loyalties that are with you now. If you wish me to release the Great Hunter to find her, I will."

Peter sighed. He glared at the iron cage. "No, she will be alone. She will miss us and regret leaving. We killed the fairies and destroyed their homes, so I do not know who she will run to. She has no one."

"Without their magic bones, we would never have the power we do. Sacrifices had to be made. Let her go and let her be alone. We have such plans and will make more friends when we get to the colonies. Grand parties and dinners. Our plan is wonderful. Can you imagine? A boy and a black-skinned, runaway slave woman being the richest, most powerful in the port city? They will bow to us like royalty. We will change things, Peter. We will rule and grow our empire. Together, we will make a better world, destroying those who try to stop us," she reassured the pouting boy.

He placed his hand on hers. "I know we will. You are right; the goal is ahead of us. If she leaves, let her be alone."

"She will be alone, and she will regret it," Mama Laveau promised.

Peter thought back to how he and Belle met, him running in the darkness, exploring, lost and alone. She found him in the dark, crying. Belle was the one who showed him the caves and introduced him to other magical creatures on the island. She took pity on him. She showed him around, and he was not alone anymore. He looked at the cage once again, his heart hardened by dreams filled with greed. She had left him. He wondered, if she was not in the cage, would she have left him years ago?

"I placed her in that cage to protect her and keep her safe, and this is how she repays me," he mumbled.

"You did all you could, Peter. Let her go," the witch replied.

Peter smiled. "Indeed, I shall. Now, what to do with that man in your cage?"

"Captain Farrell?" the witch asked.

"I thought using him as bait would lure Hook back, but it did not. So much for loyalties. Maybe he is a pirate after all," Peter remarked.

"We have three grand ships and need a captain. Perhaps he can be bought, or perhaps he can be changed," the witch suggested.

"I doubt he can be bought, so maybe changed would serve us better. As for my other friends, I need to speak with Niviene." He stood up and took a large, blood-soaked cloth sack from the floor. "You are right: keep my friends close and keep them loyal. I hope my actions tonight will keep her and her sirens with us until we begin our voyage."

Niviene stood on the deck of a half-sunken ship in the lagoon. The moon was full, and its light reflected off the waters as they rippled lightly back to and from the ocean. She had not spoken with Peter or any of the others on the island, and she forbid any of her mermaids to do so. They needed to get away from them, a new start and a new life.

Peter was going to leave the island, and they would be on their own once again.

It had been over 100 years in this place. The lagoon, the parties, and the place they called home. It was Peter who had changed. Maybe humans could not adapt to living so long. Her kind lived well over a thousand years, living, feeding, and playing in the oceans. Maybe Peter was not able to handle this due to the age of him losing his mortality. So many thoughts came through her mind. Had she made a mistake?

Where would they go, and how would they stay away from men's cruel nets and spears? The lagoon was a safe place and feeding was simple enough.

"It's a beautiful night, isn't it?" Peter's voice pierced her thoughts.

She turned and saw him standing on the shore with the cloth sack in his hands.

"I am surprised you came here to see me. What did you bring?" she asked.

"A gift. A token of our friendship." He poured the bag out on the cold sand, and five human hearts rolled out. "There are five less men on her side of the island to hunt you. They are for your girls. I know how they like the hearts the most. I sent a message to her as well."

Niviene walked from the ship into the water and then to the beach. She looked at the hearts, bleeding onto the moist sand. She glanced up to Peter. "So, she finally knows of your alliances?"

"My alliances broke years ago, you know that. When I leave this island in a few days, you and your sirens are more than welcome to stay. Without the witch's magic, I can't promise men will not come, but you are very resourceful. I think you will be able to keep this place a home for your kind," Peter replied.

"She may want vengeance and come back for war," she said.

"She does not have the manpower to do what she wants. Even if she does rally a small army, we will be gone," Peter replied. "You and the others should be safe for as long as men do not inhabit this inside of the island."

"Thank you for coming here tonight. I would not like to think that a friendship of so many years, even with a former human, would be wasted," she said, smiling.

Peter returned the smile and began to walk away, then stopped and turned back around. "There is one thing, just a small favor."

She smiled. "Of course, seeing how we are such friends."

"If you could bring one more ship into the harbor? We need more crew. It would be a fair split, half for you, half for me."

"I will talk to the others," she informed him.

"Preferably a slave ship, we need more bodies than riches. All three of our newly acquired vessels are in wonderful working order, but without the crew to get us there, they are worthless. We only have a few days until we embark, so if you could keep your eyes and ears out, we would be grateful," Peter stated.

"We will see what we can bring in," she assured him.

"Excellent. Then I will bid you good evening. Oh! One last thing. We are having a grand celebration the night before we leave. A great party, a going away, goodbye party, if you will. Lots of activities and fun. I would like you and the others to join us," he said.

"One last party to say goodbye. We will be there, Peter," she replied.

Peter walked over and hugged her close. He broke away.

"You do not think of me as a monster, do you, Niviene?" he asked, his voice cracking. The look in Queen Wolf Lilly's eyes still haunted him. "I know I can have more. More friends, more chances to play, more everything. Is that so wrong?" he continued.

"No, Peter. It's what your heart wants," she replied.

"Good. I thought I may be losing my nerve. Well, I must get back to the others. Enjoy the night, Lady of the Lake, or do you prefer Queen of the Seas? Glad we could clear the air." He started to whistle and walked off down the beach.

Niviene looked back to the human hearts. She was still bitter. She knew he was trying to bribe her and her girls with them. It was not what a true friend would do, but she knew they had lost Peter years before when the Voodoo priestess began to whisper in his ear. Maybe the island would be better off when he and that foul, dark magic woman took their evil with them.

Chapter 20

BUSINESS OVER BEDROOM

James sat across from Molly's desk. A large roll of paper sat squarely in between them. Molly was dressed well in a black corset dress, and her hair was styled as if she was going to a grand ball.

Hook was worn, sunburned, and his clothing looked as if a peasant had robbed a corpse. Downstairs from her office, music played and people laughed, drinking and wishing their cares away.

"You do always surprise me, James," she said.

"As do you," he replied. "Now is it all there? My supplies and my ship? My debt cancelled?"

"Yes, but why so forward? Do you not trust me?" Molly asked.

"You took my ship! I know I was late, but you took my ship and sold me out to Farrell!" Hook retorted.

"It was business. He is yet to come back and sign the final contracts, so I will sell you back your ship. Call it bad business decisions on his end. Have you spoken with him at all? How did you escape his clutches?" Molly asked.

Hook took the two red rubies and placed them on the contract. Molly's eyes opened wide as the gems sparkled back. "My word, where did you get such gems?"

"That's my business." James took the contract and signed it quickly. He handed it to Molly, who was still looking at his cloth-wrapped stump.

He cleared his throat, and she proceeded to take a quill and ink to sign as well.

"Where is Farrell?" she asked "How did you get away from such a clever captain? Did he take your hand?"

"No, he could never take a fingernail from me, let alone my hand. I have my ways. Still my business." James stood up.

"Leaving so quickly?" Molly asked.

"I will show this letter to Farrell when we meet again. I must be ready for my trip," James replied.

Molly stood up and stepped from the desk. She caressed his one hand. "You seem different now, James, something in your eyes. You still have one good hand. Maybe it could use some extra attention now that it must do the work for two?" She leaned in and kissed his sunburned neck.

"Sometimes, the thought of cold vengeance is more powerful than the heat of a beautiful woman," he said. He brushed her aside, softly took her hand, gave it a kiss, and left her office.

Chapter 21

More Plans Coming

Peter watched as nearly fifty dark-skinned men were walked from the deck of a Spanish slave ship to the island. Their heads were down, and they were chained together. In the distance, the crew of the slave ship shouted and screamed as many were taken deep into the water by the mermaids' attack. Peter watched the moon in the sky.

"In a few days, we will be looking at the beautiful moon from another port," he said.

"She is beautiful from any port," Mama Laveau added.

The zombie pirates pushed and led the trail of slaves down the beach towards the caves as the boys ran and played. One of the smaller children ran to Peter, his dark eyes glassy from feeding.

"Peter, is it true that we will be leaving and have a new home?" the boy asked and wiped his bloody mouth with his sleeve.

"Yes, Puck, my little brother, we shall. But do not worry; we will still play games and hunt and feed," Peter reassured him.

"I do not want to go back to the cold streets. I was always hungry and so cold at night," the boy whined.

"It will be wonderful once we get our new home built. We will have an even larger family and more lands to play on and things to do," Peter continued.

Puck wiped the blood from his small chin.

"I think it will be wonderful, a new place to play."

"Oh, it will be," Peter promised. "They have swamps and caverns, beaches for miles. You will see."

Puck smiled and ran off behind the line of slaves.

"Another boat," Peter said. "Now, we could bring four ships if we desired."

"I would rather have the three and the manpower to keep them moving. Though, we could use that slave ship as a decoy or leave it to be taken in case we run into pirates or the Queen's Navy," Mama Laveau suggested.

"Place a small crew of about five to ten and see if fate allows it to make it to port? Maybe put that Captain Farrell on it. Ha, ha! Everything is coming together so splendidly. I may have to write my memoirs on how this all came together. Maybe a play?" Peter asked.

"Let's worry about getting established, getting land, and fitting in before you worry about your play, my friend," Mama Laveau said.

"I know, business before pleasure," Peter said. "I hope these slaves turn out to be good. Sometimes those ships come in with weak, unusable men."

"I will have them turned and ready in a few days. How is our business partner in New Orleans doing?" Mama Laveau asked.

"He is expecting us at the end of the month; all properties and papers are being signed and prepared," Peter replied. "This new country, filled with rumors of war, will never know what hit them. Lots of opportunity for us."

"We will be the talk of the region, and when all is in place, I will have my vengeance on that wretched slave owner. I will put him in chains and watch him until his last days," she said with conviction.

"Maybe we will buy his lands to be used as a vacation home?" Peter offered.

"Oh, Peter, that would be lovely," she said. "Can you imagine, owning the land you once were forced to work?'

"Yes, let's do that. Ah-ha! We will throw grand balls! People will come from miles. You can host and control the land that enslaved you. I like it!" Peter exclaimed.

"Oh, I do too," she said. "But enough fantasy, we need to keep our eyes on the prize. First, get into New Orleans and get a hold on the territory. Lots of work, but it is fun to dream about such things."

"You need to come play with us. I think being cooped away in your cave with your magic has darkened your soul too much," Peter said.

"One of us must work. You can play if you want. I will play when we own the land and I have my revenge," Mama Laveau replied.

"I will not tell you how to live; it's only a suggestion. I won't push you away with all this work and planning," Peter said.

"You cannot, Peter. Let's get these fresh bodies ready for our trip, and I promise to have fun before we leave, during our farewell party."

"Excellent," Peter said. "It will be my grandest party yet!"

Chapter 22

Ghost Pains

Hook was sore but healing well enough. He stood outside a large pair of wooden doors. There was a creak as they opened into a blacksmith's shop. He peered inside, and Captain Huxley was speaking to a large, burly man next to the fire pit. Several tools and weapons hung on the walls of the shop. Huxley turned around and saw Hook.

"Ah, good, my dear boy, step inside," Huxley said.

"I got the message to meet you here," Hook said.

"Yes, indeed. We need weapons, and you need one more thing." The grizzled pirate walked over and grabbed him by the forearm, lifting his bloody, wrapped stump. "You sir, need a hand, or better yet, a hook!" Huxley remarked.

"Yes, I know I need to replace my hand. I was thinking I would do it later," Hook replied.

"No, you need to do it today," Captain Huxley ordered.

Hook backed up.

"It's not coming back, James," Huxley said. "It's gone. It won't grow back. It will never be like it was."

Hook's teeth gritted as he looked down at the rags on his arm.

"You still have not thought about this, have you? The loss? It's not real yet. It is not easy losing a limb," Captain Huxley said.

"I knew men in the Queen's Navy who suffered casualties of war. I just didn't think..." Hook started to protest.

"No man ever does," Huxley exclaimed.

"I do not want a Hook, the irony of my name and a twisted piece of iron attached at the wrist. Maybe a claw or blade. I do not want a piece of black, junky iron strapped to my arm. I refuse to look like a wounded animal," Hook said.

"James, it is not a loss you can get back, but you can make it work to your advantage," Huxley replied.

"I doubt that," Hook sighed.

"You need to be less stubborn and more open-minded, even for a pirate," Huxley said.

"And what do you know of loss and strapping metal to your body? You have your hands and fingers and can still wield a blade," Hook said angrily.

Captain Huxley laughed, "Secrets, good secrets." He walked back into the blacksmith's workstation and grabbed two large cannonballs. He looked at Hook and placed his leg out. He dropped a cannonball, and it bounced off his boot. Then he dropped the other, and it made a small clanging sound. He walked to Hook and pulled off his boot. His leg stopped short on a stump. "Had this made ten years ago. It's an iron, hollowed-out boot. Bet you didn't know that?"

Hook looked down at it. "No, I did not."

"Well, now you are one of only three people who do. Me, Lars over there, and you. I never take my boots off, even in bed with the ladies," Huxley said with a grin.

"Well, it's amazing, but a foot can be covered, not a hand," insisted Hook.

"No, but you can build something that will work like a hand, or like a weapon. You can make something that will give you some of what you lost, maybe not all, but some. Most men have a wooden stump or a small black hook but not you. No, no, no. If that island has the treasure you claim, we can afford to make something wonderful and deadly."

Hook looked down at his rag-covered stump.

Captain Huxley smiled and lifted his boot, shaking it in his face. "We can make you stronger and make that creature of the night pay."

James looked at the wrapped stump once more. He swore he could still feel his hand somewhere, but it was truly gone. He had to face this demon who changed his life and took his crew.

"I can swing a sword with my left hand almost as well as I did with my right. It will take training. I don't like it, but a hook it shall be," James said.

Huxley looked back at Lars, who was laying out several tools on a shabby, wooden table. Coal burned in the forge near him.

"He is aboard, my friend. Let's see if that idea we had will work," Huxley said to Lars.

"Idea?" Hook asked.

"Oh, you will love it ... if it works," replied Huxley.

"If it works?" he said sheepishly.

"Trust me. You may have lost a hand, but you will gain a war machine." The captain placed his hand on Hook's shoulder and led him to the blacksmith's table.

"I planned for this in case someday I were to lose my hand to a fight or gangrene, but for the treasure you claim and the chance to collect it, I will share my idea with you. If you're strong enough?"

"Strong enough?" asked James.

"Well, we did some testing, some good and some bad. Relax, you're part of my crew now, Hook, and I take care of my men, especially ones who have a way to great fortune," said Huxley.

Inside the forge, the flame grew, and Lars began to heat the iron. He shouted out to Huxley, but James did not understand what he said. Huxley laughed.

"What did he say? Was it a joke?" asked James.

"No, my boy, not a joke at all but truth," replied Huxley.

He turned James towards the forge, and they both watched as the big man moved the iron in the burning coals.

"When the iron is the color of the sunset, that is when your hook will receive its soul," Huxley said.

Hook stood still, looking at several targets that were propped up like soldiers made of straw and sackcloth. Behind him, Lars mumbled in Swedish as Captain Huxley rubbed his chin patiently. Hook looked down at his forearm. A crude-looking iron cast with leather straps was firmly affixed to his forearm. It was tight and heavy. A large reel was jutting from the inside. There was a keyhole at the end of the metal device with a crude, metal trigger below it. Hook raised it with some effort.

"That's it, practice moving it. Practice becoming one with it," Huxley said. "It's like steering your ship, James. Become one with it. Feel her with every movement."

Hook raised his arm and began to move it, rotating his shoulders and bending his elbow, trying to get used to the extra weight. It was clumsy. He felt a pinch in his shoulder and dropped his arm. He turned to look back at the two men watching him as they sipped rum.

"This is not going to help me or us," Hook said.

"He killed your crew, James. He took them from you. You wanted my help, and I am offering it. You don't like my help? Then maybe you are not the man I thought you were."

James looked down at the iron monstrosity and raised it. He moved it slowly back and forth.

"No rush, but you only have one week, so you best get used to it quickly. We can train on the way to this cursed island, but here is the only time we will be able to test it," Captain Huxley barked.

Lars spoke up in his native tongue. Huxley grunted.

"Fine, ya old sea dog," Huxley said. "You're right, all or nothing." He grabbed a long blade which was welded to an iron holster and took it to James. "May as well try these out while you get used to it. Dive in head-first, look for the sharks when you're swimming."

Huxley handed him the end of the blade. "Now click it into place."

With a shaking hand, Hook took the blade and latched the round cylinder end to his iron stump. He pushed and turned, and it locked into place.

"It will take some time for your forearm to get used to the weight," Huxley said, "but now you have a weapon in your hand."

Hook looked down at the long, shiny blade jutting from the metal device. With a small struggle, he raised his hand and began to move it back and forth.

"I will still be better with my left than if I train for months with this blade attached to that hook!" James blurted out. It was still too heavy.

"See that, now you can have two blades, one for defense and one for offense," Huxley said. "Until your arm is strong enough."

Hook began to speed up his slashes. He walked to the targets, slicing down and across into the straw and wood. The sword stayed hard and rigid in its holster. He turned to look at Huxley and asked, "Anything else?"

"Oh, James, I would not be a legend if I had not prepared for more than a blade." He then shouted to Lars, "He wants to see it all. Bring it out!"

Lars smiled, showing his two missing teeth, and the big man scurried away, disappearing into the workshop. He returned with a large, wooden box and set it down on the small table, knocking the wine and glasses to the grass below.

Hook and Captain Huxley made their way over as Lars began to unload the box. Hook looked down at the table as all kinds of blades and strange devices waited.

"These are prototypes, James, so do not get too excited," Huxley said. "They have not fully been tested. We kept this our secret until I needed them, but if we're to take this island, you'll need more than a stump."

Hook picked up a huge fist. It weighed as much as a large cannon ball.

"That's the smasher! Strike any door or hull, smash windows or skulls, blades or stone! It has an anvil of a strike," Huxley grinned.

Hook picked up a small, canister. It had a wick and appeared to be a mini cannon.

"That was my idea; it's a flintlock hand cannon. Put anything in it: rocks, glass, nails, anything. Light the fuse, take aim, and fire. It only can be used once."

"What is that?" Hook asked, pointing to a two-foot-long iron harpoon attached to a rope.

"Ah, the dagger. It launches like a harpoon. You crank the handle to tighten the gears, pull the trigger, and it fires. It's very similar to the first one we made but surpasses anything you've ever seen!"

Captain Huxley pulled a monstrous, black iron hook from the table. "This beauty can hook a ship, or you can use it as a rope, a grappling tool. At least that was the plan. It still needs some modifications."

The hook was thick, heavy, and had a long, thick rope attached to its metal base. Two small, sharp daggers stuck out from the base and curved upwards.

"It's an all-in-one hook, club, lasher. We have not tested it enough to know if it will work, but we have a week," he remarked.

Hook took the base of the sword hilt and gave it a turn. It unlatched from his forearm, and he placed it on the table. He took the hook and slid it on; a quick turn locked it into place. He raised his arm and studied the large, black hook. It had great balance and felt very sturdy. There were rune symbols engraved near the base.

"What does it say?" Hook asked.

Lars spoke English for the first time, "May God and vengeance light the path for your soul."

"He's a bit of a poet," Huxley added.

James turned the hook and swung his arm. It was still heavy, but it was beautiful. He smiled at the two men.

"I have a few ideas to add," he said. "To kill that monster, we will need a few small changes."

"Then let us make them, so we can go after that treasure and get your revenge," Captain Huxley stated.

"We will need several pieces of silver and a lot of holy water."

The two men looked at one another and smiled.

"Do I get to rob a church?" Huxley asked. "It's been a long time."

James rolled his eyes.

The sun was setting across the deep blue ocean waters. It was peaceful in the harbor of the cove. Several ships were docked, but very few men walked the boardwalk. Tranquility. Molly stood looking at the small, one-mast ship. She would miss her, though she never got to sail her. She had not spoken with James since he stormed out with the focus of a hungry tiger. *Maybe I was too hard on him,* she thought. She had feelings for him. In her business though, feelings never led down good roads. She was lost in the thoughts of the past when he approached

"She is a fine ship, isn't she?" Hook said, smiling.

She turned and smiled. He was covered in sweat, and his face was red. He looked exhausted.

"Have you been fighting a dozen men or just drunk?" she joked.

"I wish it was both," he smirked.

"James, I want to apologize. I treated you wrong with all that happened. I was out of line."

"No," he disagreed, "you were just being Molly, and you did offer me comfort."

She smiled back. "I did not want you leaving without us... being us."

"There is no woman or scoundrel I would rather share my bed or my heart with than you, Molly, even with my debts to you. But my ship is now mine again."

"I hope you find what you are seeking, and I hope you tell me all about it when you get back."

He leaned in and kissed her slowly on the cheek. He pulled back. She quickly kissed his cheek and walked off.

James rubbed his cheek and sighed. She was beautiful, sleek, and sitting in the harbor, waiting. His ship, his home, his best friend. He shook his head and walked up a plank to board his ship. He walked the deck proudly; she was his again. He walked to the railing and slid his left hand against it, slow and smooth. He looked down at his wrapped wrist, the bandages grey and tattered from trying the attachments.

"Don't worry, my friend, soon I will have a new hand, as sturdy as you, and it will help me sail you again. He turned and saw a shadow inside the cabin. He stepped quickly and peered inside. A thin, older man in black had his back turned and was thumbing through a large book on his desk.

"Father Bob?" Hook asked.

Father Bob smiled gracefully and leaned against the desk. "Yes, my captain, it's me. I did all you asked. I snuck into the church on the island and took, or rather *borrowed*, the holy water and brought it to the blacksmith's. He did not tell me what it was for, but he seemed happy that I brought it to him."

"Thank you for aiding us with this. Not all men can wield a sword or command a ship; some men are blessed by other skills," said James.

"That is true," replied Father Bob.

James slid his sword away and eyed the old man carefully. "I think it would be best if you stayed at The Cove," Hook said.

Father Bob chuckled. "I think it's none of your business where or how I conduct myself," Father Bob said. "You are my captain, and I respect that in you, but you're my friend first."

"I do not want to lose another," James started to protest.

"You won't! You need every man you can trust on this journey. I truly was a man of God at one point in my life. I have never told anyone, but I fell in love, left the church, left everything. We were married. We owned a small tavern. We had a good life until she got sick..." he tapered off. "When she passed away, I blamed myself for leaving the church, for choosing the love of a woman over the love of God. I found the alleyways and looked through the glass of wine bottles a poor substitute, but I had lost my way. I remember when you met me, drunk, covered in filth. I was lost, and you and Black Jack took me in. An old man with no skills of the sea, but you let me learn. You let me help. You let me have a life again. I cannot stay here when you risk your life to help others," Father Bob said.

"I knew you had a past. I just wished to not pry. Men have dark secrets and not all need to be shared, even to friends," James said.

"Well, I decided if you were willing to give it all for me and your crew, I needed to be honest about who I was, in case it can help you as well. You will need help from the good Lord to take on such a creature. Maybe the stories of holy water and crosses are true. If so, I will help you wield them," Father Bob assured him.

"I appreciate your help, but will He listen?" James asked.

"We will see. I have renewed my vows, asked for forgiveness, and believe I have found His favor. I still wish to be your cook on this voyage and your religious helper," Father Bob said.

"So, a man of God wishes to sail with a band of pirates and sinners?" James grinned.

"Someone needs to pray for your souls and keep the darkness at bay," Father Bob replied with a smile.

"I am glad you're with us. We set sail tomorrow at dawn," James said.

"To the ends of the earth, my captain and my friend," Father Bob promised.

"And the end of a dark creature, to avenge our friends," James swore.

"Amen," said Father Bob.

Chapter 23

The Open Sea Again

The sun set high in the soft sky, blazing its warm light on the cool, blue waters. Four ships cut through those waters as the breeze from the south pushed their sails gently forward. The lead ship was small, with only one large mast. On its deck, James stood proudly behind the wheel. The other three ships were medium-sized, with two sails and nearly twenty men on each. Captain Huxley stood behind James, taking in the ride.

"You guide a ship well, James, I must admit, I am surprised. I thought all the tales of your exploits meant you could not sail. I was wrong. She is not a big ship, but she moves very nicely on the water."

"You learn from mistakes; I have made many," James replied back.

Huxley stood up. "Your first mate, the priest..."

"You mean Father Bob?" James asked.

"Yes. Is it wise to have such a man with us? We are going to a most dangerous place, and it will be very bloody and very horrific. I do not know if a man of God will be welcome or want to be part of our quest," Huxley remarked.

Father Bob was at the front of the ship, helping several pirates, gathering ropes, and moving supplies.

"Father Bob has seen everything that I have, well almost everything, and maybe he will bring us luck," James said.

"Luck from God? You, James, are very humorous indeed," Captain Huxley chuckled.

"From what I have seen on that cursed island, we will need all we can get," James added. "We should reach the far point of the island by morning. There is only one way to approach the lair, the way I was able to escape."

"I just hope the treasure room which you boasted of is true, or this will be a one-way trip for you, James," Captain Huxley stated.

"The jewels, the gold, and other treasure that this boy-like creature has gathered will make you a richer man than you could imagine," James said. "We have to get there before he sets sail for the new world."

"He is not a vampire, James; he is just a boy, or your mind played tricks on you. Losing a crew and your arm was quite tragic. I have seen some wild things running the waters these twenty years, but your stories..." Huxley pondered.

"They are not stories," Hook promised, "and we will need your men, my priest, and luck to get to the treasure room to kill this vampire-boy and his witch." James adjusted Black Jack's gris-gris bag around his necklace.

"The witch I believe, but her magic? Ha! More of the fear of what men do not understand than of real dark magic," Captain Huxley said.

"When you see the walking dead, do not hesitate," James insisted.

Huxley sighed and shrugged his shoulders. "We never hesitate, whether it's cannon fire or monsters," he joked.

"Good," James spat back.

"Now, let's train some more with that hook of yours," Captain Huxley said.

James signaled Father Bob over, and the priest took the helm as James and Captain Huxley went to the rear of the small ship. Captain Huxley pulled his blade and attacked, and James used his sword and new, monstrous hook to strike and fend off the pirate's swings. Sparks shot from the hook as it knocked the blade away.

"I am done being easy on you, adventurer!" Huxley bellowed.

"Then send me to Davy Jones' Locker, you used up strumpet!" James shouted.

Captain Huxley unloaded again, swinging and clashing with the iron hook. The pirates chuckled with every blow.

Chapter 24

CHECKING THE LIST

Peter was sitting at his desk. The broken, iron birdcage sat in the corner next to several sacks of gold and gems. He was reading a letter and making notes on a piece of paper.

The witch walked into the cave with three large guards behind her. One of them was Black Jack. His eyes dull but wet as if he had been weeping.

Peter looked up. "Everything moving forward?" he asked.

"Yes, the ships are almost ready, and everything is running according to plan," she said.

"Well, the good news is, according to this letter and our private investors, as of last Thursday, we own a large building and some port area in New Orleans. We can sail in and take charge of the land and property when we wish," Peter said.

"How many of our crew will we keep? We cannot house and hide so many," she protested.

"We will disband our group the closer we get. We will keep most of the lost boys and release much of the living-dead into the ocean. We will keep our ship's crews light and coast into port with half of what we have," Peter replied.

"Which of the boys are you leaving here or feeding to the sea?" she asked.

"I made a list. I am not happy about it, but some of them ... as fun and rambunctious as they are boys who may cause issues once we land in the new colonies. On the island, they have been wonderful and great friends, but things need to change, and I do not know if these boys can change. Also, the blood feeding can get tricky, so we will have to leave them here or put them aboard that slave ship. We could leave it at sea or even sink it if needed," Peter said and handed her a list. There were a dozen names, some scratched off then rewritten. Some had a question mark near them.

"Hard decisions," she said.

"If it was not a new location, there would not be a list. We cannot risk one of them sneaking out to feed or being sloppy, or we lose our new life," Peter said. "Some of the children should never leave this island though. We must make a special plan for them; it's only a small group about six or so. They are a bit of a handful, even for me."

"I agree. What do you wish to do with Farrell? He is looking bad. Should we kill him now?" she asked.

"I am hoping as the journey draws near, he will break and join us. If he breaks, he could guide one of our ships," Peter replied. "Also, he could help us infiltrate when we pull into port. I am hopeful every man has a price, and we can break him and find it. If not, then maybe one last hunt during our celebration party."

"I think the boys would enjoy that," she agreed.

"I have also reworked our travel to New Orleans. Since many of us cannot be sailing at day's light, we need to keep clear of shipping lanes and other troublesome situations. It may take us another day or two, but the goal is to not be seen; we will pull into port at night, with less attention. This is why I am hopeful that Farrell will join. I know gold talks, but a young boy and a woman, particularly one with dark skin, will not be taken as seriously when buying and selling, even in the darkest, seediest places," Peter said.

"You underestimate this dark-skinned woman and New Orleans, the Voodoo magic, and the people. We will be fine, Peter," she reassured him.

"I just want to be prepared," Peter said.

"We will be. In a few months, we will visit my old master's land so that I can watch him suffer and beg for his life and the life of his family," she said with an evil grin.

"It will be a grand day for you; it will be wonderful. Speaking of wonderful, the party, it is planning itself. I swear it's becoming a living thing! Everyone is pitching in. It will be the greatest since I came to this island, the food, the music," Peter said. "I swear if I were a human, I would reign as a master of parties because no one can throw one and play like I can. Maybe we will throw another when we get settled, to welcome us to the new world?"

"Yes, a grand ball to show everyone our power and strength," she replied.

"Well, now I must plan another party. This is wonderful!" Peter smiled gleefully.

"Plan it on the journey, my friend. One party at a time," she said, caressing his cheek.

"Won't it be wonderful? This new life, this journey? We will rule like kings and queens. And if war breaks out, oh the life we can make for ourselves," Peter said.

"One step at a time, Peter," she cautioned.

"I know. You always have wise words for me, and your council is so needed," Peter said.

"I will go attend to the ships and the mermaids. They are very sad you are leaving," she informed him.

"Bah, it's business with them. They know once we leave, they are back trolling the sea unprotected, feeding on drunken men," Peter dismissed.

"I hope you will not miss this island too much when we go," she said.

"I will miss the beauty, the nights of stars walking the beach, the smells of the roasted boar, fish and salt in the air. But I am hungry for new blood and new adventures. Feeding will be so much easier for me and the boys as well, not bringing in a ship and milking every drop of blood like water on a deserted island. To feed freely is something I have not had in years. This will be best for me and my family, and you are part of my family," Peter said with a smile.

"And you are mine, so you better not make an excuse to not come with me when my vengeance is complete," Mama Laveau stated.

"I would not miss it for the world," Peter said with joy.

"He has a large family; you could feed on them for weeks," she added.

Peter laughed. "You are making me hungry. Now, go, before I daydream for hours, and nothing gets done."

The Voodoo priestess shook her head, smiling, and left his cave, her living-dead garrison walking behind her.

Chapter 25

WELCOME PARTY

James helped the pirates pull the small boats to the shore. Captain Huxley and his men continued to place large palm branches and shrubs over the dozen wooden boats. It was close to noon; the sun was high in the sky, warming the beach. Captain Huxley watched as his ships and *The Conqueror* sailed away from the coast.

"They will return to the far side of the island by dawn to aid us or retrieve our bodies," Huxley said. "I hope all this secrecy and work pays off, Hook, or you will be facing my blade. I am getting too old for this kind of work." Huxley leaned back and stretched.

Hook joined Captain Huxley and bent down. "Your sword will feast on this island if it does not feast on you."

"Then let us explore this hungry island. Where are these hellish caves you claim to have survived?"

James straightened up and pointed.

"We just go about one mile into the jungle. There is a cluster of rocks, a reef; we go in from there. They patrol the isle at night. If they do not find our boats or come this far across the island, we will have the element of surprise."

There came a rustling from the jungle. Captain Huxley's men drew their swords and formed a wall.

"So much for a surprise," Captain Huxley murmured.

It was Huxley who inhaled in surprise as Queen Wolf Lilly stepped into view, her tan, curvy form making him raise an eyebrow. Her black hair was draped over her strong shoulders.

"This is not your vampire?" Huxley asked, noticing her savage green eyes.

"Hardly, but she's just as dangerous; I can assure you," James noted.

"Like a wild jungle cougar," Huxley muttered.

She stepped to the beach; a dozen warriors stood behind her, holding spears and bows. She pointed to James.

"You, foolish one, you returned?"

"Well, she obviously knows you," Captain Huxley jested.

James stepped quickly to the warrior and bowed low. "Yes, Your Highness, I have returned to free my men and rid this island of the monster you know as Peter and that hell-witch."

"It's a foolish quest. He is very strong, even against all these men," she replied.

James stood up and smiled at her, hoping his charm was intact. "Perhaps a queen as beautiful as yourself could assist us."

She grinned, but it fell back quickly.

"You can have protection on this side of the island, but I will not lead my people into such a quest. I will not break our treaty with him, even though he breaks it by killing our men like the few I lost last week. He is a jackal who does not keep his word. I will aid you, but my men and I will not cross to his side of the island. You must fight him and his creatures on your own."

"We appreciate your aid," James said.

Captain Huxley walked over to her and bowed.

"You must introduce me to such a lovely creature, young James," he said.

"Ah, my apologies," James laughed. "This is the Queen Wolf Lilly. She and her people control this side of this enchanted island."

Queen Wolf Lilly looked the pirate commander over. "Raider and pirate, thief and barbarian," she said.

"Guilty as charged," Huxley smirked, "but you can call me Matthew."

Several of the men, including James, looked at Captain Huxley strangely.

"Matthew?" James muttered.

"Tell me, Your Highness, do you enjoy sweet drinks and walks on the beach?" Huxley asked.

"I enjoy leading and protecting my people from harm," she said quickly and looked away.

"Ah, good to know. Then if we return in one piece, I will request, as a victor, a walk on this very beach and a drink with you for helping to protect your people," Captain Huxley said and gave her a wink.

"If you return from that side of the island and live through Peter and his monsters, you are not just a thief or pirate but a true warrior," she said.

"So, it's a date," he replied.

She shook her head. "This is why we do not like visitors to our isle. Follow us to the caves where I met James at death's door. Keep your eyes open for the mermaids; they patrol the waters during the day while Peter rests."

Queen Wolf Lilly and her warriors led the way into the jungle.

"Okay men, follow the locals, mind your step, and keep your swords hungry!" Captain Huxley ordered. He leaned over to James. "She didn't say no. I think she likes me."

"I think you're dreaming," James replied.

"Call it a hunch," Captain Huxley said.

"Call it a foolish thought," James added. "When you see the beasts we are fighting to gain that treasure, you will forget her."

"Forget the treasure, my dear boy. That woman, that queen, is priceless. You fight for what you want, but now my blade will fight for something most men can't find: the affections of a woman like that!" Huxley said with conviction.

James stopped, taken back by Huxley's comment, and Captain Huxley marched on stronger, pulling his sword from its sheath.

"Onward, men! We will take on these creatures and send them to the seven hells!" Huxley yelled. "We will free this island from the vampire's grasp!" He looked at Queen Wolf Lilly, who smirked, then continued forward.

They arrived at the cove where James had escaped the vampire's grasp just weeks before. The lagoon was still and quiet. Dried blood from the battle remained on the nearby rocks and stone walls. The scent in the air was of fresh water and the beach, but a strong breeze brought the subtle scent of rotting meat. The light was cut short due to the thick cavern walls, and the pirates began to light torches, sending flickers of light and shadows around the stone-encased lagoon.

Belle stayed hidden behind several black rocks and shrubs. She had never witnessed any group of men entering that side of the lagoon or walking into the Pits of Despair. She had never heard of anyone escaping it, let alone traveling deeper inside. Even Queen Wolf Lilly's warriors never set foot in that cove. She was very curious why such men would try. They were coming for Peter. Should she go back to warn him? Why did the men, these horrible outsiders, submit to and act so patiently with Queen Wolf Lilly and her people?

The one-handed pirate, James, was leading them. For a human, he was very nice to her when she was in the cage, even if it was only for a few minutes.

Maybe he and the others were not as bad as Peter made them out to be. She waited until the men had completely vanished into the caves. Belle had already betrayed Peter. Maybe if she warned him, he would take her back. It had been several days since their last fight. They had always been friends and maybe the cage was for her own good. Her head sunk. She needed to go somewhere and think. She needed to go home. She flew off quickly into the jungle.

Peter watched as the men controlled by the witch's magic moved tables and chairs in the great hall. They were slow but obedient. Maybe in New Orleans, he could find men who would work faster. He could still control them by adding gold to their pockets. Several of the lost boys ran around with beads around their necks and flags. Some tried to set up tables for the grand event, but most still played, chasing one another. Peter didn't mind; they were hours ahead of the party's schedule.

"Peter!" came a young cry.

The vampire-boy-king spun around and looked at Julian, one of his most recent converts. The boy's eyes were black and beaming.

"Are you sure you want to leave this wonderful place?" Julian asked.

"Oh Julian, you have been here but a few weeks. We will have everything and more when we reach America," Peter assured him.

"I heard they have war in America. A few orphans told us of losing their fathers due to the war," Julian replied.

Peter stepped up and placed his hand on the boy's shoulder.

"You do not need to worry about war or anyone harming you. You see Mama Laveau's big men? They do the fighting, and we finish the fighting with the gifts I passed on to you."

The boy's face sunk. "I wish more children could enjoy what we have. I have a brother, and I do so wish to see him again."

"Do not think of him right now. You have brothers and family with us now," Peter replied.

Peter sank down to one knee and looked the small boy in the eyes.

"Tell you what, after we get to America, I will reach out to the orphanages and try to locate him in England. Maybe he can join us."

"You would do that for me, Peter?" the boy asked, his eyes beaming with delight.

"Yes, in time. But you must help me with this move, and do not bring it up again until we are established in New Orleans. Agreed?" Peter asked.

"Oh yes, Peter! That would be so wonderful," the boy replied happily.

"Now, please go see if you can help with the food and drinks for the party," Peter said.

Julian gave a quick nod. "Yes, Peter, whatever you wish!"

Julian ran off, and Peter looked around the grand ballroom.

"Yes," he said aloud in the empty room. "It will be a fine feast, a grand send-off."

In the cage, Farrell awoke to the sound of men snoring. He had dried, caked blood on his hands and face. The aches in his body reminded him that he was not dreaming. He pulled himself up using the bars in the cage and watched as Mama Laveau threw plants into a bubbling brew in a large, black cauldron.

"Ah good, you're awake," she said without even turning her head. "I heard you rise from sleep, leaving the world of dreams to now."

"The Queen's Navy will come. You took out two of their largest ships and killed off its crew," Farrell stated.

"We won't be here by the time they arrive. We leave at dawn's light for the new world," she replied.

"And what of me and the rest of the men?" Farrell asked.

The witch stopped throwing herbs into the pot. She turned and walked to the cage. "We're saving you for much later. You and this group will be the entertainment, and the lucky ones will be dead before it begins. The men need meat, and you and these traitors will feed the mermaids and the lost boys, providing great nutrients. For creatures like Peter and the others, the blood of beasts is fine, but it's the blood of men that gives them strength. I can also give your soul's essence to my Iwa. The spells and knowledge he will give me for that will be unmeasurable. A few good seasonings and proper cooking and human meat will be as good as a boar or deer. "

Farrell's face was blank.

"Ah now, do not be so sullen. You still are alive. Maybe Peter will have a use for you. If we run into Navy ships on our journey, we may have use for you other than to fill our stomachs," she informed him.

She turned and walked back to the boiling cauldron. Near her, stood a large, hulking zombie with a large staff in his hand. It was Black Jack. His eyes were cold, looking out into nothing.

"Do you like my newest bodyguard?" the witch asked. "Strong as a bull, this one, and he seems to be much more understanding than the others, as if he has had hexes or blessings put on him before. He was hard to break but so worth it. Whoever he knew had strong Voodoo magic, just not strong enough."

"Is it true that the pirate, Hook, escaped your grasp?" Farrell teased.

The witch stood straight up and gritted her teeth. "He is dead; the island has taken him." She lifted the pale rotting hand that hung from her bone necklace.

"Did you find a body?" Farrell asked.

In a rage, the witch stormed back to the cage. "Yes, we found his body and his head in the sand, being eaten by the gulls! He is dead! He is gone!"

Farrell smiled slyly. Only James Hook could make a woman so furious. "So, I guess all hope is lost," he said and sat back down. "So, how do we get past the Royal Navy with your ships and crew?" he asked.

"Too bad you killed James; the man could get past anyone. I remember one time a Spanish warship was coming up on us years ago..."

"Enough talk of Hook! The man is gone. He will not come back to save you or anyone! He is a pirate, and even if he had left of this place, he would never come back to rescue anyone!" she answered angrily.

"You evidently do not know James," Farrell said, laughing. "That hand that you wear as a trophy, he will be coming back to claim it. Whether here or when you arrive in the new country. If he still has a breath in his lungs, he is thinking of revenge."

The witch looked down at the hand hanging low across her neck along with several bones. "He is not a vengeful man. His aura was light and of whimsy."

"That's what people thought, but I have seen him in war when blood-lust set in. It was not a side he liked to show, but if you crossed him, James Hook would think of a hundred ways to kill you if given the chance. And if you hurt his crew, you signed your death note," Farrell said with a grin.

"You say these things to get into my mind," she hissed.

"He was not kicked out of the Royal Navy for just his passions with women but for crimes unbecoming an officer. His savageness, when brought to a boil, was animalistic. The blood lust was monstrous," Farrell replied.

Farrell's head sunk just for a second before continuing. "I recall a battle years ago. James would not respond to my voice but continued to butcher a man. It frightened me when I saw the look in James' eyes, no control, only wrath. You would have thought he had gone insane."

"Enough of your talk and foolishness! He is dead!" the witch shouted. She stormed from the room, and Black Jack followed behind her.

"Only James Hook could make a woman storm out of a room like that," he said, smiling.

Hook was very much alive, but would he come back for his men, for Farrell, and for vengeance? Time would tell. He had planted the seed in her mind. Even if Hook was off the island, drunk in a brothel, Farrell knew one day the witch would wake up with a sword in her gut, and James standing over her.

He would enjoy that fantasy in his mind. It would have to be enough to keep him going for the next few hours until he was either cooked, eaten, or prepared for slavery.

Chapter 26

Is Your Head Clearer Now?

Belle arrived at her fairy village after several wrong turns as the heavy, dense vegetation had changed the jungle since her departure. It had been years since she had come here. The small trees and hollowed-out log homes were rotting. The air smelled like fresh dirt and plants. The memories of many lingered in her mind, along with the life that once thrived in this hidden village, so beautiful before. The stars would shine down, and the fairies would dance and light up the sky. They played music and made wonderful drinks to relax and laugh.

She walked the moss-covered trails. Almost everything she remembered was overgrown now. As she looked around the remains of the village she once called home, the realization came that her memories were almost gone. The very last time she was here was of fire and stone. The remains burned and the bodies of dozens of dead fairies were laid out, scattered around the village.

It was the humans from the other side of the island. They had found and destroyed them. If she had not been with Peter that evening, she may have been killed too. That's what started the war with the other side of the island. She continued to walk around the garden. Her life was so confusing now. Change. So much change.

It was darker than she would like, and she lifted a hand to the sky and mumbled. A bright light came from her slender fingertips, and light flooded the area. More moss, more vines, and suddenly, a sharp light caught her eye. She walked past several small mounds of moss and earth to find a coin jutting from the earth. She bent down and tugged on it with both hands. She pulled out the gold coin and noticed a wooden handle in the soil under it. She tugged to discover a half-buried musket pistol. She looked over the land again. The people of the island do not trade with gold or use guns.

She walked around and began to dig in the fresh soil. A piece of leather and an iron belt-buckle became unearthed. She looked around at the remains of the village. Years before, she was in shock when she and Peter arrived. She had never studied the destruction.

Peter said he and the witch would bury the dead, and she need not be bothered; they would take care of her, and she was their sister now. She trusted them when she had nothing to believe in. She flung her clenched fists above her head and shouted a line of guttural sounds which ended with a whistle. The ground shivered and breathed for several seconds. The fairy took a large breath through her nose. She took in the smell of the woods and earth and followed the scent to a tree. She studied it. There were muskets embedded there, and the faint smell of powder still lingered in the magical trees. The people on the other side of the island did not use such things, except occasionally on a hunt for wild boar or deer; Mama Laveau's zombie soldiers did.

Her mind cleared, and horror appeared. The horror of lies, murder, and betrayal. She collapsed to her knees and began to weep. She choked, catching her breath, and then she let out a horrific pain-filled howl. Miles away, several birds fled from the jungle after hearing the sound.

Two men near the coast by Queen Wolf Lilly's village stood silent.

"What was that sound?" one of the hulking island warriors asked.

"I do not know," the other replied. "I have never heard of such a cry."

They listened, but it did not cry out again.

The Caves of Despair were alive with light as the pirates forged ahead, torches and swords at the ready. The dozens of hard, battle-trained pirates marched through the stone caverns. They did not speak, listening as noises, cries, and the sound of phantoms swirled and echoed around them. They heard the echo laughter of small children, then cries and howling in the tunnels. The men pressed on.

"I have witnessed horrible, disgusting things in these caverns," James said, tightening the grip on his sword.

"My men won't run! They strike first and will make whatever foul things that are following us, stalking us, wish they had never woken from slumber, "Captain Huxley boasted.

Movement came from the shadows, and three small creatures, resembling pale, sickly children, grabbed one of the pirates and pulled him into the darkness. He screamed, but his horror turned to rage, and he cursed, swinging his sword. He fell backwards into the line of men as a small head, covered in brown, stringy hair, rolled between his feet. Two pirates lifted him up.

"You screamed like a woman," one teased.

"Bugger off!" he shouted. "They surprised me!" He kicked the small head back into the shadows.

Huxley raised an eyebrow. "We swing at anything: man, woman, child, or creature," he ordered.

There came a rush of wind and then the sound of small feet running, echoing down the cave.

"Archers ready, flintlocks ready!" Huxley bellowed.

Several of the men huddled up; some drew their muskets, others small crossbows. It went quiet. The small army men stayed back-to-back in a two-row column, staring into the torch-lit caverns.

"Time to eat the yum-yums," something squeaked in the shadows. It repeated it again and again.

Suddenly, more voices rang out. A chorus of small voices, "Time to eat the yum-yums." The chant got louder, seeming to come from all sides.

"Steady, men!" Captain Huxley shouted over the chorus of the cannibal, child-like creatures. A pounding added to the chant as the creatures beat the walls with bones and small stones. This went on for several dark seconds, like drums played by deaf demons, striking, smashing. The men held their weapons still and squinted to the darkness. Then, silence. The chanting stopped. The only sound heard was the crackling of the burning torches.

They attacked from the top and the ground, from the left and right. Coming forth from the darkness, dozens of small, pale, half-dressed creatures hissed and screamed. They lunged, grabbed, and swung at the human chain of pirates, but the men stood strong, blocking with small, wooden shields and their steel swords. A small blast of musket fire followed, sending smoke into the darkness. Every few seconds, the swords would connect, and the child-like creatures would howl and fall back into the darkness. Another wave of the little ghouls came, but small arrows from the crossbows met them quickly.

"They are testing us, men. Stay strong! Stay ready!" Captain Huxley bellowed. "Steady now."

He had seen impatient men attack due to frustration before, and these creatures would not be any different. James stepped up. As a small attacker leapt through the air, he knocked it to the ground with his iron hook and sent his sword deep into the thing's round belly. It kicked and hissed before it died.

The creatures retreated again as a dozen of their bodies lay sprawled out, dead, and bleeding on the cavern floor. The pirates stepped over them, continuing on as James led the way.

"Well, you were right about these creatures, so maybe the vampire and the other creatures of darkness are not in your sun-stroked mind!" Captain Huxley said.

"Did I mention the giant alligator? Snapped one of my men in half," Hook said.

"No, you forgot to mention it, but that is something I have seen before," Huxley replied.

"Wait until you see this beast," James said.

"Oh, you never met my ex-mother-in-law," Huxley laughed.

James chuckled a bit, but then looked around, partway confused. The caves looked a bit odd with the shadows moving the walls. He led confidently, and right when he was about to stop to question his direction, he saw his bloody handprint on a stalagmite. He grunted and smiled. He turned slightly to his right, and they forged ahead with the hissing and laughter of the creatures in the darkness.

Chapter 27

PARTY FOR THE AGES

The grand hall was filled with candlelight, food, and laughter. The children drank wine, some with blood and other drinks with sweet sugar and exotic fruits. Peter sat on his throne made of bones and sculpted wood, overlooking the festivities. A goblet in one hand and a turkey leg in the other, he smiled and hummed as a couple of the boys played a piano and a fiddle in the corner of the large hall. The melody was simple and rang strong in the cave room. Mama Laveau strolled in calmly with Black Jack behind her like a shadow.

"Come now, my queen. You have not begun to even try and enjoy our last feast," Peter said with a full mouth.

"My mind is cloudy. I have been to the shore. The ships are nearly loaded with the gold and guns. I think it would be wiser to leave before dawn, possibly within the hour," she replied.

"Within the hour! I should say not. This party just got started, and we still have the play to put on," Peter protested.

"Peter, the target for us is America. We have the money and power," she stated.

"I know what we have. I know our plan, and our plan is to leave right before dawn. Now, try to enjoy your last night on the island," Peter insisted.

"Did you say goodbye to the mermaids? Did you bring them any of the feast?" she asked.

"No. I should, but I hate saying goodbye. To be truthful, ever since we spoke of our plans," Peter replied, "Niviene and her friends have been a bit of a pill and seem bitter."

"They should not be bitter; they can run this entire half of the island once we leave. They can feed on pirates and soldiers. They will never have to take an order from anyone," she said.

"I know," he agreed with a shrug. "If you like, we shall make a few plates and bring them out to the docks, see if they will take part."

The witch watched as the boys ran. Some played, some stuffed their faces with sweets, and others tossed food at one another.

"What do we do with the remaining prisoners?" she asked.

"Oh, that captain and those sailors? I will need blood for the journey. Keep them alive for now. We will take them on the trip and, if need be, ransom or use them to bargain if we run into any of the queen's ships," Peter replied.

"As you wish. I will bring the mermaids some of this feast and return before your play begins," she informed him.

"Did you bring the...?" Peter asked.

"Yes, the drink for the boys who need to stay here." the Voodoo priestess took a large flask from her robe and placed it on the pillow of the throne next to Peter. He glanced at it, then back at her.

"Just put a few drops in their drinks, and they will get tired and never wake up," she said. "Did you choose the boys who will stay on the island?"

"I only chose four. I need to choose several more," he replied.

"Well, this is your choosing. I would get rid of the weakest and most disobedient," she replied.

"Have you seen Belle?" Peter asked, trying to change the subject.

"I thought you were done thinking about her and her kind. You will never see her again once we begin our trip," the priestess replied.

Peter sat up and let out a sigh. "Sad. Could have done so much more, she could have been part of this."

"She cares too much for humans and has no need for what we crave. You will be better without her, being the traitor she is. We will not need her or her magic in the new world. I still have many fairy corpses packed away, and their ashes and bones are much easier to use than a whiney, weak, living one," she explained.

"You are right. It is just that she was one of my first friends on the island after that scavenger fed on me and changed me," Peter said, revisiting the incident in his memory.

"Do not feel for her or any of them, Peter. They will keep you from your goal. Be strong. Soon, you may rule the new world, not just this island." The witch bowed, kissed his forehead, and walked to the tables of food and drinks as the children laughed and played.

Chapter 28

Caves with Cannibal Children Are the Worst

James led the band of pirates deep into the Caves of Despair. Even with the laughing, hissing, and attacks, the men under Captain Huxley's charge were fearless. Two men had been attacked, but their wounds were bandaged quickly, and death came for the creatures who were brave enough to attack the marching column of rogue men.

They arrived at a large break in the caves, and light pierced the darkness from above. Below was a massive pile of bones, broken plates, and discarded furniture. Hook pointed to the hole in the top of the cave.

"There is where we crawl out of this death dungeon. It is only a few minutes' walk from here to the throne room.

Huxley looked back at his men. "Ropes, hooks, let's have at it, men!"

Three pirates stepped quickly, preparing their ropes so that the men could climb from the pit. The laughing and hissing had gone away. Dozens of creatures now watched silently from the darkness. Several of the pirates stood guard, making a circular wall with their torches and blades, but no one crept from the darkness. A small, short pirate was the first up the rope. Carrying a blade in his teeth, he was quick to the top. He popped his head up from the Pits of Despair just a couple of inches and gazed around the area. It was empty, finding only a few shrubs, a tree, and cavern walls.

The smell had changed from the cold, foul salt and stink of the pits and now was of cooked meats and even sweets. He climbed out from the hole and pulled a pistol from his hip.

"'Tis clear, Captain," he said in a loud whisper.

Below, the men started to climb all three ropes.

"The treasure will be in his office. It's more than I have ever seen," James said.

"I will find the treasure, whether it's in his office or in his bedroom. Just remember our deal," Captain Huxley said. "I get two-thirds of this treasure that can buy a small country, and this revenge business is all yours."

"And I will have it!" Hook said, grabbing hold of the rope.

Chapter 29

THE SHOW MUST GO ON

Peter watched with delight as the boys performed their last play on the island. The boys wore costumes: pirates, soldiers, and dresses. The small crowd of onlookers laughed and threw pieces of pies and cakes at one another. Heckling the actors made it only a bit more amusing. The young actors played their parts singing, belching, and even mooning the audience. There was a story, but improvising was heavily cheered on. Peter would chuckle and clap as he watched his small army of blood-thirsty children enjoy themselves. Mama Laveau let out a sigh. She had her fill of the child-like debauchery.

"Go if you must," Peter said. "I know this bores you incredibly."

"I will go check on the ships one last time," she said. "When we arrive and are settled in New Orleans, I will take you to a real theatre, Peter."

"Oh, now come on, I wrote this next bit for you," Peter replied.

She turned to the stage, and a boy dressed in a woman's garb began to dance, then bent over and passed gas so loudly that you could hear it over the crowds chanting.

Mama Laveau looked over to Peter and rolled her eyes. "Really?" she sighed.

"It was supposed to be a poem; I think the boys have lost some direction," Peter replied.

"I think this party and having your last night on the island has you ill-concerned of our next steps," she said.

"Just enjoying the entertainment and the wine," he replied.

"I will return soon," she informed him.

She walked away quickly with three zombies behind her. Peter turned back to the stage as a boy unrolled a piece of paper.

"And behold, under the moonlit sky did the hero emerge!" the boy cried.

The crowd suddenly chanted, "Peter, Peter, Peter!" The vampire-boy-king took a bow from his throne, smiling as the play continued.

Chapter 30

LAST-MINUTE THOUGHTS

In the harbor, away from the racket and folly, Mama Laveau cleared her head, watching as her zombie pirates moved slowly with boxes of treasure, furniture, and crates. They had three ships now and the crew, though mostly consisting of walking dead, could still command the ship as the vampire children slept during the day and sunlight hours.

The plan was simple: Peter would command the largest of the group and she the second. The third ship would have the least likeable, unruly children and most rotted of the zombies. In case of a fire fight, the last ship would be used as bait from pirates or the Royal Navy. It was just a few days sailing to New Orleans, and with the Americans and English fighting, she and Peter had hoped to slip into port almost unnoticed. Her contacts there would bring everything to plan.

She turned to her zombie bodyguards. "You stay here; I will return."

She stepped away and began to walk along the beach. It would be her last stroll with the cool sand between her toes for some time. If Peter can take time for himself and gluttony, maybe her simple pleasure of a moonlit stroll on the beach one last time would be her reward.

Finally, she smiled. She would have her revenge on the plantation that took her mother, her sisters, and her young daughter. She would make them pay for the pain by beating the slave owners who abused her and dozens more when she was just a young girl. She would free them, and they would join her. She would have a new family and a new start in New Orleans.

Her fantasy of revenge was quickly interrupted when splashing from the water broke through. Niviene and another mermaid crested above the water.

"Enjoying your last night on the beach?" Niviene asked with a crooked smile.

"I would think you would have found a way to attend the party," the Voodoo priestess shot back.

"Peter knows where we are and where we can go. I think he is too scorned to say goodbye," she replied.

"Well, you will now have this side of the island. You can feed on whomever you wish," the Voodoo priestess said.

"Did Peter mention anything about two of my friends, the ones killed by Queen Wolf Lilly's men a few weeks ago?" Niviene asked.

"No, he did not. He has been very focused on our departure," the Voodoo priestess replied.

"Yes, I am sure. Well, two of them went missing. I told Peter to ask if anyone had seen them, and a week later, we found their bodies rotting in the sun near the Caves of Despair," Niviene said.

"Why would Peter know anything of that? That is very close to the land of Queen Wolf Lilly. Maybe her tribe killed them," the Voodoo Queen suggested.

"Possibly, but they have never bothered us, not in nearly a decade, for we avoid their lands. Maybe it was a grievance or them sending a message. Treaties have been made. Thoughm I question how strong they are and who abides by them, like the way you and your dark creatures took care of those fairies years ago," Niviene said.

Mama Laveau smiled. "Lies and rumors from a jealous creature of magic who cannot understand how the world is changing."

"Still, one wonders how long it will take that little sprite to find out the truth of that night. I was not there, but things on the island sure did change quickly once they were gone," Niviene said.

"Things change. We evolve. We move forward while others live in the past. Belle has been gone for nearly two weeks. She will not be coming with us to the new colonies," Mama Laveau said. "She can stay here and live in the old ways, the ways of a dying island."

"She is a smart, little fairy," Niviene said. "She will figure it out, and if not, maybe I will tell her reasons to think you and Peter were behind the murder of our small, winged, magic sisters."

"We did not kill your sisters!" Mama Laveau spat. "It was Queen Wolf Lilly's tribe!"

"The muskets of men and booted footprints make me question your truth," Niviene said and splashed her tail. "I have visited the village and sensed great aggression and confusion there. First trust, then chaos. The trees and earth tell the secrets. You and Peter sent our island into chaos for power and stronger dark magic. Oh, but this is no matter for you now; you will leave, and all of us will be defenseless against pirates, armies, canons, musket fire, and warships. The magic of this place will not protect us here forever. So go and find another home. Go live with the damn elves. They left, and you can leave if you choose as well!

"This was our island," Niviene continued, "our home for all ancients and magical creatures. Even Queen Wolf Lilly's tribe is deep in ancient magic and comes from a line of gods. This was a great island for centuries, hidden until you came here!" Niviene added angrily.

"We leave before dawn, and you and your sisters can have the harbor and whatever we leave for you. You can live like you did before Peter or I came to this island," the priestess replied.

The Lady of the Lake was very irritated. This woman, this human, using the dark magic, treated her like a common dog. She had no respect for the ancient ways and thought her magic entitled her to be a god. She had put up with it for years and had enough.

"Pray you do not ever find yourself afloat in these waters, witch," Niviene growled. "You're the one who filled Peter with such noble ideas and poisoned this land with your quest for revenge and whispers in his ear."

"He wants what I want, and we will have it!" Mama Laveau turned and stormed from the beach, back towards the loading docks. "To hell with this island!" she muttered.

Chapter 31

Hide and Seek

Once all of Captain Huxley's men were freed from the Pits of Despair, they followed James down several large caverns. The smell of the feast still lingered, and from far off, the sounds of merriment continued to bounce off the cavern walls.

"My mind was very cloudy last time I made my way back here. I was lucky to get out alive," James whispered to Captain Huxley.

They crept down a small hill in the ground and found Peter's office in a hollowed-out doorway. James signaled the men to stop. Huxley turned, gave a quick smile to his men, and signaled them to stop again. The men knew who was really leading the mission, but they also knew James had to feel needed.

James stepped into the office, not seeing what Huxley had done, still feeling in full command of his mercenaries. Huxley followed James into the small room. The walls were bare and the desk was empty, but in the corner was a pile of gold, jewels, and coins. It looked like it could fit into a medium-sized suitcase.

Huxley eyed it. It was a good amount but not the enormous booty James had gone on and on about for days. "So, that be the treasure of the vampire-boy-king? I mean, it's good; it's a good haul, but..." Huxley stated, slowly rubbing his dark beard.

"No, the pile was ten times that. In fact, this office was full."

Suddenly, they heard boots clomping and sliding from outside. Huxley's men fell back as the noise grew. James and Huxley had no place to hide, so they stepped up against the wall closest to the door of the cave. There was a strange smell, like old, sweaty socks, which floated inside the room. A zombie-pirate carrying a small chest trudged inside. He did not look around, just ahead. He groaned and walked to the pile of treasure. His skin was grey, and the wounds from a battle or two still looked to be healing on his half-naked body.

Huxley looked at Hook, who just shrugged his shoulders. The zombie placed several handfuls in the box and picked it up, turned, and stopped. He looked at the two men leaning against the wall. His mouth full of yellow teeth was open just a bit, and his dull, grey eyes stared at them. There was a moment of confusion, and the creature started to open his mouth when Captain Huxley's blade came crashing across the rotting man's neck. The body began to fall as Hook reluctantly reached out and caught it, keeping the small chest from spilling and causing much unwanted noise. James' face turned pale as the cold, grey skin touched his cheek, and he laid the body down.

"What manner of witchcraft is that?!" Huxley asked.

"It's some form of Voodoo; I do not know. The men are alive but only capable of doing what they are told. Some are rotting corpses; some still have souls," James replied.

Suddenly, he remembered Captain Farrell. His mind raced briefly, and he thought the poor captain must be dead by now. It had been two weeks. Or at least he was a creature like the one lying in front of him. He was frozen in thought. He remembered Black Jack, the Spaniard, and the other faces of men he only knew a short time on the ship. Their fate was like the man who lay on the ground underneath his hands.

"What is it, James?" Huxley asked.

"Nothing. Just, I believe... I fear we are here too late to save anyone."

"Then we kill them all and take the gold. That's what we do. I have a feeling if there is that much treasure, this vampire-boy-king is planning an escape, so his ships have even more booty for us," Huxley said.

"I do not want the gold. I just..." James said.

"You will have what you came for. Hell, boy, if there is that much booty, I may even give you enough to afford a new crew and fleet of boats instead of that small raft you call a ship," Huxley replied.

"I wish I could have saved them," James said with a look of despair.

"Well, wish in one hand and spit in the other; see what fills up first, lad! Let's kill this boy-king, that foul witch, and these damned creatures and take their treasure!" Huxley shouted.

James let out a small smile.

"There ya go! Now lead us to battle and glory," Huxley said.

The two men left the cave and joined the small army of pirates outside in the cavern.

Chapter 32

Sitting Pretty with Zombies

Captain Farrell was starving. He sat in the hanging cage, just a foot from the ground. There were three zombies standing close to him. A fourth was Black Jack, who stood near the cave entrance leading to the beach. He held a giant, wooden club in his thick hand. They did not move but would groan every few minutes.

"If I have to command a ship of living-dead to America, they had best plan on feeding me!" he shouted. Two of the zombies moved their heads and looked at him.

"Oh stop. I will be your boss in a few hours, and if you want to eat, you had better show some respect!" he shouted.

Farrell sniffed the air as the smell of the feast lingered. "Bullocks and balls, this is worse torture than beating me! If I ever get to eat again and do captain the ship, I will break away and sail to an island of rum and fruits. Do you wish to join me?"

The closest zombie sneered and growled.

"Well, fine, stay on the island, but I am getting out of here, even if the witch herself has to kill me! I will be off this island and out of this box. Unlike you poor fellows, I am not expendable. I have a talent, and they need me," Farrell said.

He looked around the large cavern. The cages were empty. The large cooking pot had no fire under it, and the walls seemed colder than normal. His fantasy and bragging faded quickly. He glanced back at Black Jack. "I suppose you do not remember me?"

The big man grunted but looked away, back to the caves.

"I do not know what I shall do, but I'll be damned to let that witch and boy-king think they can own me," Farrell stated with conviction.

Hook had led the men past several turns and caves. Now, as they continued, the smells of the feast and sounds seemed to get farther away. Hook stopped and looked around. It was not that there were multiple tunnels, but there were one or two forks on the path back to the throne room, and frankly, he was not remembering.

"Lost your way, James?" Huxley whispered.

"I think we may have to turn back and go left at that last cavern," James replied.

"Well, this tunnel shall lead somewhere. May be best to follow a few more yards. Maybe we will end up on the beach or a better area for an attack," Huxley suggested.

"I wish I could remember," James said.

"I can smell salty air and the caress of the beaches, so we may be heading out towards the sea. Maybe we can get a look at those ships with the treasure that the creature was trying to return to," Huxley suggested.

From his spotty memory, James vaguely remembered that the path to the throne room from the beach was very direct.

"Aye, could be helpful to get my bearings with some fresh air."

"As long as we get this done soon. My crew will hit the beach in under two hours, and they do not strike lightly," Captain Huxley noted.

Hook let out a sigh and continued leading ahead through the caverns.

They crept ahead steadily, and then James stopped in front of a large cave opening. He knew he had been here; there was something familiar. He peered inside the cave to find hanging cages, three zombies, a half a dozen tables, and a large cauldron. It was the transformation room, the Voodoo priestess' lair!

"And another thing, if you walking flesh bags think for one minute..." a voice trailed off.

James looked, and there was Farrell, sitting, sulking in the cage, blathering on like a madman.

"I will take the third ship. After I eat, I'll toss you all to the sharks, and then trade the wooden, cursed boat for a small ransom. Then I will start farming!" he bellowed.

Hook stepped back into the caverns and looked at Captain Huxley. "Captain Farrell is alive? I wonder if anyone else, anymore of my crew, lives."

"We best be getting your friend with us. He may have a bigger knowledge of this vampire-boy's plan and of this island than you," Huxley stated.

"Yes, we could use his help," James replied.

"Also, if he is a captain of the Queen's Navy, good ransom money," Huxley added.

"True," James noted. "That is the pirate thing to do."

Huxley gave a nod and smile.

James walked into the room, stumbling and wandering. The zombies took note and stared at him. He staggered and groaned a bit more and stood in front of the three walking dead. Farrell sat up but said nothing. He looked at James quickly, and he gave him a quick wink.

"Balls!" James shouted, taking his blade and striking down the closest two zombies. The third was knocked back to the cage, and Farrell grabbed the creature by its tattered shirt. James slashed hard with his blade one last time, raking it across the zombie's neck, and it fell to the sandy floor with a half-hearted screech.

"You forgot one, James!" Farrell shouted.

Black Jack came trotting like a bull, swinging his club. James ducked. "Black Jack, stop," he whispered.

The big man growled and swung again, sending James back to the cauldron.

"You may have to kill him, James," Farrell said.

"Not if I can help it!" James replied.

Black Jack swung again, and his club smashed the cauldron's rim, splintering bits of iron and wood. James charged and threw a quick upper cut with his hook. It stunned the big man, and he fell back into Farrell's cage. Farrell tried to grab Black Jack by the neck, but his arms were too short, the cage too small, and the bear of a man too big. Black Jack's eyes were raging with fire and blood dripped from his jaw.

"Listen, my big friend, it's me. It's James, James Hook."

The zombie stopped for just a quick second, then raised the club again. He swung and missed, collapsing into Farrell's cage a second time.

"Well, it was worth a try," James said.

From the cave entrance, Huxley and his band of pirates were now stepping in. "Do you want aid?" Huxley asked.

"No, no, I think I have a plan," James replied. He then swung and hit Black Jack again across the jaw, and he fell into the cage again.

Farrell grabbed him by the neck. "Hurry James, I can't hold him long!"

James reared back his iron hook and sent repeated blows to the back of Black Jack's head. With a sudden whimper, the giant man collapsed to the ground. James fell to his knees and listened. He could hear him breathing.

"Good, good job, Farrell," James sighed.

"James, you have no idea how glad I am to see you," Farrell said.

Hook began to break the small chains which held the cage door closed. "Yes, well, there was a price for my freedom," he said. He slid his hook in between the door and chains and gave a pull. The chains and lock broke away from the iron cage.

He helped Farrell from the cage. Farrell crouched over, barely able to stand as his muscles and back were still quite stiff. "They are leaving tonight, within hours. They were going to give me a ship, make me captain. It was a pretty good deal, and you had to come in and ruin my opportunities once more."

Hook shot him a look.

"I'm jesting," Farrell said with a smile. "I've been going mad for days. They took the other prisoners. They tortured me, that witch! Do you have any food?"

"Food?" James asked.

"Yes, food, James. I have not eaten in a week. I almost ate my belt."

"We will find you some food," Hook said.

Farrell stood up. "Who is we?"

Huxley and his fifty men walked quickly into the chamber.

"Oh, I see," Huxley said. "You brought an army of pirates. Very well, very good indeed."

Huxley approached Farrell.

"What do you know of the plan and the layout of this island? James here remembers very little other than the ghouls and blood-feeding boy-king."

"As a member of her Royal Navy, I am not supposed to aid pirates, but I want food and have been smelling their feast for over three hours. If you swear not to kill me, and maybe feed me, I will help," Farrell replied.

Huxley looked at Hook.

"He may be more pirate than you, Hook!"

Huxley reached in his coat pocket and tossed Farrell a small apple. Farrell took it and bit into it like a wild dog on a mutton bone. With his mouth full, Captain Farrell pointed back to the cave's entrance. James looked around and found chains and rope. He tied Black Jack's hands and feet quickly and gagged his mouth with a bloody cloth he pulled from one of the cages.

Huxley came over. "This is your plan?"

"Just help me move and hide his body," Hook said. "Maybe we can bring him back to us."

"I admire your loyalty, even to a walking dead friend, but it is not a very good idea," Huxley stated.

"Just help me move him. You will get your treasure. I want my crew. As few as it is, they are my friends," James replied.

Huxley and James moved the big man's body to a corner. James removed the gris-gris bag necklace from his neck and placed it back around Black Jack's bullish throat.

"For luck, my big friend." He tossed old clothing and small pieces of wood on him. It looked like a trash heap in the corner. They returned to the cages quickly as Farrell finished the apple.

"The banquet hall is about 500 meters back the way you came," Farrell said, pointing to another cave. "That way is a short walk to the beach. They have been loading up supplies for the last several days. The witch is smart and has said very little. She only threatens me to control me. They need me to command the third ship."

"Three ships with gold, crew, and supplies," James said.

"Aye, but the crews are made up of small, blood-feeder children and these walking dead. If your plan is good, and the men strong enough, we may get the drop on them," Farrell said.

James looked around. "Who are your most stealthy men?"

"They are all stealthy, James. My men are the best; that is why the Queen's Navy has not taken us."

"We can send a dozen to the beach to sabotage the ships?" James suggested.

"Cut off their chance to leave the island, trap them between the caves, our swords, and our ships coming into the harbor. Good idea," Huxley said.

"Beware the mermaids," Farrell added. "If you get too close to the waters, they may take your men to the grave. That's why so many ships are weak or wounded, trying to retreat this place when the fighting starts."

"Mermaids?" Huxley asked. "I thought James was drinking too much rum in the sun!"

"Yes, they have helped Peter previously, though the witch has been very foul in her speaking of them. Just keep your eyes on the waters," Farrell warned.

Huxley looked back to his men. "Cooper, take eleven men to the beach. Do what ya can to the ships. Take out whoever you can, so when we start our attack, they will have nowhere to go but to the end of our blades."

Cooper nodded and said, "Aye, Captain!"

He pointed to different men, and the group of pirates quickly left the chamber to the caves.

"So, what is the plan, James?" Farrell asked. "If the witch returns with her men, it may be all for nothing."

"Take off your clothes," James said.

"What?" Farrell asked, startled.

"Put one of these dead fellows in your clothes in the cage. If she pops in, she will think you're asleep."

"That is actually brilliant!" Farrell exclaimed.

"Prop those other two near the tables," Huxley added. "Do it quickly. We may not have much time."

The pirates began to move the zombies to the tables, and Farrell took off his shirt.

"Is any of my crew alive?" James asked.

"The only one I know is the big, dark-skinned man who we moved, but she changed him. He is one of them," Farrell replied.

"Then she will have to change him back," James stated.

"James, if her magic is that strong?" Farrell worried.

"He saved me. If there is any chance that I can save Black Jack, I will do whatever I can to return the favor."

"Now you're talking like a pirate!" Captain Huxley said.

"Let's go kill that vampire-boy-king!" James said.

Chapter 33

Birds of a Feather

Belle found her way back to the beach after much soul-searching. She made her way to a cluster of jagged, sturdy, black rocks and sat down, staring into the night sky. She could not cry another magic tear. The crashing of the waves below was mesmerizing, a dull but gracious hum to fill the view.

Peter. Her mind continued to fall back to the vampire-boy. They had been so close. They had done so much before her tribe was butchered. Why did he do it? How long had he planned it? She had so many questions and knew he would never tell her a straight answer, especially not now. He would leave soon, and the only way he and that witch were going to allow her to go was if the witch used her magic and Belle stayed in a cage, pretending to be a bird so humans would not know of such magic. She was invited but only as a prisoner to her own skin.

Maybe it was best she found out. Maybe she should not even reach out to him one last time. She should let them leave so that she could enjoy the island without them. Maybe the humans of the tribe of Queen Wolf Lilly would allow her to spend time with them, and she would not be so alone. Her mind raced until a splash of water came up the rocks, almost knocking her from where she sat. She stood up and shook the water from her wet, blonde hair.

"Did I interrupt the pixie dream?" came a strong voice.

Belle looked over the rocks below as Niviene and two other mermaids splashed about below.

"I am not a pixie; I am a fairy!" Belle shouted back.

"In a world of magical creatures, I do not see a difference," Niviene said, smirking.

"Well, I guess you Sirens would know," Belle replied.

Niviene's face bent downward. "Sirens, really?" she said back. "So, are you staying with us or going back to your precious boy-king who has enslaved you for years?"

"What difference does it make to you? You're all liars. You tricked me and lied to me about my village," Belle replied.

Niviene splashed around. "Yes, we are liars to men but not to others of magic."

"You could have told me what they did, what Mama Laveau had done. I know we are not friends because of our differences and how much Peter controlled me, but honesty would have helped me so much. Being sisters of magic, I always assumed you would never betray me," Belle said.

Niviene stopped. "We are sisters of magic. We are creatures from the times of old, not of the human time. I do not know what you speak of. What did the witch do?"

Belle fluttered down from her stone perch and sat closer to the water's edge. The mermaids moved closer. "It was not Queen Wolf Lilly's tribe that killed my people. It was the witch. It was..." she paused, "it was Peter."

Niviene swam to the shore and leaned against the rocks.

"So, you are saying that the witch killed off the fairy tribe and blamed it on the Wolf Lilly's people? Thus, we began assaulting their fishing and waters?" The mermaid thought for a moment. "Then came the small war, truce, and the treaty of the borders on the island. Without the fairy magic, their power and council, the elves leaving, and their vote on life here ... it was for control and power of the island the whole time."

"We creatures of magic lived in harmony with everyone, even Peter and the Wolf Lilly tribe until a dozen years ago. I think the witch became jealous of Peter's relationship with her. I saw them swimming many nights in the lagoons, and they were not wearing clothing," Belle noted.

"Do you have evidence that Peter and that witch killed the fairies?" Niviene asked.

"I went back to my village. I found musket balls in trees, metal belt buckles, a pistol, and some gold coins. Wolf Lilly's people have no use for any of those things," Belle explained.

"I have always had my suspicions, and there were rumors, but I did not want to hurt you with such gossip. I visited the village years ago, but Peter had become so mean to you," Niviene stated. "The witch was in his ear, ridding good magic from the island. Then, she put us against each other to gain more power. The control of the west side of the island was to form an army and move on after using this land ... and us."

"We lost close to a dozen mermaids that summer to Queen Wolf Lilly's hunters, all over a lie!" Niviene raged. "I must go to Queen Wolf Lilly now. If we explain our side and there is proof, maybe we can find real peace and work with her tribe after Peter and his folly leave this island. We can make a new treaty and way of life for us all. No more luring ships to the island, no more feeding on the meat of humans, no more killing under a lie of self-preservation!"

"Niviene, I know you care for Peter, but he knew. He always knew. He led me astray, forbid me to return home, locked me up in that cursed cage. He hid his sins. Tell her that it was not just the witch who brought that ugly time to our island, but him as well," Belle said.

Niviene was saddened, though her eyes were sharp. "Peter made his choices as we all have. But now, we can restore this island once they leave. A new future and peace for those of magic and the ancient times."

She kicked up her tail, and she and the other two mermaids disappeared into the deep, blue waters.

Belle flew back to the rocky post and sat back down. She wanted to say goodbye to Peter but knew it was poison. Maybe now, if the mermaids and the people of Queen Wolf Lilly found a common bond to live by, she would have a new family. She thought about her cage and about the lie, and a small fire burned inside her. Maybe she did not want to say goodbye. Maybe she wanted to help send them off so that they would never want to return. She gritted her teeth, shot straight up into the sky like a flash, and twinkled out of sight, disappearing down the beach.

Chapter 34

THE LAST ACT

James and the small army of pirates had moved back through the caverns. As they did, the sound of debauchery and laughter grew louder. The sweet smell of charred meats and cake was noticed mostly by Captain Farrell. There were only a couple of zombies guarding the caverns, and being much slower, the pirates found them easy to dispose of. They came to the edge of the throne room. The top cavern had dozens of steps down into the throne room. James and Huxley looked past the doorway, down at the activities below. The young boys were throwing food and breaking plates as others stood on stage, dining and performing.

"What in the seven hells?" Huxley whispered.

Peter was not on the throne but stood onstage in a robe and crown made from white bone. He kicked and danced with the other children.

"Do not let their size or age slow down your blade, Huxley," James said. "They will cut your throat and drink your blood before you draw your sword."

"That's why my blade is already drawn, James," Huxley smiled.

They continued to watch. Three boys brought a long plank with a man tied to it. He looked terrified and confused. Ropes and chains kept him pressed to the lumber. The crowd got quiet, and Peter clapped and stood to address the boys.

"Yes, yes! Our last night on the island, and now for the best part of the meal: dessert!" Peter shouted.

The boys clapped and raised their glasses. "Peter, Peter!" they chanted. They placed the man in front of the boy-king. The chanting continued as he leaned towards the man. He lunged, biting down into the man's neck as blood sprayed on his face; the vampire-boy-king fed. After several seconds, with the chanting raising to its loudest, he stood up, his face red from the blood of his victim.

"Come join me, my friends. Feed with me. No more blood mixed with wine, no more food with blood. Where we travel, we will have fresh blood every night and cake for breakfast!" Peter roared.

He flipped the corpse on the board into the throne room, and the boys scrambled to eat the body like feral cats. Some bit, others fought, while others ripped at the man's flesh with claw-like fingers.

"I have lived long and lived hard and seen my share of debauchery, but this is an abomination to man and beast," Huxley whispered. "Some call me evil. Yes, I have done evil things, but this..."

"He will bring it to the American colonies if we do not stop him," James said.

"It could bring darkness to all. What if they take command of a fleet of ships, even just being boys? What if that abomination decided to infect grown men, trained pirates and soldiers? There will be no freedom. There will be no life, only destruction," Huxley stated.

Captain Huxley looked back at his men. "Be ready, men, we will advance and send this evil back to the bowels of hell."

Back in the harbor, the last of the zombie pirates moved a piano onto the lead ship. They grunted and strained, but they set it down on the deck of the hulking ship. Mama Laveau was still angry from the lecture from Niviene. She walked past the ships and her dozens of controlled living dead.

The sea air was still calming as she took it in. There was a hint of something in the air. She could smell the scent of men, and it was not of those when controlled or the smell of those gritty vampire boys who always fought and only bathed when playing in the water. She paused and looked around. Everything sat still and looked calm. It faded quickly, and so did her guard.

She wandered around the harbor, inspecting the boats. She turned her attention to the water. There were no mermaids swimming or patrolling the bay. She was not surprised, however, knowing their hatred for her, and they were not happy with Peter leaving them to fend for themselves on the island.

She called up to several of her zombies on the closest ship. "Be ready. We leave port in under four hours," she stated.

Groans and moans came back from the living dead crew. Her mind flashed ahead, knowing in just under three weeks, they could be set up in New Orleans. New opportunities and new power awaited. She could use their newfound power and have revenge on the plantation that hurt her so deeply. She would gain more power, learn more dark magic, and have that slave master and his family in chains soon enough. They would never see it coming!

She had visions of her hordes of the dead burning the grand house and the children feeding on the others who worked the plantation. Chaos and destruction were going to be her glory to them. She walked back to the caves and disappeared.

From along the cave entrance near the crest of the jungle, the pirates were waiting. Once the witch had disappeared, the pirates, with quick and silent feet, emerged to the beach and crept around the harbor, hiding behind boxes, rocks, and even the ships. Silent like a quick death, they began to set up their stealthy attack.

Chapter 35

We Welcome Your Death

Captain Huxley gestured to his men, and they spread out along the caves to descend into the great throne room. They had crept and killed all the guards near any doorway. The vampire boys continued to drink, and Peter sang as the band of pirates were now at every doorway, waiting for the word to storm the room.

Huxley looked over at James. "This is your party; you make the toast!" Huxley said.

James stood in one of the doorways and raised his right arm, his iron hook pointing to the ceiling. The dozens of men watched with hungry anticipation. Peter was laughing when he turned his head and saw Hook in the doorway. Peter's mind began to race but was quickly interrupted.

"Attack!" James shouted like a thousand demons screeching.

The pirate raiders stormed the room, catching the vampire children off guard. Pirates crashed into the tables and furniture. The first wave of children was able to show their fangs, but blades swiftly removed their heads from their bodies. The zombies began to swing their swords and clubs to keep a few of the pirates back, but it was only a matter of time before more pirates cut them down.

Peter gritted his fangs, leapt from the stage as if he could fly, and landed near his throne. He grabbed a huge hammer and slammed it hard against a large, hanging bell. The ring echoed through the room and down the caverns. He struck it again and again.

Reinforcements would be coming. For every pirate who fell under the attack, two of the vampire children were cut down. The boys were tired, drunk, and had never fought men of such training and barbaric tactics. Most battles were on the beach against British soldiers who fired muskets and fled in the chaos of being bitten. These pirates did not fire muskets or flee, even when bitten.

They fought on, hacking, swinging, and sending blood to the floor. Farrell ducked the blade of a zombie, then struck him with the short sword. The zombie groaned but swung again. Farrell tackled the creature, took the sword, and plunged it deep into the man's neck. He rolled off him and looked down. A turkey leg was resting near a pile of broken glasses. He grabbed the leg and stuck it in his mouth before running back into the fray with a muted battle cry.

Mama Laveau heard the clanging of the bell and ran past the hanging cages. She paused and looked at who she thought was Farrell.

"Your friends will not save you." She raised her hands as a green mist floated around her fingertips. She approached the cage, and the lifeless body of a zombie guard in his white shirt and military pants stared back.

Her eyes burned in a fury. She stormed from the dungeon with a shriek.

Peter was not like the others; he was stronger, wiser, and had fed on many men the last 100 years. He leapt from the throne, attacking, stabbing, and cutting down every pirate who stood in his way.

From one of the doorways, a dozen zombies clambered in but were met quickly by Captain Huxley and two of his men.

Mama Laveau arrived just as Peter tossed a body he had fed on to the floor. She raised her hands and sent a mist out over the room. The pirates began to stumble as the poison hit their lungs.

"You must get to the docks, Peter! We can still get away!" she howled. "Get to your boat, and I will join you after I kill these men!"

Peter was driven by anger and hesitated, still fighting.

"Peter, get to the beach!" she howled again. Then, the witch was stuck by a bullet in the arm and fell back.

The mist fell away as James lowered his pistol. "Damn!" he mumbled.

Peter bolted past pirates and dead soldiers and disappeared into a cave. The witch staggered to her feet, pulled the whistle from her bone necklace, and blew. She blew it very hard and ran to the caged wall at the back of the throne room. A horrendous roar belched from the darkness of the cage.

The witch ran to the cage and threw open the door as The Beast once again was allowed to play and feed. The alligator thundered into the room, thrashing, biting, and clearing paths from every living thing. Pirates fell, zombies fell, and even the boys who tried to get away were snapped in half. The chaos was infectious as all creatures, man and beast, ran for their lives.

James ran to the throne and picked up the large hammer that lay near it. He tossed it at the great lizard and struck its nose. It turned towards him.

Huxley ran to join Hook.

"We cleaned out this mess," Huxley said, "but that beast will tear my men to pieces. We must get to the harbor to stop that vampire-boy and witch from getting free!"

"I think I have a plan for the beast," James said.

"You think?" Huxley asked.

The scaly creature began to slowly walk towards them.

"Do not wait for me," James said.

"Oh, I'm not planning on it," Huxley shouted and ran quickly from the throne as the lizard gained ground.

James took a goblet of wine and tossed it, striking the beast again in the snout, spilling wine in its eyes. The room was quiet now as it cleared out. James grabbed a silver tray from the ground and ran from the throne room. The beast followed with a fury, knocking over tables and bodies in its wake.

Mama Laveau looked at the chaos and the remainder of her army.

"Everyone to the harbor!" she commanded.

Only a few boys remained as they fled the room. The pirates struggled to get to their feet, still affected by the poison. Farrell saw James running from the room, the great beast chasing just yards behind. The witch saw Farrell and stepped up to kill him. He turned, and she knocked the large turkey leg from his grasp.

"Now you die!" she roared.

"I was eating that!" he shouted back.

He swung his sword, but she laughed and knocked it away as well. She went to grab him by his neck, and three pirates tackled her, trying to overpower her. The pirates screamed as their arms burned, engulfed by blue flames. The pirates scattered as their clothing caught fire. She took off running, striking anything in her way, setting them on fire as she fled from the great room and continued to the docks.

James had never run so hard in his life. Sure, he had fled from musket fire and the thought of jail time. He had even fled through a window a time or two, running from an angry boyfriend or husband who caught him with a beautiful woman. But now, this was hell's fire on his heels. He turned down corridors, trying to stay balanced as the great beast gained. *How could something with such stumpy legs move this fast?*

He ran past Peter's office with relief, knowing he was running in the right direction. He could hear the lizard gaining, and after a quick left turn, he ran into a large, open cave. He stopped for just a second to peer over his shoulder, and the great beast turned the corner and began to close. He ran across the room to the opening of the Pits of Despair and stood near the edge.

The lizard thundered harder, and Hook began to move the silver tray, hoping the torchlight would reflect and hit the beast. It did, but it did not slow him; it only aggravated him more. The beast charged, his thick jaws open. James dove to his left, jumping into the hole as the mighty beast followed but was unable to turn. James slammed the iron hook into the cliffside and held fast to the ledge with the other hand. He watched as the creature tumbled dozens of feet below, crashing into the trash pile with a sound like a cannonball hitting an iron beam. The ground shook for a second as James tightened his grip and hoped the hook would hold.

Below, in the filth and garbage, the scaly creature rolled and found its footing in the pile. It looked around in the darkness and cried out. It started to move but stopped. Its back leg and hip were shattered. It crawled off the pile and howled again.

Hook pulled himself up over the ledge and rolled over. He lay there for several seconds, wishing it were hours. His lungs burned, and he listened to his heart race. He didn't want to get up, but he had too. He had to get to the beach. As he was lying there, he heard voices from below.

"Yum-yums?" a child's voice barked.

Then another screamed, "Yum-yums!"

James crawled to the edge and watched as dozens of the ghoul-like children came from the shadows and circled the giant lizard.

"Yum-yums! Fresh yum-yums!!" the ghoulish children shouted.

The scaly creature let out a deep hiss. The small ghouls attacked. The first few found out how big the creature's teeth were as they gnashed in anger, but eventually, they swarmed it, covering the beast with knives and forks. After being struck several times in the eyes and through its thick neck, the beast was losing steam. With the broken leg, it tried to get away from the piranha-style attack of vicious, little cannibals, but as it moved from the trash pile, more of the little ghouls attacked.

Edward emerged from the darkness. He ran full steam ahead, holding a rusty sword and small torch. The other creatures backed away as Edward jumped on the creature and slammed his rusty sword deep into the creature's neck. Edward raised his sword and torch, letting out a battle cry. He looked up and saw James peering down at the battle below.

The beast let out one last gargled roar as four more of the child-like monsters leapt on its tail, biting and stabbing with broken cutlery.

"Yum-yums for days!" Edward shouted. "Yum-yums for all of you!"

The small, child-like creatures began to chant and bow to Edward near the gator's lifeless body.

"He gave us yum-yums!" one boy shouted.

"He protects us from the bad things!" cried another.

"Yum-yums!" another boy shouted. "We get fresh yum-yums!"

They continued to chant and worship Edward, who stood on the back of the dead beast, shaking his sword in the air. The small, ghoulish children continued biting and ripping into the giant beast.

"I am king of the yum-yums!" he shouted.

James got to his feet and shook his head, hoping to get the image of the last thirty seconds out of his mind before running from the cave.

Chapter 36

BLOOD IN THE SAND

When Peter arrived at the beach, the battle had already begun. One of his ships was on fire, sending smoke into the night sky. Across the beach, zombies and pirates exchanged blows, striking one another to see which one would fall first. The remaining vampire boys attacked, leaping from pirate to pirate like wild animals, but unlike their previous prey, the pirates became more aggressive. Every few seconds, he could hear the wail of a child as pirate steel pierced their bodies or removed a limb. Peter had seen enough. He pulled his blade and ran forward. He cut down two pirates near the docks. He scanned the waters, but there were no mermaids. His first line of defense was nowhere to be seen. He continued, slicing down a pirate with every couple of steps. His eyes were red with rage.

"Peter!" shouted a voice. Mama Laveau was on the largest boat. "Get aboard. We must flee while we can." She then turned and waved her hands, sending a green mist around the boat. Several nearby pirates fell, clutching their throats.

Peter was torn, for he was loyal. He ran by the invading pirates and cut several of them down as they choked on the magic mist. The largest of the three ships started to pull from the harbor. Peter continued his assault on the beach and port, running, slicing, and cutting down the pirates, trying to give the witch more time to get the ship underway.

Three of the vampire children ran to the ship and jumped to his hull, trying to climb to escape. A volley of arrows and musket fire took two of them down, and they dropped into the water below. Peter saw the direction of the gunfire and arrows; four pirates were huddled near a cluster of rocks. Peter was there in less than a blink. As they tried to reload, they were met with his hatred and steel.

James found his way from the caves and ran onto the beach. The chaos continued as James squinted and tried to find Peter in the smoke and fog of the battle. Peter had just finished feeding. He tossed the body of an unlucky pirate to the beach and looked across the war-covered sand as James stepped out.

Their eyes met. Peter gritted his bloody teeth, and James replied with a smirk.

In the chaos of the battle, the two ran at one another. When Peter's sword and the mighty black hook met, the clang was so loud that it echoed across the harbor. Many men stopped fighting to see what caused such a ringing. Peter swung quickly, and Hook was forced to step back and parry the blows. He used his hooked hand to knock several of the blows away, causing sparks to strike the air.

"You killed them all!" Peter shouted. Drool launched from his curled lips.

"You took my crew and my hand. What do you expect a captain to do?" James shouted back and swung wildly, causing the vampire-boy-king to fall back.

Peter began to circle him. He had beaten him easily before; he could kill this one-handed sea dog and get to the ship. His eyes glanced over as the ship was now pulling away from the wooded docks. James saw his eyes shift and swung with his blade. Peter dodged it easily, but Hook threw an upper cut with his new iron hook and caught Peter across the jaw, sending him backwards.

Peter was furious. No one had ever struck him because of his vampire speed. It was as if something was slowing him down, making him weak. He attacked again, and James blocked, parried, and countered. The battle was not showing favor to either of them. Peter looked once again to the ship. The Voodoo Queen continued to fight as pirates scaled and assaulted the ship. Zombies tossed men overboard as she steered.

She looked at Peter and signaled for him to run. "Get away! Go into the jungle! I will find you!" she screamed.

Peter looked around as the remaining zombies fell. His band of vampire children lying in the sand and blood were but a memory. Peter gritted his teeth, and in a quick strike, almost like a shadow, he was behind James. He slashed him across the back, and Hook fell to his knees. Peter took off running down the beach. James felt the tear in his back and staggered to get to his feet. He saw Peter running quickly towards the jungle.

Captain Huxley saw it too. "Go boy, go finish this!" Huxley shouted.

Hook took off running. His legs pounded with adrenaline, but Peter was yards away. He could not compete with his vampire speed. Peter looked over his shoulder, and James was losing ground. He smiled as he ran, knowing he could escape. They may have lost the battle, but they could still win the war.

If Mama Laveau got away, they could still regroup and take what they could to the new world. He looked over his shoulder once more at the main ship leaving the harbor.

James continued to push, and suddenly, his legs felt like feathers. He was flying at a great speed. Belle was behind him, covering the one-handed pirate with sparks of magic and light.

"If he gets into the jungle, he will enslave people again. I can get you to him, but only you can kill him!" she cried.

James' eyes were wide in confusion.

"Thank you?" he said questioningly, and he crashed down just a couple yards from the vampire-boy-king.

Peter grimaced at seeing Belle fluttering over James' shoulder. "So, the ultimate betrayal is at hand," Peter said. "You choose him over me."

"You betrayed me and the island! You and that witch!" Belle shouted. "You killed off my people, my family!"

Peter said nothing.

"You turned the mermaids and the others of magic against us to change this island!" Belle screamed.

Peter let out a sigh. "Oh, poor Belle. You will never understand. I did everything for you. You complained about the other fairies. You complained about the tribe of Queen Wolf Lilly and her magic. You complained about everything, so I helped make your problems disappear."

"You took away my problems? You gave me new problems and murdered everyone!" the fairy screamed.

"There is always a cost for getting what you want," Peter replied.

James listened but focused on Peter's blade. He let them continue.

"I took away all your problems and gave you a chance at a new life and even a chance to come with us!" Peter shouted.

"Yes, and you put me in a cage? You used me and my magic to hurt others. You controlled and used me!" she shouted back.

"It was for the greater good, Belle. I thought you would understand that, but your simple mind cannot. Now, you have this one-armed hooligan waiting for a chance to kill me, which he won't. Our plans will continue on a lesser scale without the boys, but we will go to America and do as planned." He shifted his eyes to James. "Unless you think otherwise?"

"I think you underestimate vengeance, and I plan on teaching you the importance of it," James said.

"Then try it, you helpless one-handed wretch! I grow tired of you and that damn hook!" Peter swung, and James stepped back, knocking the blade away.

Back on the ship, Mama Laveau watched as she pulled away. Her small, five-man zombie crew stood close as she watched the docks get smaller. She could see the magic fog just yards ahead. She was nearly free.

There came a whistle, and she turned her head. Farrell pointed his pistol and fired, striking her across the cheek and jaw. She staggered to the deck of the ship. The zombie crew began to walk towards him, but three other pirates fought them back.

The Voodoo priestess crawled to the edge of the ship, her face bleeding, bone and teeth exposed in her seething face. She tried to get to her feet, but Farrell swung, striking her across the chest and right arm.

"You like to put men in cages, but there will be no cage for you," he said.

The sound of cannon fire erupted, and four ships were cutting through the morning fog. *The Conqueror* broke through first, leading the charge with the three warships of Captain Huxley behind her. Father Bob was smiling at the helm.

Cannons roared again, and the movement on the beach slowed as all eyes looked to the oncoming onslaught. Mama Laveau was cornered. She leaned back against the side of the ship, still looking for a way out.

Farrell looked over the side. Below, violent water swirled; the mermaids had returned. Niviene looked up.

"Son of Adam, toss her to us so that we may end her dark magic!" Niviene shouted.

The Voodoo priestess put her hand up to beg, but then stopped and spat at Farrell.

"So be it!" she hissed.

Farrell grabbed her by the throat and tossed her down into the blue waters. She sunk into the water, thrashing and screaming as the mermaids clawed and bit into her bleeding flesh. She started to use her magic as she thrashed and fought the mermaids. The waters grew dark with black and red blood. The commotion and fighting stopped. There was no sign of life, not a splash from a tail fin. All went quiet.

Farrell looked up as the sun began to rise over the horizon. He could see Captain Huxley's ships and James' small ship closing in.

Back on the beach, the sun was just a sliver, but its light was strong. Peter had his back to it as he kicked James and sliced quickly, striking him across the thigh.

"You fool, what can you do to kill someone like me?" Peter roared.

James rolled away, and Peter turned and saw the sun. He froze.

James threw sand quickly into his eyes and picked up the boy-king, slamming him into a thick palm tree. He took the hook and latched it across Peter's neck, pinning him to the tree. Peter looked out to the ocean as the sun was cresting.

"I can stall you until the sun rises," James said, keeping pressure on his hooked hand.

Peter grabbed at the hook and tried to pull it away, but it choked him. His hands clawed at it. Why was he so weak? The sun was making him weaker, and his head pounded. He looked at the black iron hook.

"I'll give you anything. Release me from this iron thing!" Peter demanded.

Hook smiled. "Oh, it's not only iron; it's silver, painted black and forged in holy water. Only parts of it are iron."

Peter began to tremble as the sun rose. His eyes burned, and his strength was now gone. Hook leaned into his ear and whispered.

"All you ever were and all you could have been, I am taking from you forever."

Peter's eyes watered, knowing death was closer than it had ever been. The sunlight began to burn his flesh, and it flaked away. His hands still tried to wrestle the great hook from his throat. He let out a scream as his head burst into fire, and James fell backward to the sand.

The frail, boy-like frame burned in blue and yellow flames. Within seconds, all that remained was a pile of small, scorched bones and ashes near the base of the tree. His father's ring lay half-buried in the pile his grey ash. An outline of Peter's shadow was burned into the tree bark, the last place his shadow would ever be again.

Belle wiped a tear from her eye. She was done with his abuse. Still, memories of the boy who used to play on the beach with her and the others welled up inside her. He was so innocent then, even with his vampire curse. It felt like only a few days ago, but it was over a century. Time never seemed to show its true reality. It never does.

James looked at the fairy. "I would like to thank you," he said.

"I think this island would like to thank you. I will warn you, however, if those other men, your friends, get too wild, this island will make sure you do not leave the harbor," she informed.

"Duly noted," James said. "Let's go see who is still alive and who we need to bury."

Belle sat down on James' shoulder. He laughed and began walking down the beach.

"We could just fly back, right?" Hook said.

"Yes, but I prefer this. Keep walking, child of man. We fairies are very particular when using our magic dust," she said.

"Ah I see," James replied.

"Oh, do not be down. I just have to know if I like you," she said, grinning. "I have not made up my mind."

James laughed. "I will try to be as honest and forthright as I can with you, fairy"

"That is a good start," she smiled.

Hook could see Huxley's ships and his own coming into the harbor. His ship, the smallest ship, made him smile.

"That's a tiny ship. Why would anyone use that? What is that for? Fishing?" Belle asked.

"Oh no, that is the most wonderful ship a man can have. It is small but has memories of friendship and the open sea. A ship like that is worth more than any treasure, but it's nice to have treasure to spend with your friends," Hook said. "That damn vampire and witch took most of mine."

"They did mine as well," the fairy said.

"Well then, we both need to make new friends and remember memories with the old ones," James said.

"You're not too bad for a human. There may be hope for your kind yet," she said.

Chapter 37

Rest for the Wicked

Captain Huxley looked around the blood-soaked beach. The bodies of the zombie slaves, small vampire boys, and his men were scattered from the caves to the shoreline. James stood with him. Belle still sat on his shoulder.

"Still liking the life of a real pirate, James?" Huxley asked.

"Yes. It's the same as a soldier or any man wanting to hold onto anything in his life worth fighting for. I have seen this several times, but the clothing was under a flag," James replied.

"True enough. What about that creature who took your hand?" Huxley asked.

"He is dust," replied James.

"And the world will be better for it," Huxley said.

Farrell walked down the plank of the lead ship, now returned back to port. He joined them on the beach.

"I shot that evil witch in the face, and the creatures of the ocean finished her off," Farrell said with a sense of pride.

"You savage, shooting a woman? And after all she did for you," James joked.

"No more cages for this man," Farrell said boldly.

"Well, I did promise Captain Huxley you could be his for ransom," James said.

"What?" Farrell asked.

"Aye, the Queen's Navy will pay me well for your hide!" Huxley said.

There was silence for a second before James and Huxley erupted in laughter.

"I did not find that amusing," said Belle.

"I agree with the fairy. Is that a fairy?" Farrell asked.

"Yes. She is a fairy and very helpful in our victory," James added.

"Well, James, 'tis time we bury the dead and take our plunder," Huxley said.

The sun was now in its full glory, rising over the deep blue water.

"You can take your ship, split the booty, and be on your way. Maybe find another adventure," Huxley said.

Farrell pointed. On the beach, hundreds of armed tribes, men in loin cloths and feathers, were marching towards them.

"Oh, this cannot be good," James said.

Huxley gave a sharp whistle, and three-dozen tired, worn pirates ran, walked, and staggered to their captain. The small army of island warriors stopped just yards from them and stood in formation.

"They look to outnumber us three to one," Farrell said sadly.

"Just stay ready," James said.

From the ranks, Queen Wolf Lilly broke into view, a spear in one hand and a golden goblet in the other. She approached them, walking confidently.

"You have saved this island from a growing evil. Though we do not like intruders to the island, and most humans from the lands of man are considered beasts, you, pirate, still owe me a drink."

James smiled, "Yes, Queen, I..."

"Not you, boy. Him, the pirate!" she exclaimed.

Huxley laughed and took the goblet from her. He bowed and got down on one knee. "Whatever my queen wishes, I will give her."

"You will stay with us for one night to celebrate the victory and leave at dawn with your men and your ships. Allow us to take back what that boy-king and his witch took from us, including objects of wealth and magic alike."

"This island is yours. We only wish for the trinkets of man that he stole from other men," Captain Huxley said, smiling.

"Rise, bury your dead, and tonight, we will feast," she commanded.

Captain Huxley rose to his feet, and a pirate quickly handed him a bottle of rum. He poured into the goblet and handed it to the queen. She smiled.

"So, you want to celebrate our win even though you didn't really help?" James asked.

The queen's eyes rolled.

Captain Huxley leaned in, "Do not blow this for me, boy. Look at her; she is beautiful."

Hook corrected himself. "I mean, sure why not? We won the day, it's your island, and it's a win-win for all of us."

Queen Wolf Lilly smiled.

"Return to our village at sunset for a feast. You humans will never have words to explain its glory."

"We will be there," Captain Huxley said.

The men and the queen turned and marched back down the beach.

"Your mouth does get you in trouble, James. Sometimes your battle is not everyone's, and sometimes other's battles are not worth your trouble," Huxley said.

"You fought for my battle," James replied.

"I fought for plunder and my men. Vengeance was all on you," Huxley said.

The queen stopped and looked back at Huxley. "And pirate, it would be wise for an old sea dog like yourself to find time for a nap. You could be in for a long evening of festivities."

Captain Huxley swallowed hard and smiled.

"I ain't that old," he whispered under his breath. "She will be waking up at noon."

James and Farrell laughed. The queen and her men continued down the beach.

"Humans are so beastly," Belle added.

"Okay lads, let's give our men a proper pirate burial. And for the others, let the winds, ravens, and the waters have them."

The next few hours, the pirates loaded their ship with gold, jewelry, precious stones, paintings, and furniture. Captain Huxley returned anything that may have been taken from the tribe of Queen Wolf Lilly. Even if it looked questionable, made not by man's craftsmanship, he left it.

James loaded a couple of medium-sized wooden chests onto his ship and looked around the waters. Far in the distance, he saw the mermaids splashing about. He had his ship, but the loss of crew would not be quickly replaced. The treasure would allow him total freedom if he was wise with his newfound riches. He could even buy a tavern and a new bigger ship, maybe with three masts. He laughed briefly at the thought of the large ship. He liked his small ship. He would not replace her. Maybe he would give her a friend?

Farrell lumbered up the walkway. They had placed Black Jack on their ship, and the big warrior still fought the disease in his body. He would have moments of clarity, but then the dull eyes took over again.

"So, James, or should I say Captain Hook, where do you go now?" Farrell asked.

"I am unsure. I do not have my crew, my men and my friends," James replied.

"You still have some of them," Farrell noted and pointed.

From the beach, Father Bob walked with Black Jack who seemed to stumble as he walked. His hands and feet were shackled.

"He is back?" James shouted and ran to the two men. "I thought he was gone, I thought..."

"James, he is still not himself. That witch's magic was deep and dark," Father Bob said softly. "I thought some fresh air and the walk could do him well after being tied down in the darkness of the ship for so many days."

Black Jack groaned, and some spittle dripped from his mouth. His eyes were still very much dilated.

"How do we help him? Can he be cured?" Farrell asked.

"He talked about his aunt in the Caribbean; she knew a lot of Voodoo magic. Maybe if we can find her, we can get him back," Father Bob suggested.

"Well, then that's our first stop," James stated.

The big man coughed and looked at his captain. His speech was slurred. "You have a hook for a hand," he grunted.

"We will get you back and get that poison out of you, my friend," James added.

"Belle instructed me to give him some rum and some roots and berries to help him sleep. It could take weeks or months for him to return to his former self as we knew him," Father Bob cautioned.

"Then that's what we do. He is our family," James replied.

"Agreed!" Father Bob said and began to walk the big man to the ship.

Farrell walked back over to James and watched the priest walk the zombie away.

"Well, you have some of your crew. It's a good start," Farrell said.

"Aye. Half a crew, some treasure, and the open sea is about all I can hope for now, and that is good enough for me. What do you do, Farrell?" James asked.

"Well, your pirate friend, Huxley, has advised me that he won't use me for ransom or kill me. I am going to take the admiral's ship back to an English port, give a report of the incident, and wait for accommodations," Farrell replied.

"Still a company man," James said with a grin.

"Just a little bit less. A few bad apples should not make you throw out the whole barrel, James. I still believe in the Queen's Navy," Farrell replied.

"You won't mention the island, correct?" James asked.

"Oh no, I will mention another island. One far away from this horror. Heaven forbid anyone comes here again. Let's leave the magic and monsters away from our world," Farrell assured him.

"Will you be going to the party this evening?" James asked.

"Of course! I would not miss that! I am a company man, James, but let's be honest, blowing off steam with the creatures and things on this island will be good material for my memoirs when I am an old man. It will be thought of as fiction, and I cannot wait! Also, I am still hungry!" Farrell exclaimed.

Belle flew down and landed on James' shoulder. "So, you humans are departing in the morning?"

"Yes, we are," James answered back.

"I grow weary of this place, lots of dark memories," Belle said.

"It's bad luck to have a woman on board your ship, Hook," Farrell joked.

"I am not a woman; I am a fairy," she said.

"I cannot promise you fortune or fun," James said.

"I just want adventure and freedom," she replied.

"Now that, my magical lass, I can give you in spades!" James exclaimed with a smile.

"Then I will go and pack." Belle sped off, flying away quickly.

"Ha, what a crew you will have James!" Farrell said. "A drooling zombie, an old priest, and a magical fairy."

"Your circle of friends can be what makes life an adventure, my friend," James replied.

"Indeed. Speaking of circles and adventures, where is Huxley?" Farrell asked.

"Last I saw of him, he was wandering back to his ship for a long nap," replied James.

"Could be a good idea," Farrell said.

"For his sake, I hope so," James replied.

Chapter 38

VICTORS AND THE SPOILS

The celebration was the largest Queen Wolf Lilly's tribe had ever thrown. Hundreds of the tribe set up a grand feast of wild boar and deer, with fruits from across the island. The smell of the feast drifted nearly two miles down the beach. Torchlights lit up the land like a living bonfire as men and women danced, laughed, and ate. The pirates drank from wooden mugs and glass bottles. The beverages were of both alcohol and fruit of the island. Both the pirates and islanders laughed and shouted stories to one another. Queen Wolf Lilly sat on a large, wooden throne, overlooking the party; next to her, three large bodyguards stood holding spears. Captain Huxley and James sat close by.

"The island is free; my magic can help heal it once again," the queen said.

"We appreciate the hospitality of your people," Captain Huxley said and raised his wooden goblet.

"The witch woman, she changed Peter. She changed many things over time, but now we can heal this land. It's a new dawn for all of us," she proclaimed.

James watched Farrell, his arms around an island girl who laughed at his jokes, the ones that were never funny. The drinks were obviously very strong.

Belle drank from a small thimble and let out a great belch, which caused the queen and the others to laugh.

"Excuse me!" the fairy said. "I have not drunk such things in years."

"It is okay, Belle. We have not had a reason to celebrate in years," the queen added.

Belle smiled and flew high into the night sky. She waved her hands and sent clusters of sparks and lights showering down. The party goers watched as shades of yellow, green, and purple shot into the air, exploding and sending glistening fairy dust down below. The queen laughed and gave a wink to Captain Huxley, who smiled, then suddenly understood her wink, and sat up. The queen stepped from the throne and took his hand.

"We shall go for a walk while the fairy entertains our guests," she said. "I will show you things on this island most mortal men have never dreamed."

The two of them walked from the beach into the jungle.

James took a deep sip from his mug and smiled as the party continued. He glanced to the water as the mermaids splashed about, cheering the fairy on as she zigged and darted in the sky, sending rainbows of color from her magic hands. Father Bob sat nearby, clapping with merriment as the sky show continued.

James' eyes were fixed on the night sky with its new colors and booming sounds. He glanced at his hook-like hand. He was free to do whatever he wanted with whomever he wanted, and his ship would be there waiting for him and his friends in the morning. Pirate or swashbuckler, he was feeling like a lucky man to have lived through it all and had those around him join in this adventure in his life.

He glanced to the water, the lights above shimmering on its reflection. Niviene and a few of the mermaids were more inland. They watched the lights and relaxed in the waters near the rocks.

This island was a magical place indeed, and now it was free to be the way it was centuries ago. The laughter continued, the air still sweet with roasted food, and James smiled. Niviene swam to the beach and stood up on her mortal legs and walked to James. She sat down near him.

"You are quite the adventurer to survive all that this island offers," she said.

"I had a lot of help," he replied.

"It is a great island. It was once a paradise," she reminded him.

"It still can be," James acknowledged.

"Not the way it was. Time is changing, things along with man, travel, and technology. It's a time where magic and the gods are fading," Niviene replied.

"If you were human, you would understand change and how things fade so much faster."

Niviene was put off by his response. After a quick scowl, she grinned. "Perhaps. Our time away from humans may have slowed us down as well. I hope to gain favor with Queen Wolf Lilly and the people of her tribe. We have had bad blood for so many years. Maybe we can have a new start on the island. Keep it hidden a bit, but maybe allow for some to visit if need be."

"I dare say I may never want to, as beautiful as it is," James said back.

"Truly not return as the hero and take in such a place?" she asked.

"Maybe in time, but my memories of this paradise have some very dark shadows as well," James replied.

"Then we shall hope time helps heal them. Trust me, good humans are hard to find and keep close. I have known a few and seen them come and go," she said." I hope you will come back to us in the time."

"I will keep that in mind," James said and glanced back to the lights that Belle was casting in the night sky.

Chapter 39

CAPTAIN JAMES HOOK AT YOUR SERVICE

The next morning, Hook watched Farrell launch their two ships from the harbor. Both great military ships set off in the ocean. *The Argonaut* crew was made up of pirates wearing navy uniforms, and the plan was simple: return the ship, have the pirates leave in row boats before the Royal Navy got close, and another ship would return them to Captain Huxley's small armada. Captain Huxley, still very tired, stood near James and watched as well.

"If we would have had arrangements, that ship would have joined my other three. Now, I could buy three of them with the booty on this island," Huxley stated.

"Did she sleep till noon?" James asked.

"She was still sleeping and snoring when I left around 8:00 a.m. That wonderful woman gave me a magic ring and said it will always guide me back here if I ever want to spend time with her and her tribe. Like a man such as myself could ever return and settle down... in a tropical paradise... with a beautiful, magical queen. Nope, I need dark taverns, blades, cannons, and the open water," Huxley replied.

James laughed and looked down at the ring which Huxley's was wearing on his left hand.

"So it's a pirate's life," James said. "You could give me the magic ring."

"Are you daft in the head?! The things she showed me, the lost places, the creatures of legends. This island is incredible. There is much power and magic here. It truly is paradise. I touched the sword of Arthur! The real sword, Excalibur itself! The Lady of the Lake had it hidden, or so she thought! Lilly knows where she hid it," Huxley replied.

"Oh, it's just Lilly now? No Queen, no Wolf?" James noted.

"Well, she is my Lilly, but I have said too much. I would be a fool to never return. I just do not know how long until she would kick me out," Huxley laughed.

"She is a magical demi-god queen, and you're a pirate. Maybe it could work," James replied.

"I think my heart stopped twice in our... adventures... last night, and I would have welcomed death in her passionate arms," Huxley confessed.

"Good thing you took a nap," James said.

"Indeed!" Huxley exclaimed.

They both looked out to the ocean, the deep blue water and light blue skies.

"Good friends, good adventures, and the freedom of the open sea," James said, smiling.

Father Bob waved from James' small ship. Belle fluttered around the mast. It was time to go. He shook Captain Huxley's hand.

"Maybe another adventure at another time," James said.

"Aye, my boy, but how about with less magic and monsters next time?" Father Bob asked.

"What kind of adventure would that be?" James said.

Huxley smiled. "Agreed. May the wind always be in your sails, Captain James Hook!"

James smiled and walked back to his ship.

In the cove near the Pits of Despair, Edward stood in the sunlight. He wore a hooded grey cloak and tattered, black pants. A necklace made of the giant alligator teeth was draped across his shoulders. In his hand was a long spear. He stepped out into the sunlight. It did not burn. His eyes adjusted to the sun, and behind him, the other child-like creatures stayed in the shadows. He watched as some of the ships left the harbor until they were well off from the island. He walked back to the caves and lifted his spear.

"I am Edward, King of the Yum-Yums! The evil men have left us, and I am the protector of this island and you, my brothers!"

The hooting and chanting of the creatures smashing bone against rock walls echoed through the caves.

"King of the Yum-Yums, King of the Yum-Yums!" the chant began. He walked back to the sunlight and stood like a statue awaiting any threat.

The Conqueror was breaking free from the island's coastal waters. A couple mermaids swam playfully alongside the small ship. It was a perfect day to be back on the water. The warm sun and the soft breeze helped clear James' head from the previous day's events.

"We head west to the Caribbean," James said. "Hopefully, we will be there in a few days."

Father Bob was tying a knot on a rope near the mast. "He is still asleep down below," Bob said. "I pray we can bring him back to us."

"You pray, and I will sail, my friend," James said.

Belle flew up from the cabin area. "My magic is not working. I tried to help him, but it's not the kind of magic we fairies do."

"I appreciate it, Belle," James said. "We will get to his homeland in a few days and hope his aunt can break the witch's spell."

"A few days? I can do better than that. Try hours," Belle replied.

Belle flew across the deck, and fairy dust fell across the ship. It shook and slowly rose from the waters. "You said west?" she said, smiling.

Hook held on tightly, as did Father Bob.

"Yes?" Hook replied, unsure what was going to happen.

"Then west it is!" Belle shouted, and the boat hovered over the waters and shot across the ocean.

"Is this safe!?" Captain Hook shouted.

"Sure! Where is your sense of adventure, human?!" Belle shouted back. "Let's go save your friend and find you a new crew, Captain James Hook!"

James smiled and gripped the wheel tighter. Freedom and adventure were calling once again!

Meet the Author

Mark Tarrant is a creative powerhouse who knew he wanted to write and create from his first encounter with *Star Wars*.

Born in Lansing, Michigan, and growing up in Massachusetts, Tarrant grew up loving books about monsters and the unknown.

A big fan of comics, especially those of Robert E. Howard's Conan character, his reading eventually included the master of horror, Stephen King. His storytelling is also influenced by his passion for Western movies, particularly *The Good, The Bad & The Ugly*.

His artistic talents have received recognition in *The Boston Globe*, *USA Today*, *The Valley Advocate*, *The Republican*, *The Herald*, and *The Buzz*.

Mark strives to continue to create unique characters and situations for entertainment, whether it be in film, comics, books, or short stories. His favorite two words are, "What if..." or for those who know him, "Cigar time..."

Tarrant's personal life is a sharp contrast to the fantasy world that captivates his readers. He lives in New Mexico, loves history, particularly the wild west, and gets especially excited during NFL season.

Learn more about Mark at **www.MarkTarrant.com**

Book Club Questions

1. How did the writing bring you into the world of pirates and horror?

2. Did you feel that James Hook should just deal with his choices and give up on his crew or was it more adult to go back to fight for them?

3. What characters did you feel were most manipulative toward each other?

4. Would there be any redemption for Peter if he could break the cycle he is in and the path he is on with the witch?

5. Was the pace of the story easy to follow?

6. If you were on the island as a friend of Peter's, how long do you think you would live until something may have gone wrong by his own hand?

7. Would you prefer to be in the world of Peter or of James Hook? What would you do when those two worlds collided?

8. Who was your favorite female character in the book? Why?

9. In what ways was Peter's character different from other vampire stories and myths?

10. Was the Voodoo Queen's magic too powerful for the story? Do you think she is truly dead?

11. If Peter was able to return by magic, could he find redemption or would he continue his quest for power?

12. In time, what do you think Belle will do since she is free from Peter's clutches: stay with the pirates, return to the island, or have her own adventures trying to find her fairy kin?

13. Would you like to read more of this series, and what would you like to see happen with your favorite characters?

14. What would you say if Peter could return from the land of the dead with dark magic and there is much more to the story?

15. Do you enjoy true historical events and social aspects with the fantasy story? If yes, what more would you like to see in this time period and locations with monsters and magic?

16. Who between Hook and Peter would you want fighting for your life in a bad situation andwhy?

More books from 4 Horsemen Publications

Fantasy, SciFi, & Paranormal Romance

Amanda Fasciano
Waking Up Dead
Dead Vessel

Beau Lake
The Beast Beside Me
The Beast Within Me
Taming the Beast: Novella
The Beast After Me
Charming the Beast: Novella
The Beast Like Me
An Eye for Emeralds
Swimming in Sapphires
Pining for Pearls

Chelsea Burton Dunn
By Moonlight

Danielle Orsino
Locked Out of Heaven
Thine Eyes of Mercy
From the Ashes
Kingdom Come
Fire, Ice, Acid, & Heart
A Fae is Done

J.M. Paquette
Klauden's Ring
Solyn's Body
The Inbetween
Hannah's Heart
Call Me Forth
Invite Me In
Keep Me Close

Jessica Salina
Not My Time

Kait Disney-Leugers
Antique Magic

Lyra R. Saenz
Prelude
Falsetto in the Woods: Novella
Ragtime Swing
Sonata
Song of the Sea
The Devil's Trill
Bercuese
To Heal a Songbird
Ghost March
Nocturne

Paige Lavoie
I'm in Love with Mothman

Robert J. Lewis
Shadow Guardian and the Three Bears

T.S. Simons
Antipodes
The Liminal Space
Ouroboros
Caim
Sessrúmnir
The 45th Parallel

Valerie Willis
Cedric: The Demonic Knight
Romasanta: Father of Werewolves
The Oracle: Keeper of the Gaea's Gate
Artemis: Eye of Gaea
King Incubus: A New Reign

V.C. Willis
The Prince's Priest
The Priest's Assassin
The Assassin's Saint

Horror, Thriller, & Suspense

Alan Berkshire
Jungle
Hell's Road

Erika Lance
Jimmy
Illusions of Happiness
No Place for Happiness
I Hunt You

Maria DeVivo
Witch of the Black Circle
Witch of the Red Thorn
Witch of the Silver Locust

Mark Tarrant
The Mighty Hook
The Death Riders
Howl of the Windigo
Guts and Garter Belts

Steve Altier
The Ghost Hunter
Romasanta: Father of Werewolves
The Oracle: Keeper of the Gaea's Gate
Artemis: Eye of Gaea
King Incubus: A New Reign

Fantasy

D. Lambert
To Walk into the Sands
Rydan
Celebrant
Northlander
Esparan
King
Traitor
His Last Name

Danielle Orsino
Locked Out of Heaven
Thine Eyes of Mercy
From the Ashes
Kingdom Come
Fire, Ice, Acid, & Heart
A Fae is Done

J.M. Paquette
Klauden's Ring
Solyn's Body
The Inbetween
Hannah's Heart

Lou Kemp
The Violins Played Before Junstan
Music Shall Untune the Sky

R.J. Young
Challenges of Tawa

Valerie Willis
Cedric: The Demonic Knight
Romasanta: Father of Werewolves
The Oracle: Keeper of the Gaea's Gate
Artemis: Eye of Gaea
King Incubus: A New Reign

Discover more at 4HorsemenPublications.com

Lightning Source UK Ltd.
Milton Keynes UK
UKHW012242060223
416577UK00010B/667/J